ADVANCE PRAISE FOR
YOUR PERFECT LIFE

"Filled with relatable characters who made me laugh out loud, and sweet and surprising insights about how the perfect life may be the one you've already got."
—**Jen Lancaster**, *New York Times* **bestselling author**

"Sassy, heartfelt, and smart. A clever take on switched identities that will make you think about the choices you've made and what matters most to us all in the end."
—**Amy Hatvany, author of** *Safe with Me*

"Clever, quirky, fresh, and ultimately empowering! Liz and Liza remind us that even though the grass often looks greener in our friends' lives, nobody gets *happily ever after* unless they go *after* it."
—**Claire Cook, bestselling author of** *Must Love Dogs*

"Liz and Lisa's voices are warm and comforting, like a relaxed chat with great friends while wear~~ing cozy pj's and~~ sipping wine. I highly recommer~~d~~
—**Beth Harbison, author of** *S.~~~~*

"For every woman who's ever w~~ondered about~~ the path not taken . . . humorous and insightful."
—**Emma McL~~aughlin and Nicola Kraus~~**, *#1 New York Times b~~~~*

your
perfect life

your
perfect life

a novel

liz fenton
and
lisa steinke

WASHINGTON SQUARE PRESS

new york   london   toronto   sydney   new delhi

Washington Square Press
A Division of Simon & Schuster, Inc.
1230 Avenue of the Americas
New York, NY 10020

First Washington Square Press trade paperback edition May 2014

WASHINGTON SQUARE PRESS and colophon are registered trademarks of Simon & Schuster, Inc.

For information about special discounts for bulk purchases, please contact Simon & Schuster Special Sales at 1-866-506-1949 or business@simonandschuster.com.

The Simon & Schuster Speakers Bureau can bring authors to your live event. For more information or to book an event contact the Simon & Schuster Speakers Bureau at 1-866-248-3049 or visit our website at www.simonspeakers.com.

Designed by Akasha Archer
Cover photography © Benjamin Edwards Photography
Cover design © Connie Gabbert Design and Illustration LLC

Manufactured in the United States of America

10 9 8 7 6 5 4 3 2 1

Library of Congress Cataloging-in-Publication Data

Fenton, Liz.
Your perfect life : a novel / Liz Fenton and Lisa Steinke.
p. cm.
"Washington Square Press fiction original trade."
Includes bibliographical references and index.
1. Female friendship--Fiction. 2. Identity (Psychology)—Fiction.
3. Life change events—Fiction. 4. Psychological fiction. I. Steinke, Lisa. II. Title.
PS3606.E5844Y68 2014
813'.6—dc23
2013017485

ISBN 978-1-4767-3057-8
ISBN 978-1-4767-3058-5 (ebook)

To Mike, for being my soft place to fall
For Reese, Dain, and Harper, always dream big

your
perfect life

CHAPTER 1

....

casey

My mouth tastes like ass.

Rolling over, I grab for the water I always leave on the night-stand and silently pray that there are also two Advil waiting for me to help numb the pounding in my head. Why did I think that last shot of Patrón was a good idea? I rack my brains trying to remember what happened after that, but it's just a blur.

"Hey, sleepyhead."

I startle at the sound of a man's voice next to me and in-stinctively pull the sheets over my naked body as memories of last night come crashing back. Being sent a tequila shot by a good-looking twenty-something. Motioning for him to join me. Four drinks and two shots later, us, fumbling in the back of the cab, making out like two teenagers. Coming back here, to my penthouse apartment in the Wilshire area of Los Angeles. And now, waking up to him in my bed, unable to recall his name. Was it Cody? Carl?

"Hey, you." I decide a *you* will have to do as I run my fingers through my hair and glance around the room for anything I can put on. Our clothes are strewn everywhere, my bra is lying on the TV, and my underwear is ripped in half on the floor. Wow. Cody or Carl or whatever his name was didn't mess around last night.

"Come here." He pulls me by the waist into the fold of his body and I feel myself stiffen, my inhibitions no longer blunted by alcohol. He kisses my neck and I smile despite myself, suddenly remembering the reason I let him rip my La Perlas last night. But I don't have time for a repeat performance, I think, as I glance at the clock. I'm due in the studio in less than an hour. And at thirty-eight, I don't bounce back from these nights the way I used to.

I detach myself from him gently. "Sorry, I'll have to take a rain check," I say, knowing I'll never see him again. "I'm late for work."

"No worries," he replies and rolls out of bed and grabs his pants from the chair in the corner. "I've got an audition later anyway."

That's right. He's an actor. I vaguely remember discussing his role as "man number three" in the next Will Smith movie. I sigh. My penchant for twenty-something struggling thespians has always been my downfall.

Stepping out of bed with the sheet wrapped tightly around me, I kiss his cheek. "Thanks, and sorry, I don't mean to kick you out of here." But we both know that I do.

He wraps his chiseled arms around me. "It's fine."

"Great. Well, I guess I'll see you around?" He lingers by the front door, his shirt still unbuttoned, his jeans slung low on his hips revealing the Calvin Klein waistband of his boxer briefs.

I know what's coming next. Happens every time. "Hey, so, in

case your agent is looking for fresh talent, would you mind talking to her for me?"

"Sure," I reply, cringing at the thought of pitching my latest sexual conquest to my agent. "Just email your résumé to my assistant." I write down her email address and swiftly escort him out the door and lean my head against it.

I'm getting too old for this shit.

I rush out of hair and makeup and toward the *GossipTV* set just as the taping is about to start. "Three minutes!" my producer, Charlie, calls to me as I sprint past him expertly in my high-heel ankle boots.

I hurry into place and glance over at Dean Anders, my co-host. He grimaces at my tardiness without looking up from his notes. "Nice of you to show up."

"No problem," I answer sarcastically. "What would you do without me?"

He smirks and opens his mouth, but before he can speak the stage manager cuts him off. "Four, three, two," he says before pointing at me as the red light on the camera comes to life. I may have been flustered a minute ago, but now I'm in my element.

"Welcome to *GossipTV*! I'm Casey Lee and we've got the freshest scoop coming your way right now!"

Thirty minutes later, the relenting red light turns off and I pull off my boots. "Why do great shoes have to hurt so much?" I say to no one in particular.

"That's the price you pay for high fashion." My assistant, Destiny, sweeps by and takes the boots out of my hand, twirling them by their four-inch heels.

"Ain't that the truth?" I mutter as I make my way back to my dressing room. I glance in the mirror. Even after an hour in hair and makeup, I can still see the circles under my bright sapphire eyes and the lines around them when I smile. Like always, there's a small part of me that hates that I've chosen a profession where age forty is considered ancient, where the Kelly Ripas of the world are the exception not the rule. This past year, I've felt the clock start ticking. Not my biological clock—I'm talking about the clock that exists in the minds of all the executives who determine when on-air talent gets stale. I'd been pretty fortunate in my career, starting right out of college as a researcher at *Entertainment Tonight* and eventually working my way up to on-air correspondent. And for the past three years, I've been the cohost of *GossipTV*.

But I know that I'm only as good as my last sweeps number, and I'm starting to live on borrowed time. It's a fact that Dean likes to bring up often. He is twenty-eight and arrogant because he doesn't have that damn clock ticking in his ear.

I lie on the couch in my dressing room and close my eyes, practicing the meditations my yoga teacher taught me. But I can't concentrate—it feels like the walls in my painfully small dressing room are closing in on me. I might be on-air talent, but it doesn't afford me much more than a nameplate on the door, a pleather couch, and if you ask me, way too many mirrors. And then there it is again—the tight ball of anxiety lodged in the base of my throat. *Breathe, Casey. Just breathe.*

Destiny glides in the door a moment later, iPad in hand. "Ready to go over your schedule?" she asks.

"Am I ever ready?" I joke and take a sip of the water she wisely brought me.

"Oh, did Colby wear you out last night?" The sides of her

mouth curl up as she tries unsuccessfully to keep a straight face.

Colby! So *that* was his name. I knew it started with a C.

"He emailed you already?" I groan.

"Yes, he sent his résumé and said he had a *very productive* meeting with you."

I put my hands over my face. "It's the last time, I promise."

"Like I've never heard that one before," she says with a snort.

Destiny has been with me since my first on-air job and is more than just an assistant to me. From the minute she strutted into her interview, I knew she was the one. She told me that if I hired her, she'd always have my best interests at heart, I'd never be late for anything, and, most important, she'd be the best damn gatekeeper I ever had. Ex-boyfriends from hell? No worries. Bad dates? She had me covered. My mother? Piece of cake. Having already called her list of references, I was well aware of those facts and then some—she'd been given a five-star review from each. I needed someone who wasn't going to call *Us Weekly* when I had a meltdown over low ratings, someone who wouldn't feed damaging information to people like my cohost Dean's assistant and rumored lover, Fiona, a long-legged ex–beauty queen who'd do just about anything to take me down. I needed someone I could trust. When I listened to Destiny, sitting cross-legged in my worn leather chair, telling me a story about putting herself through college by working two jobs, I knew in my gut I had found a hardworking assistant and someone I could trust. Only later would I realize I'd also found a lifelong friend.

"Okay, so let's talk about the next few days," she says as she taps on the iPad and pulls up my calendar. "You've got an interview with the *L.A. Times* Calendar section after lunch today. Tomorrow the car service will pick you up at five thirty for your high school reunion."

I groan. I'd forgotten all about it, or more likely, I'd just blocked it out. It would be a ballroom full of people triggering memories that I'd been trying to forget for twenty years. "Why am I going again? And who schedules a high school reunion in the middle of winter?"

Destiny sighs. "Is it ever really winter in Southern California? We've been over this. You know you need to go. People will be expecting you to show up—you're a celebrity now." She laughs and I roll my eyes. "Plus, you promised Rachel. You haven't seen her much lately." She shows me the calendar on the iPad like it's exhibit A in a courtroom. "Three months is a long time not to see your best friend. What's going on with you two anyway?"

I wish I knew. Our last few conversations had been filled with awkward pauses, and I'd felt more like I was suffering through a bad date than talking to someone I'd known forever.

We'd been friends since the day she walked into my seventh-grade English class. She was the new girl, but stood tall and had an air of confidence that was unusual for a girl in middle school. It wasn't until we'd had our first sleepover, when she scrutinized her flawless face in my vanity mirror— the side that *magnified it*—that I realized she'd been putting on an act that day, probably hoping she, as much as her class-mates, would believe it. While the teacher introduced her, she'd caught my eye and smiled, and I noticed a worn copy of *All Night Long* from the *Sweet Valley High* series under her arm, a book I'd read countless times. We'd been best friends ever since, surviving junior high, high school, and even college together. And when she'd called about the reunion, I'd promised I wouldn't flake on her, even though I had absolutely no desire to go.

"Hey, I can feel you judging me over there. We've *both* been busy, you know."

Destiny raises her eyebrow. "Mmm . . . okay."

"Oh, come on. You know how insane my schedule's been and she's got *three* kids." I crinkle my nose at the thought of her domesticated life. I love Rachel. But she always seems so . . . *frazzled.* "And I may have had to cancel the last few times we had dinner plans, but I'm not going to flake on her, she's my oldest friend. It will be good for us to spend some time together. And John too," I add, referring to her high school sweetheart and husband, also a friend of mine.

Destiny nods her head with approval. "And it will be good for you to flirt with some men your *own age.*"

"We both know that's not going to happen!" I say with a laugh, but there's a part of me that hopes there will be someone my own age to flirt with. Someone mature and kind who doesn't care if I can get him a job. Someone who wants to know the part of me that has nothing to do with TV.

CHAPTER 2

....

rachel

The house is quiet. The bedroom is dark. When it's peaceful like this, I can almost convince myself that I'm satisfied with my life.

I look over at John, the light coming through the blinds hitting him across the face. He still looks like the man I fell in love with over twenty years ago, just a little bit older. His brown hair is graying slightly at the temples and there were more lines around his blue eyes. His jawline is still strong, his body still toned from his daily runs. He's aging well, the bastard. Me, on the other hand, not so much. My age shows in the lines in my forehead and the stretch marks on my belly.

I feel every one of my thirty-eight years. I reach for John's hand, but just as I do, his alarm goes off and he's in the shower before I can even muster a hello. My hand is still resting where his body used to be. The baby cries as if on cue. The day has officially begun. And this is a day I'm not ready for at all. Because at the end of it, I'm going to be wearing a *Hello My Name Is* sticker and feeling fat in a prepregnancy dress.

"Don't you have your high school reunion tonight?" Audrey, my sixteen-year-old, asks at breakfast.

"You must feel so old!" My fourteen-year-old, Sophie, chimes in.

"God. I can't even imagine!" Audrey rolls her eyes and fake gags.

"Can't imagine what?" John rushes into the kitchen and takes a swig from my coffee cup.

"What it's going to feel like to be twenty years older."

"It feels old." John laughs, looking in my direction. "Gotta go," he says, kissing the baby, then the girls, but not me. I run my finger over a crack in the granite countertop and add it to my mental to-do list, right below the leaky faucet in the girls' shared bathroom, the loose floorboard in the entryway, and the temperamental water heater that needs to be replaced. We've definitely outgrown our once-cozy Spanish-style house nestled on the corner of a cul-de-sac in Culver City—the closest neighborhood to John's pharmaceutical sales territory in Santa Monica we could afford when we bought it over a decade ago. But even though he had long since been promoted to regional sales manager and was no longer pounding the pavement with the latest and greatest antibiotic or asthma inhaler, we were still here.

"I'm out of here too." Audrey grabs her car keys off the counter. I still can't wrap my head around the fact she's driving. Wasn't she just a gap-toothed seven-year-old? And now she's taller than I am with legs for days—legs that cause John to get a frightened look in his eyes whenever he takes notice of them.

Her hair falls down her back in long, loose natural curls and her eyes are a piercing blue, like John's.

"Ready?" she asks Sophie.

And she's driving my fourteen-year-old, who looks almost older than Audrey, her beautiful long hair recently chopped off, without my consent, to resemble her favorite singer. Her green eyes—that match mine—are rimmed with too much eyeliner, her lips obliterated by dark lipstick. I sigh, too tired to battle it out with her this morning.

"Bye, Mom," they say in unison.

"Be safe," I say, to the already-closed door. I pull the tie of my robe tighter and begin to feed our baby, Charlotte, wondering if any of my former classmates are unemployed, sitting in a kitchen with walls desperately in need of a new coat of paint, trying to coax a bite of banana into a fussy baby's mouth.

When I told John I was pregnant, he thought I was joking. When I kept insisting it was true, he'd asked for the proof. Together we'd dug through the bathroom trash can until finally, I'd found it. As I held the white stick with the word *yes* illuminated in pink high in the air like an Olympic torch, we burst into a nervous fit of uncontrollable laughter, finding it much easier to laugh than talk about how this baby was going to change things.

We parked ourselves on the bathroom floor and struggled with the math until we figured out that we conceived Charlotte the night of our anniversary dinner. We were drunk before our entrées arrived. Something came over me at the table. Maybe it was the second bottle of wine or the fact that I'd splurged to get my hair and makeup done and felt uncharacteristically sexy. But I'd reached under the table and grabbed him, and suggested he meet me in the bathroom. Of course the last thing we were thinking about was birth control; neither of us could remember the last time we'd even had sex, let alone hot sex.

The second person I told about the baby was my best friend, Casey. She looked at me blankly, waiting for the punch line.

I told her the part about seducing him and doing it in the bathroom but left out the part about how long it had been since I'd seen him with his pants down. I always left that kind of thing out of our conversations. Casey is happily single, goes to Hollywood parties, and regularly has sex with smoking-hot twenty-year-olds. The last thing I wanted her to know was that I could barely get laid by my own husband. Or worse, how I barely *wanted* to get laid by him. Something about not saying it out loud made it easier to justify and deny my part in it. I wish I still had the urge to have rip-roaring sex with John, or better yet, I wish we still laughed together, like the teenagers we once were, like my mom and dad still do, and they've been married for fifty years last summer.

Charlotte drops her sippy cup on the floor and giggles. Of course I can't imagine my life without her. But my life in general is not at all how I thought it would be. When I'm asked about it tonight, I won't be able to explain why I'm not in broadcasting, like Casey. None of them want to hear how, against everyone's advice, I dropped out of college when I got pregnant with Audrey. Something about my due date and graduation date being the same day threw me off. I always planned to go back and finish, but the timing was never right. And then somewhere along the way, I lost interest, or desire. Or maybe a little bit of both. Hopefully, tonight, everyone will be focused on Casey and will not even ask.

Ten hours later, John and I ride the elevator in silence as it ascends to the floor where our reunion is being held. I look down at my dress, hoping my Spanx are doing their job. As the doors open, John reaches for my hand and we walk in together, smiling. It's funny how quickly we can transform into the people we ought to be.

CHAPTER 3

....

casey

Sidling up to the still-empty bar, I order a double Belvedere and soda. A very young bartender gives me a conspiratorial wink as he sets my drink in front of me, like my boozing is going to be our little secret. I knock it back, and he swiftly replaces it with another. As I give him a flirtatious smile, I hear Destiny's words ringing in my ears: *Flirt with someone your own age!* I ignore them. "How are you?" I ask as I take my hand and pin a strand of my golden hair behind my ear.

"I'm great. These are my favorite events."

"Why? Do drunken has-beens from high school tend to tip well?" I quip, sounding a little more jaded than I intend to.

"Actually, no. You'd be surprised how regret and bitterness inspires cheapness in people," he says as he wipes the zinc bar with a towel and nods at a man dressed in an expensive charcoal suit who sits three bar stools over. I recognize him as Patrick Sanders, former science club geek who earned a full scholarship to MIT, and then went on to start his own biotech company. I smile and give a small wave before looking away, not wanting him to take it as an invitation to join me. I wasn't ready to explain why I was one of the few unmarried, childless people here. I drain the rest of my vodka and soda and swish the ice cubes around. I could use about ten more of these.

Patrick orders a Jack and Coke and I watch him sip it greedily. Maybe he's as nervous as I am. I watch him glance around the crowd, tugging at the knot of his silk tie, a distant look in his eyes. Could his past be gnawing at him as much as mine?

When I received the invitation to the reunion, I'd immediately tossed it into the trash. But then Rachel had called—talking a mile a minute. What was I going to wear? Who was I nervous to see? Wouldn't it be fun to be there together? When I didn't respond, I could hear her inhale deeply. And then in a voice that didn't even sound like hers, she'd said that *everything* wasn't always about me. I was surprised not only by her attack—which came out of nowhere—but by how much the words had stung. Still sting.

I thought about what going would mean, the unhappy memories that would try to surface, the emotions I'd have to fend off. In my day-to-day life it was easy not to think about my lack of a family, but being in a room full of people I'd known twenty years ago—people who had other halves and cars with more than two seats—would force me to focus on it. But then I thought about Rachel and all of our shared memories. Even though it was the last place on Earth I wanted to be, I told her I'd RSVP yes. She's my best friend and that's what we do; she would've done the same for me. At least I hope so.

"Ready for another?" The bartender nods toward my empty glass and I can't help but stare a beat too long at his deep brown eyes, sun-kissed skin, and sandy blond hair. If I didn't know any better, I'd think there was a surfboard behind the bar.

"Only if you tell me your name. And the real reason why you love these events," I say playfully. Patrick hears me and gives me a sideways glance, probably wondering why I'm hitting on a guy half my age, even though he looks like the type who takes out girls so young it prompts people to wonder *Is that his date or his daughter?*

The bartender begins a long pour of the Belvedere. "My name is Brian," he says as he slides the cocktail across the bar expertly. "And I love these events because it brings out the best *and worst* in people. Want to truly see inside someone? Shadow them at their high school reunion."

I take a long sip of my drink. "Do you really believe that?"

He leans in close. "See that guy over there?" he whispers, bobbing his head in the direction of Patrick. "He has everything. Multimillionaire, private airplane, trophy wife. He runs a Fortune 500 company. He could buy and sell every person here."

"So?" I whisper back.

"So, he's downing his drink like it's water because he's worried about what you and everyone else he went to high school with will think. That he's still the nerd that the head cheerleader rejected, the guy the football players bullied."

"Are you sure you just haven't been watching too many reruns of *Gossip Girl?*" I snort and cover my mouth quickly, hoping no one else heard. "Besides, how would you get all that from serving him one drink?"

"You'd be surprised what I know," he says seductively.

I'm about to ask him what he knows about me when a couple walks up, the man impatiently waving a twenty at Brian.

They survey the bar quickly and begin to whisper. *Are they talking about me?*

Not wanting to know the answer, I turn my back to them and scan the room, taking in my classmates. Some look exactly the same. Others, much older. I shudder at the thought that someone in this room could be judging me and my choice to wear a cranberry red minidress, instead of a nondescript pantsuit, like most of the women here.

The room buzzes with conversation, of which I hear snippets. "I have two kids . . ." "Then we moved to Grand Rapids . . ." "So what do you do?" And I wonder again what it would be like to be able to say I've been married for five years, have two kids, live in the suburbs.

I know I should mingle, especially because people will notice if I don't. But I hesitate. Just signing in and getting my name tag was enough to send me straight to the bar. *Yes,* I've met Jennifer Aniston. *No,* I don't know if she hates Angelina Jolie. *Yes,* I'm pretty much resigned to answering questions like this all night. But part of me is relieved. The more they ask about the latest celebrity gossip, the less they'll ask about me.

Rachel texts me that she and John are on their way up and I'm glad when I see them walk in, hand in hand. Rachel smiles apprehensively as she makes her way toward me. I take in her simple black dress and diamond earrings, the ones John gave her for their ten-year anniversary. Her shoulder-length chocolate brown hair flows freely and I can see from here that she spent considerable time perfecting her makeup, making her green eyes sparkle. She looks beautiful.

I wave them over and watch the envious glances as they walk my way, one of very few high school sweetheart couples from our class that passed the test of time. Back when I was still wondering which bar was hosting Ladies Night on Wednesday, Rachel and John were getting ready for their first baby. I'd begged her not to drop out of college when she discovered she was pregnant. She was so close to graduation. But no, she'd said, this is my life now.

I signal to Brian the bartender for two more drinks as Rachel and John approach. "Here's to officially being old," I call out as I hand one to each of them. John brings me in for a small side hug as he takes a large gulp.

"What's up, Little C?" he says, using the nickname he gave me in high school. I'd met John my freshman year when I sat next to him in Mr. Roberts's biology class. He was a total jock who'd transferred from out of state, and I'd harbored a small crush on him at first. But he was literally speechless when I introduced him to Rachel for the first time at the water tower where we used to sneak to drink wine coolers with the upper classmen. And from that point on, they were an item and I was their third wheel. But I didn't mind. John always looked out for me like a big brother and some of my best memories were of the three of us together.

I reach over and poke Rachel in the arm. "You look nice."

She touches her simple black dress self-consciously. "Thanks. You sure it's okay? I don't look old?"

"You are the one person who doesn't have to worry about that. You look exactly the same!"

"What do you mean?" Her tone lets me know this wasn't the right thing to say. But it's true. Rachel could throw on her old cheerleading uniform and blend right in, her dark hair still worn in the same style, and not a single crease in her un-Botoxed forehead. Meanwhile, I hadn't been able to lift my eyebrows properly in years.

John steps in before I can answer. "She means it as a compliment."

She shoots him a death stare. "Stay out of it."

John turns to me. "She's upset about the ballot."

"The ballot?" I ask.

"You know when you checked in downstairs and they gave you a name tag? They also handed out a ballot. We're supposed to vote—"

Rachel cuts him off. "We're supposed to vote on things like who traveled the farthest . . ."

"Well, I can see how that would be incredibly upsetting," I say, laughing.

"Let me finish. There's also other awards like most successful and least successful."

"Least successful? Are you kidding me?" Brian was right. These things really do bring out the worst in people.

"No. There's not a least successful award. That's just what Rachel thinks it is." John rolls his eyes like she's not standing there. "It's called *Least Changed*."

"Same thing." Rachel crosses her arms over her chest looking even more like an eighteen-year-old.

"Anyway," John continues. "Since the moment we checked in, people have been marveling at how she hasn't changed a bit and she's afraid she'll win the award."

"Didn't you guys just get here? Like five minutes ago?"

"All the more reason why I think I'm going to win," Rachel says, looking terrified.

"Well, all I meant when I said that you looked the same is that you look beautiful. And *if* you win, the reason will be because you haven't changed, not because you're not successful."

I touch her arm gently to let her know I mean it, but she looks away. John and I exchange a look. *Rachel's in a mood tonight.* I swallow the lump that's been building in my throat since I rode up in the elevator with two couples bantering about how lucky they were to have found a babysitter while I'd stared down at the velvet five-inch stilettos that were already pinching my pinkie toes, the pain a welcome distraction from the chatter around me. *How could she not realize that this night might be hard for me too?*

"Rachel! Casey! John! Of *course* I'd find the three of you together. I mean, how crazy that nothing has changed in *twenty* years!" Class president, head cheerleader, and resident mean girl Julie Meyers bounces up looking nothing like her high school self, an extra fifty pounds hanging from her formerly petite frame. I think about Patrick Sanders drowning his high school memories of being rejected by her in a stiff drink and want to tell him he's better off.

"Wow, y'all look great!" She grabs Rachel and twirls her around. "Girl, you look exactly the *same!*"

John and I share another look. I signal Brian for another round. He gives me a knowing look. *See, I told you this brings out the worst in people.* I roll my eyes at him.

But once the drinks kick in, it seems like everyone's having fun, even Rachel. I've been trying to follow Destiny's advice, even hauling my ass off the bar stool and flirting with a few men my own age. Apparently, this twenty-year reunion is packed with recent divorcées. I had felt some apprehension about coming here without ever having been married, but now I wonder if it was worse to come here saying you tried and failed. I try to keep the smile pasted on my face as they discuss their child custody schedule and bitterness over alimony payments and think that while twenty-somethings may be lacking in maturity, at least they don't have this kind of baggage.

I try to catch Rachel's eye from across the room. I'm trapped talking to the former chess club president and his wife and I think they're pitching me some sort of chess reality show, but I tuned out a few minutes ago when the DJ started playing Cutting Crew. She finally comes over to rescue me. She's much more relaxed than she was earlier, her cheeks are flushed, and her eyes are shiny from the alcohol. I'm reminded again of the girl who charmed John at the water tower so many years ago.

"Are you having fun yet?" I ask tentatively, looking for signs that her insecurities from earlier are gone. She'd seemed down lately and I certainly hadn't succeeded in making her feel better, not that I'd tried that hard. Our conversations only seem to go from bad to worse because I can never say—or as in the case of the phone call about this reunion—*not say*—the right thing. I definitely don't know what to tell her when she complains about Charlotte being up all night or Sophie throwing a tantrum over some outfit. I just listen, because what am I supposed to say? I don't get what's *that* stressful about her life. We were both broadcasting majors in college, but I often think that even though she was immensely talented, Rachel would have gotten eaten alive had she ended up with a career in TV.

"You know what? I *am* having a good time," Rachel says as she loops her arm through mine, making me miss the girls we used to be.

"Where's John?" I ask, glancing around before finding him leaning against the bar talking to a woman whose name I can't remember. By the way he's gesturing, it's clear he's telling a story, and by the way she's leaning in, just a little too close, it's obvious she'd listen to that story on repeat for hours. John's always been a good-looking guy who, at six foot four, has turned more than his share of heads. I remember in high school and college Rachel used to get so jealous, secretly confiding in me that she wondered if she was pretty enough for him. And of course she was—and still is.

I elbow Rachel. "Look at that woman throwing herself at John; so pathetic. I should go over there and save him." I motion toward the nameless woman with the large, hungry eyes who looks like she wants to take a big bite out of him.

She waves it off. "Oh please. Let him have the attention. We've been together forever and we're *so boring*. Boring as hell." She smiles and twirls the straw in her empty glass. "Ready for another drink?"

"Welcome, everyone!" Julie Meyers is up at the podium demanding our attention. "It's time for the awards!"

Rachel stiffens and John walks back to us and drapes his arms around her possessively. She leans into him and exhales and I feel a pang in my stomach. Even if it's boring as hell, it must be nice to be someone's *someone*. Someone you can exhale into.

Julie starts calling out the awards: Most Likely to Star in a Reality Show on Bravo; Person with the Fewest Original Body Parts; and my favorite, The Number-One MILF and Number-One DILF. People are running up to the stage with the excitement of an audience member selected to be on *The Price Is Right*.

"I think you showed less emotion when you won your Emmy last year!" Rachel whispers to me and we share a laugh.

"Okay, next up, our most successful graduate. Now I think we can all guess who this is!" Julie locks eyes with me as she calls my name. "Casey Lee, get up here!"

I look over at Rachel and John. John is whistling and Rachel's face is frozen until I catch her eye and she quickly composes herself and starts to clap. I walk up to the podium and grab my award, say a hurried thank-you, and head back down as quickly as possible, Rachel's expressionless face etched in my mind. "It's nothing," I say to her when I return, trying to let her know that she wouldn't have been so upset that I won if she understood how much I've given up to get it. She nods silently and looks away.

I look over to my right and watch Patrick Sanders walking dejectedly over to the bar. *How the hell did I win this over him?* He could buy this hotel if he wanted. Brian has his drink waiting when he walks up and looks over at me with a knowing smile that says *I told you so.*

Julie's voice shrills over the microphone again. "And now for our last award, Least Changed!"

John and I exchange a panicked look.

"Rachel Cole!"

CHAPTER 4

....

rachel

"Rachel Cole. Where are you? Come on up here and get your award!" Julie is grinning widely, completely unaware that I'd rather give birth to triplets than accept the Least Changed award.

So what if it's technically an honor for someone who still looks the same—a compliment even. I know what it really means, what everyone's really thinking: that I've done nothing with my life.

I'm not sure if I should collect my award with the dignity of an Academy Award winner or get up there and tell everyone off. The four Belvedere and sodas I've downed are pulling for me to give the crowd the finger. With each step toward the stage, I feel my anger mount. I can hear nothing but the sound of my out-of-style high heels on the linoleum floor.

I walk up the stairs to the podium and Julie congratulates me yet again and hands me a plastic award. A trinket I've seen at the dollar store. I think of Sophie's cheap soccer trophies and medals, which she recently relegated to a box in the garage, and I realize they look like Olympic medals compared to this.

I scan the sea of my classmates and see a man holding up his glass to me and cheering and it takes a moment for it to register that it's Jake Johnson, our senior class president and captain of the volleyball team. He's got a paunch and a comb-over now, but a huge smile is plastered across his face. He's obviously having a great time even though he no longer looks like an Abercrombie & Fitch model. He swings his arm over the shoulders of the editor of our high school newspaper, Nancy Myers. She smiles my way, not a care in the world, even though she looks older than her thirty-eight years, gray at the temples and deep lines around her eyes. She's having fun too—the kind of time I hoped I'd have.

I had been so excited to see my old friends and relive fun memories, never expecting the moment I walked in that I'd become consumed with insecurity, instantly transforming into a gangly fifteen-year-old who never felt she was pretty enough or smart enough *or just enough in general*. Not for John or for anyone. But somehow, back then, I was able to mask it, only whispering my true feelings to Casey late at night on the cord-less phone I sneaked into my bedroom, the darkness giving me the courage to say the words. At school, I became an over-achiever, taking on one more extracurricular activity, joining one more club, anything to prove myself. But now, standing here as a grown woman, I'm finding it almost impossible to swallow my tears. I quickly mumble a sarcastic "thanks a lot" into the microphone and stumble down the stairs, leaving a wide-eyed Julie behind, still clasping my trinket in her hand. I head toward the double doors leading out of the ballroom.

"Where are you going? You okay?" Casey calls after me.

I turn around slowly, ready to tell her how I'm feeling, until I see the Most Successful award dangling from her perfectly manicured left hand. Her hair is styled expertly, her makeup was obviously done by the award-winning makeup artist at her studio, and the designer minidress is hugging her in all the right places. Not only has she realized all of her dreams professionally, she looks more gorgeous than ever.

"I need to be alone." I turn toward the door again so she won't see my eyes filling with tears.

"Hey, don't go. Talk to me," Casey says quietly.

"Talk to *you*? *You* have no idea what I'm feeling."

I ignore the hurt look in Casey's eyes and snap, "Oh, wait, you probably have people to call for this. A life coach on speed dial, perhaps?"

I see John approaching, a concerned look on his face, but I shake my head to warn him not to get in the middle of this.

"What crawled up your ass? Don't let some silly award mess with your head. It's not worth it," Casey pleads.

"Said the most successful to the least successful."

"For the last time, your award was for still looking the same, which is meant as a compliment. You haven't aged a day since you were eighteen. You should be flattered!"

"Flattered? Just look at them." I motion toward no one in particular. "They know I haven't lived up to their expectations. I was voted most likely to succeed in high school yet my biggest accomplishment is what? President of the PTA? No, wait, I've got something better than that: I won the brownie bake-off at Sophie's school two years ago." I glare at John, still watching us from a safe distance. I think of the headhunter I'd secretly met with just days before finding out I was pregnant with Charlotte; the résumé we'd crafted; the excitement I'd felt as I thought of working outside of the home again.

I hated to admit it, but having another baby had changed us. Suddenly we were fighting about everything: who would get up with her, who *should* get up with her; another college tuition on a single income; my refusal to let John continue with his weekly poker night because I needed help. I don't remember it being this hard before, but then again, it was sixteen years ago and I was a much different mom and wife back then; more patient and less exhausted.

"No one here is thinking you aren't a success except *you*. No one is pitying you except *you*. Don't tell me you're actually jealous of *this*?" Casey waves her trophy in front of me. "You want it? Take it!" Casey tries to push it into my hand, but I step back and it falls on the floor between us and a group of classmates looks our way.

"I don't want your award. It doesn't matter. I wouldn't expect you to understand. You have everything you ever wanted."

Casey shakes her head. "Okay, fine. You want to have this out. We'll have this out. Why don't you have everything you ever wanted? Why didn't you ever go back to work? Why did you give up?" Casey challenges.

"You think having a baby is giving up? God, you have no clue what you're talking about. It wasn't as simple as you thought it was. You think I could've finished college while I was pregnant and then gotten a job at some TV station all while trying to take care of a newborn?"

"If you wanted it bad enough," she says, her words slicing through me.

"You just don't get it. You've never actually had a baby."

Casey scoffs then looks away, sadness crossing her eyes. And then I know I've gone too far.

"Okay, you two, let's end this thing right now," John says in a hushed tone as he walks up with the bartender, who is carrying two drinks. "These are from our friend Brian," he says. "He wisely suggested you two need to drink these and let go of whatever it is you're fighting about."

Brian smiles broadly, eyeing the two shot glasses full of a bright purple liquid. "I made these extra special for the two of you."

Casey rolls her eyes. "You think it's so simple. Like a couple of shots can make us forget all the BS that's gone on tonight? A lot's been said."

John puts his arms around both of us. "You guys have been fighting like sisters for years. Angry one minute, best friends again the next. Why should tonight be any different?" He gives me a supportive look, "It's just a high school reunion, right?" He kisses me on the cheek. Then he turns to Casey, "Just knock back one of these and call a truce."

Brian holds out the shots proudly. "C'mon, ladies. I promise these will make you both realize how silly you're being."

"Fine," I say, grabbing one of the shot glasses.

"Whatever." Casey takes the other.

"We might as well make a toast while we're at it," I say.

Casey lifts her shot glass and says sarcastically, "To your *perfect life*."

"No," I say, clinking my glass against hers. "To *your* perfect life."

....

casey

"Mom!" A girl is screaming. Am I dreaming? Or is that one of my neighbors? It's probably that kid who just moved in, the star of that new Disney show. She's always fighting with her mother about something. I swear children should not be allowed to be in show business; it's hard enough when you're an adult. Temples pounding, I pull the pillow over my head to block out the sound and make a mental note to complain to the homeowners' association about the thin walls in this place.

Next come stomping footsteps that sound so close. She couldn't be inside my apartment, could she?

"Mom!" I open my eyes, half expecting to see the Disney star, but instead it's Rachel's daughter, Audrey, who yanks the pillow off of me and shakes my shoulder. Did she just call me Mom? Doesn't she recognize me? I'm her fun and free-spirited Aunt Casey. I squeeze my eyes closed again, willing this bad dream to be over so I can get some serious REM sleep.

Finally, she leaves. Thank God, I was dreaming. But a few

moments later, I'm overcome by the smell of poop. I open one eye and find baby Charlotte dangling in front of me. A very stinky baby Charlotte. This dream is so real. I can smell the poop so clearly.

"She needs to be changed, Mom. C'mon."

Fine. I'll deal with the baby so I can move on to a much better dream, like the one I had the other night about Brad Pitt. I take Charlotte from Audrey and carry her to her room, fumbling for diapers and wipes. Trying to remember exactly how I've seen Rachel change one of these. Audrey looks at me strangely.

"What's wrong with you? You're acting like you don't know what you're doing." She folds her arms over her chest and even Charlotte gives me a funny look.

"Well, why don't you help me out then?" Even in my dream, I don't want to get shit all over everything.

"Fine," she says reluctantly before expertly wiping the baby's bottom and folding all the offensiveness into a neat little ball and securing it closed. She lifts Charlotte's bottom and places the clean diaper under her, sprinkling some cornstarch for good measure before cinching it up. Wow. She's really good at that. Even the baby gurgles her approval.

She holds Charlotte out to me and for a moment it doesn't register that she wants me to take the baby. Finally, I reach for her and awkwardly place her on my hip. Audrey shakes her head and walks out of the room. I wonder if she's this bitchy to Rachel in real life. I'll have to ask her when I wake up.

Rachel. We both said some terrible things last night. I run back through our fight, cringing as I recall every hurtful word. As soon as I escape from this crazy dream, I'm going to call her.

John walks down the hallway without so much as a good morning. "Hey there." I call out.

He turns around. "What?"

Okay, grouchy. I hold out the baby to him. "Can you take her downstairs?"

"Has she eaten?"

"Um, no?"

He looks at me oddly but takes her anyway. Now I can crawl back into bed and end this craziness. On my way back to the bedroom, I catch my reflection in the hall mirror and do a double take. The image looking back at me is not mine. It's Rachel's.

This can't be real. This has to be a bad dream. I pinch myself—hard. Yep, it hurts. I rush to the bathroom and wash my face. But no matter how hard I scrub, every time I look at my reflection, it's not my blue eyes staring back at me. I tug at Rachel's brown hair, hoping my blond locks will somehow be revealed underneath. I pull up Rachel's knee-length cotton nightgown searching for my body.

"How did this happen?" I say aloud, hearing Rachel's voice. I grip the edge of the white tile countertop and think back to the reunion, the awards, the fight. *Think, Casey!* What happened next? But the last thing I can remember is that bartender handing us two shots and Rachel and me making a toast.

"MOM!" The calls for me are getting louder and louder. *I'm not your mom,* I want to scream. *I'm your Aunt Casey who should be sound asleep until at least 11 a.m., maybe noon—in her* silent *high-rise apartment!* I lock the bathroom door and sink to the tile floor, not wanting to face the mirror again. What do I do? I can't hide in this tiny bathroom forever; it reminds me of my dressing room.

If I'm Rachel, then where is she? Is she me?

I start tearing through her bedroom—pulling drawers out

of her dresser, searching under the bed—desperate to find her phone. Then John reappears. "Do you hear the kids calling you?" he asks, the annoyance in his voice sharp, a look on his face to match.

"Can you handle it please?" I reply briskly, my hands inside Rachel's black evening bag finding everything except her phone. *Lip gloss, a wad of cash, the ballot.*

John's dressed in running clothes, his Nikes dangling from his right hand. He looks at his watch. "I guess I'll have to," he snaps and starts to leave before turning back. "What's your problem?"

"I'm sorry," I say, realizing I need to stop acting like a crazy person who just discovered she's in her best friend's body. "I'm just hungover. Can I have a few minutes to regroup please?" *Even though there's not enough time in this world to help me regroup from this.* I force a smile. This seems to appease him and he walks away, presumably to deal with the kids.

I finally locate the cell phone and start dialing Rachel's number before I realize that I can't call her, I'm holding her phone. *This is crazy.* I call my own cell phone number and hold my breath. Who will answer? If I've become Rachel, what's become of me?

"Hello?" The sound of my own voice answering my phone gives me the chills.

"Rachel? Is that you?" I whisper from inside her walk-in closet, rows of khaki capri pants hanging next to me.

"Casey! Thank God. Yes, it's me. What the hell is going on?"

Relief pours over me. At least I know where she is, that's she safe. And that I still exist.

"I was just calling you. Well, me," Rachel says sounding out of breath.

"I don't know what's going on. This is so strange," I say as I twist Rachel's gold wedding band and notice her ragged cuticles—chewing on them has been a bad habit of hers since middle school.

"I totally freaked out when I woke up in your bed this morning. Nice sheets, by the way." She forces a laugh. My laugh. "What are they, like five-thousand-thread count?"

"Two thousand . . . and on that note, flannel sheets? And what's with this cotton nightgown that looks like my mom's? Really, Rachel?" I pull the nightgown over my head and start looking for something else—anything else—to put on. I run my hands over the rows of bland cardigan sweaters, the stacks of Gap jeans, the shoe tree filled with slip-on tennis shoes, and debate putting that terrible nightgown back on.

"Well, I nearly had a heart attack when I woke up without any clothes on. Is that how you always sleep? I can't remember the last time I did that . . ." Rachel trails off.

Maybe that's why John's so damn cranky. Between that and the nightgown that looks like Ebenezer Scrooge should be wearing it.

I settle on a pair of workout pants and a T-shirt. Maybe I'll try to get Rachel on one of those makeover shows after we get this all figured out and switch back. *If we switch back.* But first we need to figure out how we got here in the first place.

"We need to figure out—"

Rachel cuts me off. "Why we're trapped in a bad *Freaky Friday* remake."

"Exactly . . . You're Jamie Lee Curtis by the way."

"At this point, I'll be anyone if it means I can get my life back."

"Just one thing," I say, picturing John with his running shoes in hand.

"What?"

I open the closet door and listen for more calls for Mom. "I don't know how to ask you this, but how do I convince John to take care of these kids so I can leave the house?"

"Oh God, the kids. I haven't even asked about them. How are they?"

"They're fine, I guess," I answer.

"You guess? It's seven thirty in the morning. What have you been doing?"

"Oh you know, the usual. Sleeping in. Relaxing. Realizing I'm in another person's body!"

"I need to come over there and help. They need me in the mornings. You don't understand. It's pretty chaotic."

"You can't come over here and help. You're not you, remember? And anyway, what could possibly be so chaotic?"

"You have no idea."

"Well, John's going to have to handle it. What's his deal anyway? Why does he act like you have to do everything?"

She sighs. "Careful. Don't remind me how it is. I may not want to switch back."

CHAPTER 6

....

rachel

I fling the front door open and I'm staring at myself. It's me, but it's not me. My dark hair is swept back in a neat ponytail, my cheeks flush—is that blush?—my eyelids covered in eye shadow. "Is this really happening—is that *you* inside *my* body?"

"We have to talk about this inside my apartment." Casey pushes past me. "All I need is my nosy neighbor calling Perez Hilton about this."

"Please tell me we're about to wake up from this dream." I place my hands on my new, nonexistent hips.

"I wish I could. But I just woke up at your house with a baby's diaper in my face. This is real. Shitty-diaper real." Casey slumps down on her white pillowless sofa and kicks off a pair of my running shoes that I haven't worn in months. I cringe as I notice the way the Lycra pants Casey's wearing are clinging to my thighs.

"How is she?" I self-consciously feel Casey's thighs, but they're now slim and toned, no doubt due to her daily workouts.

"Who?"

"Charlotte!"

"She has a clean diaper," Casey answers, clearly distracted, running her finger over her midcentury modern coffee table, inspecting her finger afterward. "What does my housekeeper think I'm paying her for? There's dust all over this."

"Yeah, I really hate it when that happens." I grimace, thinking about the laundry piled high next to the washing machine. Casey has a big dose of reality coming her way when she gets back to my house.

"This is insane. I'm a guest in my own home. What is happening?" Casey paces across her white stain-free rug.

I could never have a white rug in my house.

"I woke up this morning to total silence. No one was calling for me . . ."

"That's because they were calling for me!" Casey laughs. "Your house is Grand Central Station in the morning. I haven't even had coffee yet!"

I walk into Casey's sprawling kitchen, a giant island in the middle with two sinks in it—*two sinks*—and open the Sub-Zero refrigerator searching for coffee.

"I'll make you some," I say over my shoulder, the feeling of being able to take care of someone comforting me slightly.

Casey hops up on the counter and I think I see her flinch a bit, probably not used to the extra weight she's carrying.

"Did you scream when you saw yourself?"

"Bloody murder! I'm surprised someone didn't call the cops." I pour the coffee into the filter.

"A scream? It would take a lot more than that to get a reaction out of my neighbors. Nick Nolte, Wee-Man, and Dennis Rodman all have apartments in this building."

"I ran over to your full-length mirror and freaked out. My muffin top was gone!"

I watch as Casey puts her hand on my belly, feeling surreal as I stare at myself. So this is what they mean by an out-of-body experience.

"This?" Casey says, pinching at my stomach. "There's nothing here?"

There's a lot more there than should be. I was never petite, but before I had Charlotte I was in good shape and two sizes smaller. I should be exercising in those running shoes and workout pants every morning. If John can make the time to do it, why can't I? "You're sweet to say that, Casey, but I'm out of shape. You'll see. When you haul the baby up and down the stairs enough times at my house, you'll feel it." I look away, tears burning in my throat as I think of Charlotte.

Casey puts her hand over mine. "Well, hopefully I won't have to feel it. Hopefully we'll figure out how to get out of this mess and you'll be hauling your own baby in no time."

"What did we do to deserve this?" I hand Casey a cup of coffee.

Casey thinks for a moment. "I've slept with a lot of young guys."

"I'm sorry, and how is that bad again?" I smile, our banter temporarily pulling me out of the panic brewing just beneath the surface as I think about my family.

"We're two smart women. We can figure this out. Like I always say, when all else fails, turn to the movies for the answers. What happened in that body-switching flick with Matthew Perry and that kid from *High School Musical*? You should know this one; you watch crap like that with your kids all the time, right?"

Ironically it was that movie *17 Again* that Sophie and I had argued about just a few weeks ago. She was supposed to be doing her homework, but I caught her watching it. After she'd sassed me about how I shouldn't be barging into her room un-announced, I'd grabbed the laptop, slammed it shut, and then also slammed her bedroom door behind me.

"They don't switch bodies. Matthew Perry just becomes younger," I say quietly, remembering a cell phone conversa-tion I'd overheard between Sophie and one of her friends later that night. She'd called me a bitch. I'd been so upset I couldn't even tell John—things had been so rocky between us that I was afraid he'd agree with her. Maybe I had overreacted.

Am I being punished for how I treat my family?

"I guess we're on our own." Casey attempts another smile but a look of fear crosses her face, the reality now sinking in for her too, and I wonder if she's thinking what I'm thinking: what if we can't switch back?

Casey looks at me expectantly, a look I've seen before. From Audrey when she has a problem with one of her friends, from John when he's stressed about not making enough money, from myself when I worry about my marriage falling apart. She needs me to tell her it's going to be okay. "Don't worry. Like you said, we're two smart women. We've got this. Let's go over what happened last night. What's the last thing you remember?"

"The shots." Casey's eyes grow wide. "Did John spike our drinks?"

"John? Suddenly my husband has magical powers? And why would he want us to switch bodies?"

We both consider what that would mean.

"Gross," I say.

"Yeah, gross."

"The bartender!" we say in unison.

"Jinx." Casey laughs and pinches me, reminding me of her fifteen-year-old self.

"This has to have something to do with that bartender. I caught him giving me funny looks a few times last night," I say, remembering how good it felt to have a young, hot guy watching me, even if he did seem a bit off. *I really need to get out more.*

"He was also acting weird earlier in the night with me too. I thought he was just flirting at first. He was pretty hot."

"Smokin'," I say a little too quickly.

"But then he knew all these things about Patrick Sanders and was very intense when he talked about how high school reunions bring out the best and worst in people. There was this look he got on his face when he said 'the worst' like he got off on that part. On seeing people's insecurities, their failures, their longing for their lost glory days."

"And remember he was the one who brought us the shots. And what did he say?"

"That the shots would make us realize how silly we were being!" Casey says.

"We have to find him. It can't be that hard," I say, thinking that if I can track down tickets to a sold-out Selena Gomez concert, I can find him.

"At least we know his name is Brian," Casey says excitedly.

"Do you think that's his real name?" I wonder aloud.

"Bartender with magical powers or not, I know his type. He definitely gave John his real name. He wants us to find him. I can tell he gets off on all this." Casey heads toward the door. "Come on, let's go get our bartender!"

"Wait. So how did you get out of the house? Where did you tell John you were going?"

"I just told him the truth, that I needed to come over here and talk to you about last night."

"And he was fine with that?" I ask.

"Well, I didn't exactly ask him. Was I supposed to get his permission?"

"No. But Audrey needs help with her science project and Sophie has a book report due."

"And why can't John can't handle that stuff again?"

I exhale, not sure how to explain to her that I'm the reason he's so reluctant to help. That I've corrected him and nitpicked at him so much over the years about "the right way" to do this or that, that somewhere along the line he stopped offering and I stopped asking. I thought things might be different with Charlotte, but John checked out the second I challenged his arm placement while he was trying to burp her in the hospital room. But it wasn't me there now. It was Casey, someone who had a good heart, but also didn't know the first thing about being married with kids. "You have to understand, John goes to work every day so that I can stay home. And those things are my—now your—job," I say, rationalizing, even though I'm not sure how much I believe that. "So, you are going to have to suck it up, sister." I smile sweetly to take the sting off my words.

Casey snorts. "I'm not sure why your job is 24/7 and he's working bankers' hours." She looks away before asking in a small voice, "What if I can't do this?"

"You'll be fine. It's not that hard!" I lie, thinking of how exhausted I am most days. "If we're still like this tomorrow morning, and let's pray that we're not, here's what you need to know: don't let Sophie wear a short skirt to school. She'll try, she'll even fight you on it. But stand your ground. If you can, check her backpack. I caught her taking a change of clothes and some makeup to school last week. Audrey's moody. She usually wants very little to do with me. And don't give the baby any dairy. It gives her diarrhea."

"Gross." Casey frowns in disgust.

"Rule number one, you cannot be grossed out by baby shit or baby puke. It will give you away immediately . . ." She thinks for a moment. "This is going to be so hard being away from them. I miss them already."

"You even miss the shit?"

"Yes, I even miss the shit."

"You wouldn't have missed the shit this morning," she laughs. "You're going to have to give me some very detailed instructions on how to be you. I don't even know what to feed your baby." Fear washes over Casey's face.

"Don't worry, okay? For now, just go home and take care of them." I bite back the tears, my own fears taking hold. For a moment, we're frozen, both considering what it means to fake another person's life.

Casey breaks the silence. "Well, you'd better get your, I mean my, ass over to the hotel and find Brian. I'll head back to your house and try to remember something from my high school science class so I can help Audrey. Thank God for Google." She puts her hand on the doorknob but swivels around quickly. "Wait, what do I do when John tries to kiss me?"

"Don't worry. There's no chance in hell that will happen."

She looks at me, confused. Then she shrugs and leaves.

When I arrive at the hotel, I catch several people staring at me. What are they looking at? Then I remember I'm not me. I'm Casey Lee. Just twenty-four hours ago, I was cleaning spit up off my sweatshirt and now I'm a celebrity with a flat stomach in size two designer jeans.

After I'd peeled myself out of bed this morning, my head throbbing from one too many vodka somethings at the reunion, and drowsily made my way toward the bathroom, I was in a state of euphoria despite the headache. Somehow, the hangover gods had aligned, and not only was the baby sleeping in, but neither of the girls had called for me! I practically floated to the toilet as I basked in the silence. I was dreamily washing my hands, wondering when the three-piece orchestra was going to start playing, when I'd first seen Casey's face in the mirror over the sink.

I'd turned off the light and closed the door and it almost didn't register that it was *her* face, not mine, that I'd just seen. I was so fixated on getting back into my bed—I didn't remember *ever* being so comfortable (had I used a new fabric softener on the sheets?)—that I was about to slide back under the comforter when it hit me. It had not been me that I'd seen in that mirror—my brown hair hadn't been matted to my head, the dark circles that had taken permanent residence under my eyes had vanished, and was I naked? And that had not been my bathroom—I don't have a heated toilet seat, my sink is a far cry from marble, and I'd most definitely never had an official hand soap dispenser!

I'd crept back to the bathroom, my heart pounding in my ears as I turned the knob on the door. When I'd seen her face again, I'd screamed—that bloodcurdling horror movie kind—and sprinted out of the bathroom toward the floor-to-ceiling mirrored wall in Casey's closet, praying it was all just a bad dream.

I'd spun around, studying the body in front of me from every angle, my terror slowly turning to adoration as I'd analyzed my new reflection, amazed that Casey's thighs didn't rub together, her butt didn't jiggle, and her breasts still stood up on their own! Feeling creepy gawking at my best friend's body, I surveyed the closet for something to put on. Bigger than Charlotte's nursery and rivaling anything I'd seen on one of those celebrity reality TV shows, the closet was lined with shoes in every style, shelves were stacked high with jeans, hangers were draped with suits, skirts, dresses, and evening gowns—most with price tags still on them. There was an article of clothing for every occasion. So what do you wear when you've just taken over your best friend's body?

I grabbed a pair of jeans and held them up, musing that they could probably fit Sophie! I slowly slid one leg in and then the other. I prepared to do my usual deep inhale so I could suck in my stomach, but the zipper went up effortlessly. And even though I was struck by an intense fear of being trapped in Casey's body forever, I never wanted to forget the way it felt to be able to fit into a tiny pair of jeans.

I take the elevator up to the ballroom remembering last night all over again. How John grabbed my hand before we walked in. When was the last time he didn't hold my hand for show? When did our marriage take a nosedive? When did I become the woman who clicked on those online articles about how to reignite the flame in your marriage? Just the other day, I actually took one of those quizzes on the Yahoo! home page to find out if I was still attracted to my husband. I clicked the screen closed before the results appeared.

The ballroom is empty, so I ask a janitor where I can find Brian, the bartender who worked a party last night. He shrugs his shoulders and suggests the front desk.

"Miss Lee. So nice to have you back." A woman behind the desk wearing a badge that reads MANAGER gives me a toothy grin. "How can I help you?"

I smile back at her. "Well, I'm looking for an employee who worked at the high school reunion last night."

"What's wrong? Do you know the person's name? I can speak with him or her right away."

"Oh no, it was . . . nothing like that," I stammer. "His name was Brian and I wanted to personally thank him for his good service," I reply. Although I'm not sure if thanking him is exactly what I want to do.

"Was he young and blond?"

I nod. *Don't forget those brown eyes.*

The manager, probably in her early forties, smiles to herself and I wonder if she's also thinking about how handsome Brian is. As she clicks through her computer, her gold wedding band resembling my own, her brown hair also falling straight around her shoulders, her upper arms in need of Shake Weights, I wonder if she also has a husband who doesn't look at her the same way anymore.

"Here it is. Brian's schedule. You're in luck. He's in our meeting room downstairs setting up for another event."

"Thank you so much," I say and head toward the elevator.

"Oh, Miss Lee," the manager calls after me. "Can I trouble you for one more thing?"

"Of course. What is it?"

"May I have an autograph for my thirteen-year-old daughter? She'll be so excited. She watches your show all the time."

Just like my daughter Sophie. Does yours also think you're a bitch? "Sure," I say as I sign Casey's name on a piece of hotel stationery, realizing I have no idea what her work signature looks like. This could be the first of many things I'm going to have to fake.

I find Brian setting up glasses on the bar. He looks up and smiles, revealing just the hint of a dimple. Is this how all men look at Casey? I could get used to this.

"Hi. I'm—"

"I know who you are, Casey, from the reunion last night. Double Belvedere and sodas, right?"

"Uh, y-yes," I stammer, feeling the heat rise to my cheeks.

"I still can't believe you're old enough to have graduated from high school twenty years ago." His brown eyes meet mine and it's impossible to look away.

"Guilty. I'm thirty-eight. Practically old enough to be your mother." *Did I just say that out loud?*

He flashes me another smile, revealing a perfect set of teeth. "I'm quite certain my mom doesn't look like you."

I probably look a lot more like her than you realize. "So, I need to ask you a question about last night."

"Lay it on me," he says as he rolls up the sleeves of his shirt, revealing tan forearms.

"It's kind of strange."

"Try me."

"Did you put something in our shots?" I blurt out, and a woman arranging a centerpiece on a nearby table looks over.

"Like what?" Brian answers, reaching past me to grab a case of wine, the muscles in his forearms straining.

"Something magical?" I whisper, looking over again to see if the woman is listening. On my way over, I'd received a text from Casey warning me that I'd have to be discreet. That I'd have to be careful of people overhearing my conversations or, worse, taking cell phone pictures or video and sending them to the gossip sites.

"Well, if you consider purple hooters magical, then I'm guilty as charged." He breaks open the box and starts removing the bottles, lining them up neatly behind the bar.

My heart sinks. Maybe he's not involved in this at all, but I press on anyway, still praying that he is. "Something in addition to the alcohol . . . like a potion or something?"

He laughs. "What do you think I am, some kind of witch? Mixing up potions in the cauldron? Give a guy a little more credit than that."

"What do you mean?" I start to panic. The look of satisfaction on his face sends a chill up the back of my neck.

"I mean I'm a pro. I don't make a witch's brew." He walks closer to me and tickles my ear with his breath. "I cast a spell."

I grab his arm and whisper back. "So you did this to us?"

"Define 'did this to us.' What exactly did I do?" he asks.

"You hijacked our bodies," I say aggressively.

"Did I?"

"Last time I checked, I wasn't a five-foot, ten-inch woman with perky breasts and a tight ass!"

The woman arranging the centerpiece meets my eyes and I think I see a flicker of recognition. She quickly scurries out of the room and I pray it's not to call TMZ. How does Casey live like this?

"So you didn't want Casey Lee's life?"

"*No!*"

"You could've fooled me. You certainly didn't seem too happy with your own last night, accusing everyone of thinking you were the least successful when I think it was really only you who believed that about yourself." He leans back against the counter. "And Casey, she was no better, questioning her decisions while she drowned her insecurities with booze."

Casey questions her decisions too?

"Look, Brian, we both had a lot to drink and said things we shouldn't have, especially me. But it doesn't mean you had the right to fuck with Mother Nature."

"So you're saying you want your life back?"

"Of course I want it back. I have a family." My voice breaks slightly. "They need me. Don't you understand that? And right now Casey is over there trying to be me . . . doing God only knows what."

Brian narrows his eyes and frowns. "If you want your life back, you're going to have to figure out how to do it on your own. But it is possible. In fact, you already have what you need to make it happen."

"Really? That's all you've got for me? Can't we just drink two more shots and tomorrow I can wake up in my own flannel sheets with cellulite on my thighs and Casey can wake up with some hot twenty-two-year-old?"

Brian's mouth contorts into a cocky smirk as if to say, *Like me?*

"Rachel, you're missing the point. It's not about the shots. It's about *why* I brought you and Casey the shots," Brian says, suddenly seeming much older than he did only moments ago.

"Then why did you?"

"That's something you and Casey will have to figure out on your own." I start to protest, but he interrupts me.

"But listen, if you guys do figure out how to switch back, tell the real Casey to call me," he says as he flashes me a crooked smile. And even though I'm panicked, I can't help it, my knees buckle beneath me just a little.

I look down at the brightly patterned carpeting, trying to figure out how I'm going to explain to Casey that I failed. When I look back up again, Brian is gone.

CHAPTER 7

....

casey

Charlotte's cries wake me from a deep slumber in the middle of the night. *Does this baby ever freakin' sleep?* I glance resentfully at John snoring next to me. And does he *ever* get up with her?

I stumble into Charlotte's room. "What's the problem, girlfriend?" I ask her. "This is the third time you've been up." Rachel assured me the baby slept through the night (one of my first questions for her), but Charlotte has been up every few hours. It was as if she knew there was an imposter in her house. I pull her out of her crib, unsure of what to do next. When Rachel had each of her kids, I was always the first to send the latest in baby couture and a few blinged-out pacifiers. But I was so caught up in my own life that I was never around to actually help her with the everyday things. And I had a strict policy about not babysitting until they were potty trained. As I put my nose up to Charlotte's diaper to see if she needed a change, I couldn't help but think karma is a bitch.

I try bouncing her up and down against my chest, something

I could swear I'd seen Rachel do. Or maybe it was Jessica Alba. Either way, it seems to work. Charlotte calms down quickly and eventually falls asleep in my arms. I lean in and inhale her sweet baby smell. Luckily Audrey and Sophie didn't question me when I asked them to help me give her a bath earlier. At dinner, I told them I wanted to have some bonding time and they reluctantly agreed. As Audrey rubbed the shampoo into Charlotte's scalp and Sophie turned on the bubble machine, I felt there was something missing. I'd imagined them playing with their baby sister, but instead they bathed her silently, Sophie reaching back to check her phone every few minutes and Audrey braiding the same section of her own hair over and over again—something I'd have to ask Rachel about later. Although I still think they were happier to be in that bathroom than at the dining room table. Never much of a cook, I prepared a meal that was almost inedible. I could barely choke it down. Rachel always made it look so easy whenever I joined them for dinner. For a long time, I'd come every Sunday night without fail, but after I won the Emmy last year and things got busier at work, I hadn't made it as often. I'd started having Destiny call to cancel because I couldn't handle Rachel's disappointed tone; she didn't understand why I couldn't leave work on a Sunday night. I think of her having to go to work today, pretending to be me. Maybe she'll finally get it.

I was terrified to go to bed with John tonight. I couldn't remember being that scared since I had to interview Charlie Sheen during his warlock phase. What if he wanted to have sex? Rachel assured me there was no way in hell that he'd want to kiss me, let alone have sex with me. But she quickly added that if for some odd reason he did try, to tell him that I had my period. I smile as I remember back in college when he'd cover his ears like a little kid any time Rachel or I would even say the word *cramps*. Some things never change.

After the girls went to bed, I'd run up the stairs and locked myself in the bathroom. When I came out, John was already asleep or pretending to be. Either way, I was relieved. It gave me a chance to study the document from Rachel. I crawled into bed and pulled out my phone, scanning through the list of instructions she'd emailed, the subject line reading "How to be me." She'd included everything, down to when trash day was. As I read page after page, I was amazed at the sheer number of things Rachel is responsible for. *You can do this,* I told myself.

The alarm went off like a fire alarm a few hours later and I hauled myself out of bed. How does Rachel have the energy to get up so early after a sleepless night? I splashed cold water on my face, threw on a T-shirt and jeans, and scrolled through Rachel's checklist: wake up the girls, prepare Charlotte's bottle, smile if she shits.

"Audrey, get up!" I push her motionless body. "You're going to be late for school."

"Get out of my room!" she yells with a fierceness that startles me.

Is this how she treats Rachel? My protective instinct takes over. "Hey! You do *not* talk to your mother like that. Get your ass up right now, young lady!"

The word *ass* seems to snap her to attention. "Geez, stop freaking out. You're such a spaz!" But at least she gets out of bed and heads into the bathroom. Mission accomplished. Now I just have to figure out what to put in Sophie's lunch. But before I can, I hear Charlotte's cries.

"Rachel!" John calls out from the bedroom. "The baby's crying!"

Duh.

I run into her room, hoist her out of the crib, and awkwardly change her diaper, resisting every urge to call for someone, anyone, to help me. I think it may be on backward, but decide it will have to do. "Shush, shush, I'm getting your bottle right now," I mumble as I carry her down the stairs and make a mental note to Google "how to change a diaper" later.

John saunters into the kitchen as I'm trying to make Charlotte's bottle with my left hand, my right wrapped tightly around her. "Coffee?" he asks, watching me as I spill formula onto the counter. *A little help, please?*

I perk up. At least he's offering to get me the caffeine I desperately need. "Why, yes, thank you. Venti bold with sugar-free vanilla, please," I answer as I attempt to lower Charlotte into her high chair, her chubby legs refusing to bend.

He starts laughing, still watching me as Charlotte kicks the tray, clearly not wanting to sit in the damn chair. "I'm not offering. I'm asking if you've made any. And when did you start drinking Starbucks?"

My patience wears thin. "The other day," I snap, but collect myself quickly, looking around for the coffeemaker. Clearly Rachel does this for him each morning. Does everything around here, it seems. And when did she become so subservient to him? "And I guess that's where you'll be going this morning if you want coffee. I've got my hands full here." I make a wide sweeping gesture with my hands for dramatic effect.

"Fine, but you don't have to be rude about it."

I sit down at the kitchen table and look up at him. "I'm sorry, I'm just feeling really overwhelmed. I need help."

"Well, that's a first. You never seem to want my help when it comes to the kids."

"Really? I don't?" I ask. Why doesn't Rachel ask for help? Why does she think she can do it all herself? No wonder she doesn't have time to get highlights.

John puts his hand on my forehead. "Are you feeling okay? You've been acting really strange since the reunion. Are you still thinking about that award?"

I stand back up and smile brightly. "No, I'm fine, I promise. Just tired, that's all."

We're standing face-to-face and for a second I wonder if he'll kiss me. Isn't that what husbands do when they're concerned about their wives? But he turns away and grabs his briefcase by the door. "See you tonight."

"See you tonight," I echo quietly as he walks out the front door.

"Hey." Sophie comes bounding down the stairs dressed in a skirt so short it barely covers her butt.

"You're not thinking of actually wearing that to school, are you?" *When did my sweet little Sophie start dressing like a whore? I know Rachel warned me about this, but I thought she was just exaggerating.*

"What's the problem? Aunt Casey wears stuff like this on her show all the time."

"She does not! I mean she may wear a *few short things* that she can totally pull off, by the way. But she's an adult and you're a child." I think back to the minidress I wore to the reunion wondering if I *really did* pull that off.

Sophie rolls her eyes at me. "Mother, I told you, I am *not* a child anymore. I'm fourteen!"

"Well, child or not, you're not wearing that skirt to school.

Go up and change right now." I look at the digital clock on the microwave. "You guys need to leave soon or you're going to be late."

"You are *so* uncool!" She huffs out of the kitchen. "I wish you were more like Aunt Casey! I want to be just like her one day."

Oh, if you only knew.

Fifteen minutes later, I've pushed both girls out the door, wearing semiappropriate clothing, having eaten a somewhat nutritious breakfast, and with only three meltdowns between them. How have I only been awake for an hour?

Charlotte crawls over and pulls up on my legs. I pick her up and scroll through Rachel's checklist on my phone. "When exactly do I get a shower, Charlotte?" And I swear I hear her laugh at me.

CHAPTER 8

....

rachel

I stare up at the *GossipTV* offices, petrified to go inside. I begged Casey to let me call in sick, but she told me it was not an option, unless, of course, I wanted to be responsible for getting her fired. With frightening detail, she described to me how cutthroat the television business is, that even though she's been hosting the show for three years and it brings in the highest ratings for the network, there's always some twenty-one-year-old with fake boobs waiting to steal her spot. In her case, it's a bitchy little tart named Fiona. The insecurity in Casey's voice threw me off as she described how far she'd gone to prove she wasn't replaceable, once even hosting the show with a stomach flu so bad she had to run to the bathroom between every take.

How can I do this? How do I pretend to be Casey Lee? She does this every day, while I haven't read from a TelePrompTer since college. What if showing up and trying to do her job is actually worse than if I'd called in sick? Won't her cohost see right through me? She warned me Dean Anders is a total a-hole with a short man's complex who looks for any opportunity he can find to steal her spotlight and bad-mouth her to the executives. It's rumored he's sleeping with Fiona too. Just that fact alone makes my stomach hurt.

"What are you doing out here?" I recognize Casey's assistant, Destiny, a dead ringer for Beyoncé, tapping on my car window. "I've been texting you for the last thirty minutes," she says as she yanks the door open. "Ryan McKnight cheated on his wife with some stripper on their anniversary! They want you to re-cord a couple of teases about the *shocking new details* we're going to reveal on the show tonight." She rolls her eyes dramati-cally.

My head is spinning. What's a tease? I struggle to think. And who's Ryan McKnight? Isn't he in one of those boy bands?

"Why would anyone care if he cheated on his wife? Isn't he washed up?" I ask.

"Um, yeah, until he wasn't! Until he got a part in that indie film and won an Oscar and is now an A-list actor who vacations with Clooney."

I stare at her blankly. I really had been in a sleep-deprived haze since having Charlotte.

"Girl, what's wrong with you?" Destiny stares at me long and hard.

I take a deep breath as she gives me a once-over. She knows I'm not Casey. I've already blown it.

"Oh, I know what it is. You're not caffeinated, are you?" She shoves a Starbucks coffee cup in my hand and I obediently take a sip. "Come on. We've got to get you in hair and makeup and go over the script."

I reluctantly follow her, my heart pounding in my chest as I think about what lies ahead. Now's probably not a good time to reveal I have stage fright. It's been more than sixteen years since I've been in front of a camera, and I'm certain it won't be just like riding a bike, like Casey promised it would.

The next hour is a whirlwind as makeup is caked on my face, script after script is shoved at me (there's a new color for every revision!), and getting my mic pac put on is more invasive than a full-body pat-down at LAX. About ten minutes before I have to go on camera I sneak off to the bathroom to try to calm my nerves. Luckily I've been to the offices before so I know my way around.

"I look like a man in drag," I say to the mirror.

"Don't be so hard on yourself." A tiny blonde walks out of the stall. I know instantly she must be Fiona. "It's normal for older women like you to have to wear more."

Women like me. My heart sinks for Casey. She warned me that Fiona is a bitch, but I had no idea it was so blatant or hurtful.

She smiles, revealing a set of teeth so straight and bright white that they look almost as fake as her boobs.

I stare at Fiona as she fluffs her platinum hair in the mirror and I decide I'm not going to let anyone talk to my best friend like that. I don't know what Casey would do in this situation, but I know what I would do. "Well, maybe if you're ever on camera, you'll know what it feels like," I hiss, and walk out of the bathroom, momentarily forgetting all about my stage fright.

"Five, four, three, two . . ." The stage manager points to me and I freeze. Suddenly all eyes in the studio are fixated on me.

"Is something wrong?" A man wearing a headset—I decide

he must be a producer—steps out from next to one of the cameras and walks over to me. I'm momentarily taken aback because he's not acting rude and aloof like almost everyone I've encountered so far today. Even the production assistants have an attitude!

"I'm sorry. I was waiting for the . . . one?"

The studio erupts in laughter and my face burns with embarrassment. *I knew I couldn't handle this,* I think as I stare at the crew members' contorted faces, my humiliation growing. Suddenly I'm fourteen again, with a strand of toilet paper a mile long sticking to my pink pump as I walk into the freshman formal dance.

"We hardly have time for jokes," Casey's cohost, Dean Anders, says loudly, not bothering to hide his irritation. I look down at the box he's standing on, shocked at how much arrogance he has for someone so short.

The producer shoots Dean a pleading look. It's clear he's been in the middle of this before.

"You ready to go again, Casey?" the producer asks.

The crew members, no longer laughing, now seem irritated. I hear one of the cameramen mutter under his breath, "We're going to end up in overtime and lunch will be cut short."

"Want a bottle of water?" Destiny calls from the side of the stage.

I nod.

"Don't forget a straw. Her lipstick will take thirty minutes to fix if she drinks directly from it," the makeup artist says curtly.

I take a long drink, smiling at the makeup artist through my straw. The smell of the lunch from the craft service area wafts onto the stage—*is that lasagna?*—and I notice the same cameraman sigh as he looks in the direction of the food.

I hand my bottle of Fiji to Destiny, the makeup artist blots around my mouth, the hairdresser pulls a comb from her fanny pack and expertly whisks a stray strand away from my face, and the stage manager counts me down again. "Five, four, three, two . . ."

I stare at the blinking red light and start to read what's on the TelePrompTer. "Welcome to *GossipTV*. I'm Casey Lee and . . ." Suddenly the words on the screen are moving faster than I can read them and I stop, looking down at the black piece of tape on the stage beneath my feet, or my mark, as I was reminded by the stage manager when I stepped over it before we started taping.

"I'm sorry," I say quietly, trying to ignore the crew's glares.

"You've got to be kidding me," Dean chides. "I've told you people a hundred times that I should read the intro copy."

I stare at the dozens of video monitors surrounding me, some with the *GossipTV* logo plastered across them and others filled with video of the celebrities I read about in the script they gave me this morning. In the largest screen in the center is footage of Ryan McKnight performing on stage at one of his concerts. What am I doing here standing on this set, playing TV announcer? I knew I couldn't pull this off. The hundreds of lights hanging above me are hot and overpowering and a bead of sweat rolls down the side of my face. The makeup artist runs out and blots it with a sponge and the producer pulls me aside.

"You okay?" He seems genuinely concerned. I study his face. He appears to be about my age and he's cute with blond hair and kind brown eyes. Casey's never mentioned him.

"Yeah, I'm fine. Just a little out of it today," I reply, resisting the urge to scratch my nose.

"Do you need to take five?" he asks slowly and I can tell he's hoping I'll say no.

I look at Dean staring at me smugly from on top of his box, a different makeup artist applying something to his eyes—is that eyeliner? And think of Casey. I can't give Dean the satisfaction of watching her screw this up. "No, I'm ready, I'll get it right this time."

I close my eyes and visualize myself reading the Tele-PrompTer flawlessly. The stage manager counts me down again. "Five, four, three, two . . ."

"Welcome to *GossipTV*. I'm Casey Lee and we've got the freshest scoop coming your way. Tonight, we'll reveal the shocking new details on Ryan McKnight's steamy night with stripper Ashley Jones. What she says *really* happened in that hot tub." The words start to flow and before I know it, I'm finished.

"That's the Casey we know." The producer smiles at me.

"Hey, Charlie, should I run these scripts down to the booth for tonight's show?" a young kid, probably an intern, asks shyly.

So Charlie's his name. I look at his hand. No wedding ring.

"Nice job. See you later when we tape the show," Charlie says as he walks out of the studio.

"Hopefully Ryan McKnight will keep his pants on until then," I call after him. And I can't help but wonder why Casey has never mentioned the only nice guy who seems to work here.

Several hours later when I'm back in Casey's office, I'm surprised at how giddy I feel as I prop my sore feet up on Casey's oak desk. I lean back in her ergonomic chair feeling every muscle in my body finally start to relax as I look around. Her Emmy is sitting high on a shelf. What it must feel like to have an Emmy! I remember her speech—she let the F-word slip out, but quickly made a joke about not winning an award for social etiquette.

Casey's walls are covered with dozens of framed pictures of her posing with celebrities. Casey and Jennifer Aniston. Casey and Jennifer Lopez. Casey and Donald Trump. I smile when I notice Audrey and Sophie's school pictures tacked up on a small corkboard next to her computer. I run my finger over Charlotte's birth announcement pinned below the photos of the girls and wonder what would've happened if I'd told John about my visit to the headhunter. If I hadn't deleted my résumé off the computer as I thought of the pregnancy test in the bathroom trash can. Would I have my own oak desk somewhere by now? I assumed John would've told me to forget it, that the cost of day care would be more than I'd make at some entry-level job. But maybe that's just what I told myself so I didn't have to put myself out there again.

I sink back in the chair and close my eyes. I got off to a rocky start during the promo tapings this morning, but I studied the script intently all afternoon and even closed Casey's office door for a while and practiced reading it out loud several times. I really got into the groove when we taped the show that will air tonight. With each compliment from Charlie and other members of the crew (even that cameraman seemed to come around after we broke for lunch—maybe he was just hungry?), I became more confident. And by the end, I was even ad-libbing a little bit, equal parts irritating and surprising Dean, who clearly wasn't used to on-air banter with Casey.

I found a rhythm, remembering how I used to read the TelePrompTer with so much ease in college that it would get on Casey's nerves. Reading the Prompter wasn't her strong suit and I remember how she struggled with it for two semesters before she finally got it down. Now with an Emmy under her belt, it's hard to believe she ever had to work at it.

And it felt great getting so much praise and positive attention from the staff and crew. I couldn't remember the last time I'd even heard a thank-you from someone in my family.

But even so, as I drive over to my house for dinner, I can't believe how much I miss them. I felt an ache in my chest when I didn't hear the baby cry this morning. I even missed having to wake up Audrey. I was so homesick I would've welcomed a fight with Sophie over what an appropriate bra for a fourteen-year-old looks like. Not to mention the anxiety that kept me up half the night. What if Casey leaves something small on the ground that Charlotte can choke on? Or what if she doesn't tighten her car seat straps after she buckles her in? And will she make sure that Sophie isn't turning into a future member of *The Bad Girls Club*?

And then there's John. Dare I say I actually miss him too? Unless he was traveling for work, I rarely went more than a day without seeing him. And there's a comfort sleeping next to him in the bed each night. Although having Casey's California king bed all to myself last night wasn't so bad either.

I open the door to my house and hear the familiar buzz of the family chatter in the kitchen. I fight back the tears as I walk in to discover Audrey and Casey laughing in a way I can't remember laughing with her. And I'm struck by a horrible thought: Is Casey doing a better job than me? Struggling to find the confidence I had just an hour earlier at *GossipTV,* I walk into the kitchen and plaster a smile across my face. It doesn't matter how I feel. I have to be Aunt Casey now.

CHAPTER 9

....

casey

I rifle through Rachel's soft leather satchel to find the checklist I finally printed out because I was referencing it so much. I'd also given Rachel instructions on how to live my life, but mine were verbal and consisted of not much more than the warning, "Just don't get me fired." Rachel had taken her instruction list to the next level, even making me practice CPR on one of Charlotte's dolls. "I'm not an idiot!" I told her, but deep down I did worry that something terrible might happen on my watch.

The weight of being entrusted with the most important people in Rachel's life is overwhelming. Looking down at the weekly calendar she included in my packet, I find today's date and see that I have a play date at the park with someone named Hilary and her daughter, Melissa. Okay. I can do this. How hard can a play date be? I wish my life consisted of play dates all day, although I'd prefer to play with a twenty-five-year-old with a baby face, not an actual baby.

The first order of business is getting Charlotte into this

damn stroller. I've interviewed some of the biggest celebrities, clawed my way up one of the trickiest ladders in the world, yet I can't figure out how to work the buckles on a baby carriage.

After ten minutes, sweat is running down my back and Charlotte is on the verge of a meltdown, so I give up and decide to carry the baby to the park instead. How hard can it be? I put her on one hip, sling her enormous diaper bag over my shoulder, and start to walk the five blocks that quickly feel like five miles. I have to stop and readjust Charlotte and the damn bag—that weighs more than she does—every few feet. "Do we really need to put your entire house in one bag? Is the kitchen sink going in here too?" I had joked to Rachel.

But she was adamant. "Trust me, Casey. Never leave the house unprepared. It's the first rule of parenting."

And for the most part, I listened. But not all the items would fit, so I just made an executive decision on what was really necessary for a trip to the playground and I ditched the rest. I can't even imagine how heavy it would've been if it had *everything* in it.

I look around for the woman that Casey described. Tall, thin, with long blond hair. I see a woman matching her description and pick up my pace. I'm about to call out to her when I hear Rachel's name being called from behind me and I turn to see another taller, thinner, blonder woman walking toward me. She's wearing a beautiful heather gray wrap sweater and matching TOMS flats.

"Where are you going?" She looks at me like I've gone crazy. "We always sit over there." She points to a grassy area by the slide with her perfectly manicured hand.

"Oh, sorry, Hilary. I just thought I saw someone I knew."

"You're such a space cadet," she says condescendingly. I try not to judge her too quickly. From what Rachel has told me, she's one of her best mom friends. And Rachel wouldn't be friends with someone who treats her like crap, right? From my experience in her body so far, she's got John and the kids doing that.

John. I made the mistake of trying to talk to her about him on the phone this morning, but she wasn't having it. "Casey, please don't start judging my marriage. You've been there for one day, for Christ's sake."

"I'm not judging. I just want to know if he's going to lift a finger while I'm here."

"Don't count on it," she said, and quickly changed the subject back to how we could get our lives back. After her conversation with the bartender, we were no closer to figuring out how to do this and we were both starting to panic that we might be stuck in each other's lives—and bodies—for the long haul.

"Remember when Jamie Lee Curtis let her daughter miss their engagement party to go be in that band contest and then her daughter gave her blessing for Jamie Lee Curtis to marry Mark Harmon? That's how they got to change back."

"Yes, but this is real life, not some crappy remake of a crappy movie."

"True," she replied.

"Plus," I continued, "what's the lesson here? Being in your body, in your role as supermom, is just reinforcing why I haven't had kids."

"Okay, they're not *that* bad," she said defensively.

"Oh really? Does Audrey scream at you like that every morning, or was it just my lucky day? And when did Sophie decide she wants to be the next Britney Spears?"

"She wants to be like you, Casey."

"Even worse!" We both laughed.

I sit down on the colorful quilt Hilary spread out and try to relax. *Keep the topics simple,* Rachel warned.

"So how was your reunion?" Hilary jumps right in as she carefully unpacks the applesauce I'm quite sure she pureed herself. "I'm dying to hear every last detail!"

"It definitely had its share of ups and downs," I say truthfully as I set Charlotte down on the blanket.

She lowers her voice and leans in. "Oh, what did Casey do this time?"

I'm taken aback. Had Rachel talked about me to Hilary? Why would she assume that I'd be responsible for the ups and downs? "Why would you think Casey was involved?"

"Oh, come on. I know sometimes you get frustrated with how obsessed with work she is. A reunion is a place that can bring out the worst in people. Especially a D-list celebrity with something to prove."

I try to react calmly. *D-list, my ass!* "Well, first of all, since she mainly only interviews A-listers, I'd put her on the B-list at least, especially considering her Emmy win. And I know she's a workaholic, but she still really cares about me, about what's going on in my life." And that was true. Rachel was still the most important person in my life. But did I ever stop and tell her that? Or was I as bad as John and the kids were? Taking her for granted. Even being Rachel for just one day, I was realizing how out of touch I had become with her. And how little I'd been there for her over the past few months. How Destiny had been right, yet again. God, I hated *and loved* that about her.

"Well, you've really changed your tune about Casey." She adds formula to a bottle and shakes it up. "Good for you." Her words seem empty.

I'm about to ask her specifically what the hell Rachel's been saying about me when I smell something foul. I look over at Charlotte, who has a very serious look on her face. Like she's trying to come up with the answer to something really complicated, like how to solve global warming or understand why Paris Hilton is still considered a celebrity.

"Oh, someone's got poopy face!" Hilary sings in a high-pitched voice.

There's a face?

I pick up Charlotte carefully and quickly realize that this is not any ordinary poop. It's like a nuclear explosion that seeped all over the Burberry outfit I bought for her a few months back and fished out of the back of her closet this morning.

"Oh, shit!" I shout.

"Rachel!" Hilary cries out and covers her baby's ears. "Language!"

"Sorry," I stammer as I frantically dig through the diaper bag to find the wipes. I pull them out and lay Charlotte on the quilt quickly, remembering too late that I should've put a changing pad down first. As I pull her pants off, poop spills out onto Hilary's blanket and Charlotte's poopy face has turned into a full-fledged grin. I smile, remembering Rachel's warning that I'd better not let anyone see me sweat when it came to handling a number-two situation. Especially not a mom friend.

Hilary moves her things away, afraid of what might happen when I open the diaper. *You're not the only one who's afraid, sister.*

Ten disgusting minutes and a whole package of wipes later,

I've got the problem under control. But now I understood why Rachel was so insistent that I pack an extra set of clothes. Too bad I didn't listen.

After giving Hilary an awkward apology for getting poop on her blanket, blaming my amateur diaper-changing skills on a sleepless night, I grab Charlotte, clad only in a diaper, and make the walk of shame to the car, the $250 Burberry outfit I bought for her now lying in the bottom of a park trash can.

"Stop laughing!" I beg Rachel later as I tell her the story. We've locked ourselves in the den with Charlotte, going over every detail of each other's day. Thankfully, she brought take-out with her for dinner and saved everyone from my cooking. I think the kids were wondering why their Aunt Casey had A) been thoughtful enough to bring dinner and B) seemed so incredibly overjoyed to see them. It was the first time we'd all been together in many months, and given our old switcheroo, I'd say it was awkward at best.

"Mom, can you pass the pasta?" Sophie asked me.

Rachel sprang out of her seat to grab it and I gave her a look and took it myself. "Here you go," I said as I set it in front of her.

"Make sure you have some vegetables with that," Rachel added. Everyone at the table looked at her like she had two heads.

"Aunt Casey, since when do you care what we eat?" Audrey laughed.

"Yes, Aunt Casey," I said pointedly. "I'm perfectly capable of making sure the kids eat properly."

"Sorry," she said and poked her fork around her plate. "Just trying to help."

"You can help by giving us all the latest scoop on Ryan Mc-Knight!" Sophie chimed in. "Was he really cheating with that hooker in the hot tub?"

"Sophie!" Rachel and I scolded her in unison. I gave her another look. *Let me handle this. I can do it. Just trust me.*

"That's inappropriate dinner conversation," I said to Sophie.

"Whatever." She rolled her eyes at me and pushed her plate away.

I could feel Rachel's eyes burning into the side of my head. She wanted me to do something. But what? Did people still send kids to their room? I was trying to decide what to do when John interrupted me. "You are not allowed to talk to your mother that way. Hand over your cell phone for the night."

"Dad! That is so unfair!" Sophie screamed as she got up from the table, grabbed her cell phone out of her backpack, and slammed it onto the table before running upstairs to her room and slamming the door too.

Relieved, I turned to John. "Thank you," I said as I touched his arm.

He looked surprised at my gesture. "You're welcome."

Rachel cleared her throat next to me. "Ahem."

"Sorry," I whispered to her. And then when we realized the rest of the family was staring at me, I added, "I mean, sorry, you had to see that."

"It's totally fine," she'd said. "I'm sure she does it *all the time*."

"I hope not," I said out loud before I could stop myself. Thankfully, everyone started laughing and I joined in, letting them think I was in on the joke.

• • •

In the privacy of the den, I finally get the chance to find out how things went for Rachel at *GossipTV*. "So, tell me every detail about your day." I try to sound perky, not wanting to give away the fact that I'm terrified she got me fired.

Rachel bites her bottom lip and stares off for a moment. "I think I did pretty well. Like you said, it was kind of like riding a bike; it just came back to me."

I exhale in relief. "I'm happy for you," I say, although I'm happier for me. That job is all I have and I can't afford to lose it. "That must have been fun, to get back out there."

"It was," she says slowly. "It reminded me that I used to be good at something other than being a mom." Before I can comment, she adds, "Charlie seems nice."

"He is. You can trust him." Charlie and I had worked together for years. He was one of the best producers around and one of the few people on the show who I knew had my back. I decide not to mention our history to Rachel. No matter what happened between us, I know he'll still look out for me, for her.

"Why have you never mentioned him?" she asks with a look I've seen before.

"Don't even go there. Just because he's the *one* nice guy who works in the studio does not mean he's the right guy for me."

She laughs. "Okay, okay, I get it. So let's talk about Fiona then. Oh. My. God. She was so mean today. I know you warned me, but I had no idea how bad it really was."

"She wants my job. She's a barracuda. Be very careful with her," I say, trying not to think that if Rachel can't pull this off, if she can't step into my shoes and do a great job, I could lose everything to Fiona. I don't tell her this, not wanting to put more pressure on her than I already have. Rachel had always been right at home in front of the camera at our broadcasting stations in high school and college. I prayed that Rachel was right and that it all came back to her today. We were about to find out. I pick up the remote control. "It's going to start."

Rachel doesn't seem to hear me. "It just seems like a sad way to be, surrounded by people always wanting you to fail," she says quietly as she play-kisses Charlotte, who was overjoyed to see her when she walked in the door earlier, confusing John, who made a comment that Charlotte sure seemed unusually excited to see Auntie Casey. Not surprising, considering I can't remember the last time I'd scooped Charlotte up in my arms before the switch. It was much easier for me to focus my attention on Sophie and Audrey than it was to hold a squirming baby who could always sense I was uncomfortable.

"I've never really thought about it like that," I say, clicking on the TV. "It's just the way things are in the business. You can't afford to think about it too much."

"I guess not," Rachel responds, but I can tell that she doesn't really understand. The theme music for *GossipTV* starts playing. "So . . . are you ready to see my television debut?" she asks cautiously and I can't tell if she's asking herself or me.

I don't answer as the opening credits of *GossipTV* start and I try not to cringe as I see a version of myself give a megawatt smile and start speaking.

CHAPTER 10

....

rachel

The show starts and as my face appears on the screen, I nervously await Casey's reaction. This is her career. Her livelihood. What if she thinks I screwed up? After everything she's told me and what I've now seen firsthand about her job, I would never forgive myself if I did anything to jeopardize her career, or worse, if I disappointed her.

We sit in silence.

As I watch, I see the mistakes, the flaws, the places my eyes moved back and forth, making it obvious that I was reading the TelePrompTer. I see the smoke everyone was blowing up my ass earlier. I feel so stupid that I believed their praise. I hadn't so much as stood in front of a camera in forever and they called me great. Fantastic. I think someone even used the word *magnificent*. Of course the crew would never tell me if I sucked. Isn't that how this business worked? Air kisses with a side of bullshit?

Dean complained about me the entire time, but I thought it was just Dean being a jerk. Looks like he was right.

Casey grabs the remote and hits pause. "Wow," is all she says. Then she repeats it several times, looking stunned.

I wait for Casey as she tries to compose herself. But I'm ready to take my lumps like a man. I deserve them.

"You were . . ." She pauses and stares down at the frayed edge of the orange rug I'd been so proud to buy after reading it was the "it" color of the season.

"It's okay, you can be honest. I deserve it."

"You were really, really good." She says the word *good* so quietly I almost don't hear it.

"Really?" Now I'm the one who's stunned.

"Really," she says flatly.

Then where is the smile? The thank-you? The relief? "But there were so many mistakes. You saw them, I know you did."

"Well, yeah, I saw some. But it's like you've been doing it for years. How long has it been since you've been in front of a camera?" Her face contorts as she calculates.

"Since Audrey was born," I say.

"Over sixteen years and you walk out there and handle it just like me?" Her voice is shaky.

"Isn't that what you wanted?" I bite my cuticle.

"Don't do that." Casey swats my hand away from my mouth. "That's a fifty-dollar manicure you're ruining," she scolds.

I look at my image paused on the TV screen. "I don't get it, don't you want me to do a good job?"

She starts to say something, but thinks better of it. "No, I do. I do want you to do a good job. That's what we need. To keep up appearances."

I can tell she's bothered, but I decide to let it go.

"How long is this going to go on? How long are we going to be held hostage in each other's bodies?" She sighs and lies back on my faded tan couch covered with stains I've meant to clean for ages. Just days ago, I scolded Sophie for spilling soda on it. "Great. All we need is one more stain!" I'd yelled.

"The baby spills stuff all the time and you don't care. Your precious angel can do no wrong!" Sophie shot back, her eyes filled with tears. I'd sat there stunned, my voice caught in my throat, wondering if that was really how she felt.

When John and I had told her and Audrey that we were pregnant—dangling I'M A BIG SIS T-shirts in front of their faces—they weren't thrilled, but I'd been prepared for that reaction from the research I'd done online. What I hadn't been prepared for were my own conflicted feelings as the girls fired off questions I didn't know how to answer. With the shirts balled up in their laps, they interrogated us. Would I have to share a room? Would I have to babysit? And then maybe the hardest question of all: Why?

It didn't help things that my pregnancy was hard and I pretty much slept my way through it. And then once Charlotte was born, she had demanded a lot more of my attention than I'd anticipated. And I'd missed a lot: the opening night of Sophie's last play; the deadline to mail in the money for a trip Audrey wanted to take with her class to Washington, D.C. And I'd clearly missed the resentment Sophie—and probably Audrey too—had been feeling.

What I wouldn't give now to apologize to Sophie for losing my cool over a spill. I wish I'd hugged her and told her I was sorry for not being there for her, for being too hard on her.

I look at Casey, still waiting for my answer. "I don't know how long this is going to go on," I say. "The bartender was so confusing and cryptic."

"We need to go back and talk to him again." Casey sits up quickly.

"Do you really think he'll be there? He disappeared into thin air. Remember? And when I went back to the manager to find out more about him, she had no memory of ever talking to me about a bartender named Brian. She said no Brian had ever worked at the hotel. She didn't even remember the autograph I signed for her daughter."

"Let's go back over what Brian said. Maybe we can figure this out," Casey says.

I sigh. "We've been over this."

"I know, but maybe we missed something," she says.

"He didn't say much, just that it was possible to get our lives back, but we were going to have to figure out how. And that the answer is within us."

"That's helpful, Brian." Casey laughs.

"I know. What the hell?"

"But maybe if it was that easy to find him the first time, we can track him down again. And when we do we'll force him to fix this." Casey crosses her arms over her chest.

"Hey, I could flash him one of your boobs, seeing as he's really into you, by the way. He was totally hitting on you the entire time I was asking him how to switch back!"

We laugh and then both fall silent when reality sets in that it really isn't funny.

"Can I change the subject?" I ask.

"Please!" Casey says.

"I've been planning this thirty-ninth birthday party for John and—"

She cuts me off. "Thirty-ninth? Who plans a thirty-ninth birthday party?"

"I know, I know. It's kind of ridiculous. But he's so freaked out about turning forty that there's no way I can throw him a fortieth. So I'm going to surprise him with a thirty-ninth. Something he'll never expect."

She thinks for a minute. "Isn't his birthday coming up in just a few weeks?"

"Yeah . . ."

"Why don't I know about this?" I ask, feeling hurt that she didn't bring me in on the secret.

"You do; well, Destiny does. It's in your calendar according to her."

"So is it all planned then?"

"Not exactly. I haven't done everything."

"Well, you have a venue, right? And the invitations have been sent out?" Casey sits up tall.

"If a *save the date* email counts, then yes, I've told people when it is."

"Rachel!"

"We don't all have assistants, you know. I have a baby, two moody teenagers, and there's a lot going on. There are days when getting a shower is a miracle."

"Um, I know. Look at this hair." She pulls at my limp locks.

"Not so easy when your hairdresser isn't there to do it for you, is it?" I laugh.

"Whatever. Listen, about this party that I guess *I'm* now planning. It's been forever since I've coordinated more than my weekend outfits. Destiny handles all this kind of stuff for me. Maybe she can help! You can ask her for a favor tomorrow. She won't like it, but she'll do it."

"I don't know," Rachel says. "I feel bad asking her. She already seems to have so much on her plate."

"You think I can do it by myself?" Casey challenges. "You're going to be way too busy to help me. And it's not like I can ask John."

Seeing the overwhelmed look on her face, I back down. "Okay, I'll ask her tomorrow. Maybe she can at least help finalize some of the details."

Just then the television pops off pause and Dean is announcing how much Tom Cruise's movie made at the box office over the weekend. I look over at Casey, who seems tense as she watches, so I grab the remote and turn the power off.

I look at the clock. Even though I don't want to, I should leave soon so Casey can make sure the girls' homework is done and try to get them to bed at a reasonable hour. I wonder, what if Charlotte decides to wake up in the middle of the night again because she's teething? I start to get teary.

"What is it?" Casey notices my face.

"What if we can't figure out how to change back?"

"I don't know," is all she says.

·············

casey

My checklist for John's surprise party seems to be getting longer by the minute, mostly because of Rachel's urgent texts every few hours reminding me to check this or call on that. Considering the last party I threw was in college and consisted of thirty of us standing around a keg with a bowl of Doritos, I'm feeling a bit out of my league. I've attended more fabulous parties than most, but I've never had a hand in actually planning them. I would just show up with my latest man candy on my arm and drink expensive champagne, never giving one thought to all the hard work that was involved to make it so perfect.

But surprisingly, like so many other new things I've tried since becoming Rachel Cole, I'm getting the hang of it. Charlotte is no longer waking up every three hours; she seems to have accepted the fact that she's stuck with a knockoff of her real mom. She's been the only one in the family who seems to be questioning my true identity, touching my face often, and seeming as uneasy in my arms as I am holding her. Everyone else has accepted this slightly inept version of Rachel with little or no thought, and I've found myself wondering if they just aren't paying attention anymore. The thought makes me sad for Rachel and angry with myself for being one of the people in her life who hasn't been more checked in. It's easy to take Rachel for granted, to count on the fact that she'll always be there for you even if you don't call for weeks.

I accomplish a personal record this morning, not only getting the kids off to school and Charlotte dressed in more than a onesie, but even figuring out that damn coffeemaker so John could have his precious cup of morning java. It wasn't exactly a venti bold from Starbucks, but the fact that I brewed it myself made it taste even better to me.

One thing I haven't quite figured out is John and Rachel's relationship. As their self-proclaimed third wheel for many years, I always thought I knew them well as a couple. But now, living her life, being her, makes me wonder if I ever knew anything at all. And every time I try to ask Rachel about it, she blows me off and tells me not to worry about it. But I do. I worry that Rachel and John are living like strangers under one roof. When I pushed her, Rachel told me that this is just how it is, that she and John spend so much energy making sure that Audrey's grades are college worthy, that Sophie isn't a hot mess, that Charlotte isn't going to choke on something random, that they just don't have any energy left for each other. And to be honest, I can understand what she means after being here for only a week. This life is exhausting.

I reach up and touch my greasy hair and try to remember when I last washed it. For someone whose personal upkeep has always been a huge part of her life, I've really let myself—or rather, Rachel—go. I finger the list of emergency numbers that

Rachel gave me. She said I could call Jan, the babysitter, if it was a 911 situation. Well, if bad hair isn't an emergency, I don't know what is, so I pick up the phone.

Three hours later, I emerge from the salon a new person. I broke into my email account and sent an urgent message to Destiny to pull every string she had to get Rachel an appointment at Anya's for the works—ASAP. Highlights, waxing, a facial, everything under the sun. Oh, and I told her to be sure to charge it to my account. I didn't want to be responsible for giving John a heart attack. As a regional manager for a large pharmaceutical company, he does well, affording Rachel to stay home and live a very comfortable life. But Anya's Day Spa is a whole different level. The bill for all the services would definitely make his head spin.

The valet pulls up with my car and I'm so intoxicated from my spa experience that I overtip him. He looks from my dirty minivan to the twenty-dollar bill in his hand in disbelief. Glancing in the rearview mirror, even though I still look like Rachel, I feel more like myself than I have in days. *You can thank me later, Rachel.*

My phone rings and I answer the private number, hoping it's her. I can't wait to tell her how fabulous she looks.

"Hello?" I sing.

"Mrs. Cole?" an unfamiliar voice asks.

"Yes, how may I help you?"

"This is Vice Principal Stone from Oakwood Middle School. We want to let you know that Sophie did not show up to fifth period today."

I start to panic. Has something happened to her? Could she have been kidnapped? "Oh my God," I say to him. "What do we do next?" I ask. Call the police? Search the local hospitals? I think of how I'm going to explain to Rachel that one of her kids was kidnapped while I was on all fours getting a full Brazilian wax by a woman named Titi.

"Well, Mrs. Cole, as I told you the last five times she's ditched this class, she's going to fail algebra if she doesn't start coming regularly."

"Ditching? She's ditching school?" I say incredulously. "Are you freakin' serious?" First slutty clothes, now this? What was going on with her? Has Rachel lost all control over her?

He pauses. "Mrs. Cole, are you okay? This isn't the first time this has happened. As we discussed before, I called you directly without getting your husband involved."

"I didn't want John involved? Why?" I realize I've said this out loud.

Principal Stone chuckles, "I learned a long time ago not to ask questions like that. But you told me that you preferred to handle it yourself and not to bother him with these matters." He pauses and I can hear him shuffling papers on his desk. "Are you sure you're okay?"

Why would she keep things like this from John? "Yes, I'm fine. I can promise you Sophie will be attending *all* of her classes tomorrow."

"Very well," he says. "You can let her know she has a week of detention waiting for her when she does return to school."

That's not all she has waiting for her, I think. *Wait until she gets home.* I consider calling Rachel, but decide against it. I can handle this. Plus, she's taping right now and I don't want to mess up her mojo. She's been doing my job surprisingly well. In fact, there's a small part of me—make that a big part—that's hurt that no one can tell the difference. I worked my ass off, sacrificed so much to get where I am. And after a sixteen-year hiatus, Rachel steps into my shoes and they fit perfectly. Maybe I'm even more replaceable than I thought.

I drive home and pay the babysitter in a haze. What am I going to say to Sophie? Do I play good cop or bad cop? I pace around the kitchen as Charlotte watches me curiously. "What do you think?" I ask her. She smiles and claps her hands and suddenly I know what I have to do.

Later that afternoon, Sophie saunters in the door like nothing's happened, Audrey trailing closely behind her.

She stops in her tracks when she sees who's waiting for her in the living room. "Dad, what are you doing home?"

I walk over to Audrey and hand her Charlotte. "Can you take her upstairs while we chat with your sister?"

Audrey, seeing the serious expression on my face, takes Charlotte silently out of my hands, but does a double take. "What did you do to your hair?"

Thrilled that someone has finally noticed, I respond, "Oh, just a few highlights, that's all."

"Interesting," is all she says as she turns and heads upstairs.

Before I can determine if that was a compliment or not, John is already tearing into Sophie. "You better start talking *right now* about where you've been all afternoon," he says as he reaches into her backpack and pulls out a dress that looks like it could fit Charlotte. "And then you can explain what *this* is and why you were wearing it."

Sophie's eyes are as big as saucers, and it reminds me of when she was just a toddler, so sweet and innocent. I know you're not supposed to have favorites, but Sophie has always been mine. Her fear quickly turns to anger. "Nothing, Dad!

Just hanging out with some friends. I hate algebra! That's why I never go!"

"What do you mean you never go?" he asks and turns to me. "Is this not the first time this has happened?"

"No, it's not," I sigh.

"Why haven't you told me about it?" he says curtly, his anger turning on me. "What the hell? I'm their father. I need to know what's going on!"

Trying to calm him, I walk over to him and speak softly. "Well, I'm telling you now. We can discuss why I didn't tell you later. But at the moment, we need to deal with what happened today," I say, nodding back at Sophie. "Listen, I hated algebra too—" I start.

"You always told me you loved math," she interrupts.

Damn. That's right. Rachel was a math nerd.

"Well, maybe *hate* is a strong word," I begin again. "But I did struggle with it at your age. And you know who really couldn't stand it?"

"Who?" she asks, looking down. I'm losing her again.

"Your Aunt Casey."

"Really?" Sophie looks back up at me.

"Yep, she absolutely hated it. But you know what? She still showed up every day." I try to read her face, to see if my words are having any impact.

"But like Aunt Casey ever uses algebra now, Mom."

"True," I say. I can feel John's eyes on me. He's wondering how I'm going to handle this. "But if she hadn't passed algebra, she couldn't have graduated from high school. And if she hadn't graduated from high school, she wouldn't have gone to college. And if she hadn't gone to college, she wouldn't be where she is today." I think about Rachel not finishing college, not getting to where she wanted to go.

"I guess that makes sense," Sophie says, then pulls her phone out of her pocket and starts to play with it.

"I'll take that." John grabs it from her without argument. "You can have it back in a week." He puts it onto the kitchen counter and turns back around. "Do we need to hire you a tutor?"

"Maybe." Sophie seems embarrassed. "I'm just so lost. I don't even want to try. It's useless."

"Maybe your mom can help you with your homework each night," John offers.

"I think the tutor thing sounds good," I say quickly, the thought of trying to determine what X is making me feel queasy already. "Right?" I ask Sophie. She looks at me oddly but nods, obviously wanting the conversation to be over.

John gently pulls her up from the couch by her arms for a hug. "Listen, I love you. But if you do this again, I'm taking away your phone for good." He pulls back and looks her directly in the eye. "Do you understand?"

"Yes."

"Okay, go to your room and start on your homework." He dismisses her and she runs up the stairs, taking them two at a time.

"Well, that went well, don't you think?" I ask when she's gone.

"We'll see," he says. "You never know with these kids."

"Tell me about it." I laugh and walk over to the kitchen counter and grab an unopened bottle of red wine. "Care for a drink?"

"Seriously?" he asks, looking at his watch.

"It's five o'clock somewhere." I smile.

"Are you just trying to distract me from the fact that Sophie's been ditching school and you chose not to tell me?"

"Maybe." I smile again, trying to charm my way out of this the way I've seen Rachel do before. "I don't know about you, but after that, I need a drink."

It works. "Can't argue with that reasoning," he agrees.

I pour each of us a full glass and he raises his for a toast. "To not completely effing up our kids." He smiles and I'm reminded of the John I used to know. The one that used to be a lot more fun.

"Cheers to that." I toast him against my better judgment and pray we don't switch bodies too. Then things would really start to get confusing.

Then he startles me by leaning in and kissing my cheek before whispering in my ear. "And by the way, I love your hair."

CHAPTER 12

....

rachel

"Tomorrow on *GossipTV* we've got an exclusive interview with the dancer who's making some shocking accusations about Ryan McKnight."

"That's a wrap. Let's break for lunch," Charlie says into the microphone on his headset.

"What are you doing for lunch today?" I ask him.

"The usual, I'll hit the craft service table and eat at my desk," he replies with a smile. This past week, I've noticed he smiles a lot. When Dean throws a tantrum. When Fiona complains. Even when I ask for yet another retake because I know I can be better.

Again, I wonder why Casey never mentioned Charlie to me. I can tell by the way he talks to me that they have a rapport. Maybe I'll join him for lunch and try to squeeze some conversation out of him. He's always friendly, but also a little standoffish at the same time and I wonder why. I look toward the table. "I think I'll head over there and see what they have today."

"Really? It's all carbs and junk over there. I thought you had a policy against eating refined sugar."

I almost laugh out loud. If he only knew who he was really talking to. I eat what I have time to eat, which is usually leftovers off a teenager's plate.

"Rules are made to be broken," I say with a laugh.

I wait for him to laugh but instead he hesitates and scrolls through his phone. "You know what, I forgot I have a script meeting. I'll have to skip lunch. See you this afternoon at the taping." He walks away before I can say anything.

"What are you up to? You know you're only going to confuse that boy if you have lunch with him," Destiny says as she walks up.

"Really? How so?" I ask, then remembering I'm supposed to be Casey. I'm supposed to know what she's talking about. But I don't. When I'd pressed Casey about Charlie she'd told me there was nothing I needed to know about him. "He'll be nice to you. Just be nice back," was all she'd said.

She laughs. "You know how so. Do I need to remind you how things ended last time?"

I stare at her blankly.

"What's with you lately?" She gives me a funny look. "You seem different. You even come to work happy. If I didn't know any better, I'd think you actually liked this job. And now Charlie. Every time I turn around, you're talking to him. You've barely spoken to him in months and suddenly you want to eat lunch with him?"

"So, can't a girl be happy and want to talk to people?"

Destiny shifts the stack of scripts in her arms. "Charlie's my boy. Just remember he's one of the good ones, okay?"

"Hey, you want to grab a drink after work tonight?" Maybe

after a couple of cocktails I'll be able to find out exactly what happened between Charlie and Casey.

"Hell, yeah. You definitely owe me for helping with this party for Rachel. In all my spare time!" She raises her arms and a few of the scripts fall to the floor.

"Let me help you with those. The intern forgot to take them to the control room again?" I roll my eyes.

"Yes, what's with college students these days? They don't work hard like I did, like you did." Destiny frowns.

I think about college again, as I have so many times since I started coming to this studio every day. I remember Casey's accusation at the reunion. Did I give up? What if I'd finished college after having Audrey? Where would I be now?

"Thank God Casey found you, I mean, I found you." I talk faster to cover my mistake. "I'm going to buy you as many cocktails as you want to show you how much I appreciate what you're doing to help Rachel with this party. She's so busy with the kids and everything she's juggling. Even though she really wants to do it herself, the last thing she has time for is planning a party for John."

"I know you said that, but when I talk to her, it's like she barely wants my help. She's already got most of it handled. She keeps telling me that I'm in charge of making sure everything at the venue is perfect and that's it."

I frown.

"You seem surprised," Destiny says.

Must be beginner's luck, I think. "I guess I assumed she was having a harder time than she is." I think about where I was just a week ago; I was exhausted from getting up at all hours with the baby, and constantly fighting with my older daughters. I was barely able to find time to say two words to my husband. I can't image planning John's party on top of it all. If Destiny had called the real me last week, I would have fallen over with gratitude and accepted her help without a moment's hesitation. Why did Casey tell Destiny she has it under control?

Does she have a better grip on my own life than I do?

"Girl, you're lost in thought. Let's get back to work. I need you to read through your script and make your tweaks so we can do the intern's job and get these to the control room before the taping."

"I can't believe it's almost nine thirty. Where did the day go?" I say as we take a seat at a table in the bar.

"This is early! I can't remember the last time I got out of that place before eleven." I marvel at how good Destiny looks at the end of such a long day. Still fresh faced, not at all like she applied her makeup twelve hours ago. And her energy—she never runs out of it. The obvious differences between being thirty-eight and twenty-nine, I suppose.

"What do you want? I'll go order for us," I offer. She deserves a moment off her feet. She works her ass off. And even though it's felt good having someone take care of me for a change, getting me coffee, answering my phone, thinking about my needs before I can, that's always been my job, my role, what I'm good at.

"Really? Are you sure?" Even out of the office she's still in assistant mode, wanting to take care of Casey. "I'm on it," I say, standing up.

"I'll have the usual."

What's her usual? I try to remember what twenty-nine-year-olds drink. Rum and Cokes? Strawberry daiquiris? I have no clue. And I can't screw this up right now. I need her to believe I'm Casey. Casey would know her usual.

"Why don't you try something different tonight?" I suggest.

"Oh, and drink Belvedere and sodas like you?"

"Why not?" I cringe, remembering the high school reunion.

Destiny doesn't skip a beat. "Sure, I'm game."

The bar's exceptionally crowded for a Monday night. Don't any of these people have kids?

"Hey there."

I turn and a gorgeous guy with black hair and olive skin, well over six feet tall and not a day over twenty-five, is staring at me. I'm almost positive I saw him on a Calvin Klein billboard on Sunset Boulevard this morning. The same guy I fantasized about as I stared at him in nothing but his underwear. And now here we are.

"Hey," I say, instantly feeling nervous, and trying not to picture him in his underwear again.

He looks at the bartender and all the people vying for a drink. "We could be here awhile. We might as well get to know each other." He smiles, revealing two dimples. "What's your name? I'm Steve."

"I'm Rach—, I mean, I'm Casey."

"And what brings you here tonight, Casey?" he says, his blue eyes holding my gaze.

"I'm here with my friend over there." I turn and motion toward Destiny, who gives me a half wave and a disapproving look.

"So what do you do, Casey?" He flashes his dimples again.

"I'm in television," I offer.

"And so is everyone in this room," he says with a laugh. "Can you be a little more specific? What do you do in television?"

"I host a show called *GossipTV*."

"I thought you looked familiar. With that douche bag, Dean Sanders, right? Is that guy annoying or what?"

"Something like that." I laugh.

The bartender finally notices us and walks over. "So sorry to keep you waiting, Casey, I didn't see you over here."

"That's okay."

"What are you drinking? Double Belvedere and soda?"

"Make it two," I say.

The bartender looks from Steve to me. "You guys together?"

"Well, hopefully we'll be together soon," Steve says. Such a cheesy line, but he delivers it so smoothly I believe it.

"Oh, no, we're not. When I said two, I meant the other one was for my girlfriend over there," I say awkwardly.

The bartender stifles a laugh and asks Steve, "What are you having, man?"

"The same." He smiles at me and my knees go weak. "So, I'd love to get your number, take you out sometime."

I think of John. "I can't. I'm kind of seeing someone right now." *For about twenty years.*

"Well, can I still give you my number? I'd love to talk to you and get some advice. I'm a model but I've always wanted to be a host. Are you friends with Ryan Seacrest?"

My heart sinks. He never wanted anything to do with me. He just wanted to use me as a connection.

"Sorry, I have to get back to my friend," I say quickly and take off with the drinks.

"Let me guess. A model but wants to be a host?" Destiny asks.

"Yup."

"Sunset Boulevard, in his underwear, right?"

"Pretty sure," I say as I look back toward the bar and find him with his arm wrapped seductively around a petite blonde's waist.

Destiny takes notice. "That jerk doesn't waste any time, does he?" She takes a sip of her drink. "Geez, this is strong. Did you get me a double?"

"Guilty," I say, trying to play off the fact that I have no idea what she drinks.

"Girl, you know I drink white wine. A double anything is going to knock me on my ass!"

"Guess you're getting drunk tonight, bitch." I clink my glass against hers and take a drink. Then another.

"You know it doesn't always have to be like that."

"Like what?" I ask.

"Like that guy at the bar."

"It felt like crap just now. I thought that guy was really into me."

"Oh, he was. He would've slept with you and then slid his head shot and reel under your pillow."

"Ugh." I think of Casey and realize this must happen to her on a depressingly regular basis.

"You know there are guys who've liked you for you."

I know she's referring to Charlie. "Your point?"

"My point is when it was real, you didn't want it."

"That's not true!" I say, baiting her to tell me why it is.

"Oh, please. Everything was great before you screwed it all up."

What did Casey do to him?

I take another sip of my drink, trying to figure out how to pry the details out of her without giving myself away. "Before I screwed it up. Please. He had a hand in it too."

"Is that the story you're telling yourself?" Destiny purses her lips.

"It takes two to tango, right?"

"You guys tangoed all right. If I remember correctly, you tangoed quite often!"

So they slept together. And it sounds like Casey ended it. But why? I decide to take a guess.

"Well, you know what they say, you shouldn't dance where you work."

Destiny doesn't skip a beat. "So why are you dancing with him again then?"

"I'm not!"

"But you want to," she teases.

I feel myself blush. Is this how I've been acting at work? Like I wanted to sleep with him? Sure he's cute, adorable actually, but I'm married.

Destiny turns serious. "The thing is you can't just dance with him here and there. He's a nice guy. He'll get hurt. He really cared about you, you know."

"You really think he cared about me?"

"Yes. Why is that so hard for you to believe?"

So did Casey get scared? She'd never had a real relationship and there must be a reason for that. Could she be choosing these twenty-somethings because she knows these flings will never lead to something more serious? I'd always wondered that, but she'd used the excuse that she was too busy with her career to have a relationship and I'd chosen to believe her. It was just easier that way. "Man candy is easier and sweeter," she'd said.

"So are you opening this door? Are you finally ready to tell me what happened? Because when I found you crying that night you blew up at me and refused to talk about it," Destiny says, slurring her words. She wasn't kidding about the drink knocking her on her ass.

Not sure what to say, I just nod and let her keep talking.

"What I never understood was why you dropped him so quickly and refused to talk to him again. It was like one day everything was great and the next, it was over."

"I don't know why I did that," I say, telling the truth for the first time tonight.

"I never told you this, but he came to me after you ended it," Destiny says quietly.

"He did? What did he say?"

"He said he couldn't tell me what happened because you'd sworn him to secrecy, but he wanted me to make sure you were okay. He told me to let him know if you needed anything. But not to tell you that we'd talked. And that didn't surprise me. Even after he was hurt, he was still looking out for you."

I shake my head, wondering what happened between them.

"The thing is I always thought . . ."

"Always thought what?"

"That you'd end up together."

CHAPTER 13

....

casey

"And that's our show. Good night from *GossipTV!*" My voice rings through the bedroom and I grab the remote to turn off the DVR. Rachel's getting better each episode. This time, she didn't even look like she was reading the TelePrompTer. In a designer wrap dress and four-inch stiletto boots, she might look like me, but she's definitely better than me at faking that Dean isn't the most arrogant asshole who ever lived.

"Your mama's doing a great job!" I say to Charlotte, who's playing with a tub of blocks I dumped out for her so I could get ready to have lunch with Rachel today. I can't wait to surprise her with her new look. It's not a huge departure from what she had, just a few highlights and a much-needed trim, giving her hair a shininess to it that it hadn't had in a while. It turns out the back of her closet is where all the cute clothes are stashed. Just because I'm wearing Old Navy instead of Tory Burch doesn't mean I need to look frumpy. I discovered a few sassy sundresses, some leggings, and even a great pair of boots. Not that I didn't like her uniform of empire-waist shirts and cargo pants, but a girl needs some variety in her life.

I also need to talk to Rachel about Sophie. Every day she seems more and more withdrawn. John and I talked about it more last night and decided that we both needed to keep a much closer eye on her. And even though Rachel seemed to prefer keeping John in the dark about whatever's going on, I'm relieved to have his help. I'm certain she's not going to be thrilled that I called him, but it sure seemed to wake Sophie up. She was on her best behavior this morning, getting out of bed without me having to pull the purple comforter off her like I usually do, frantically trying to raise her from the dead. One morning, I even grabbed one of Charlotte's annoying musical drums and played it next to her ear until she finally raised her head. *Teenagers.*

I've gotten less sleep the last few weeks than I ever have— including back when I pulled all-nighters as a production assistant. That level of exhaustion was nothing compared to this. But I could finally feel myself adjusting, no longer waking with crusty eyes and bitterness lodged in my throat. In fact, I'd started to crave the chaos in the morning. I liked taking care of people; it felt surprisingly good considering I hadn't so much as fetched my own americano in years. I always thought of this as another perk of all my hard work, but now I wondered if it was just another way to avoid actually living my life.

I felt bad for Rachel. I knew she was missing her family so much. But who was I missing from my own life? Destiny? Yes, of course. But I couldn't think of one other person. I was an only child and my parents had retired to Florida several years ago. I hated to admit I'd been somewhat relieved. My relationship with my mom, Natalie, had been strained since high school for reasons I didn't want to get into. She was a creature of habit and called me the first Sunday of every month, but she was usually more interested if Angelina and Brad were really as nice as they appeared than in what was actually going on in my own life. My relationship with my mom had always bothered Rachel. Even though her own parents had moved to Boston three years ago, they were still very close, which was something that I now had firsthand experience with, fielding more phone calls and emails from her in a week than I had ever received from my own mom. Which was fine with me; I'd always considered Rachel my real family. She was the one I had turned to when things went sour with whatever guy I was dating; she was the one I called first when I got the *GossipTV* job.

Did I miss Charlie? Yes, there was a part of me that missed the comfort of seeing him stride into the hair and makeup room each morning in his uniform of plaid shirts and baggy cargo pants, ready to brief me on that day's script. Or making sure I never got mic'd by Wally, the creepy audio guy who always breathed heavily as he ran his hand up my dress to attach the mic pack. But I couldn't afford to have that kind of distraction at the studio. I just didn't have time for emotional attachments, or at least that's what I've told myself. But being here, in this life, makes me wonder if there's more to life than reporting on other people's lives. Rachel's life may be a complete cluster fuck half the time, but at least she has roots. Take away my silk sheets, my fifty-seven-inch TV, my view of the Hollywood Hills, and what did I have?

As I'm packing up the car to meet Rachel, Hilary prances up with her designer jogging stroller. Decked out in a striped jogging bra and matching shorts, she looks like she just stepped out of a Nike catalog, not like she had a baby nine months ago.

"Hey there," she says, coming to a stop in front of my house. "We missed you at the park a few days ago."

"You did?" I say blankly as I heave Charlotte's stroller, which Rachel found on craigslist, into the back of her minivan.

"Our weekly play date?" She looks at me oddly.

"Oh yeah," I say, hitting my forehead with the palm of my hand. "Sorry."

"Where were you?" She pushes the point as she glances into the messy van. I walk over and stand in front of the open door to block her view of the dirty diaper and half-filled bottles that I didn't remove yesterday.

"Where was I?" I repeat. I glance at my reflection in the car window and run my fingers through my hair. "I was at the salon."

Hilary gives me a once-over. "Oh, yes, the highlights. Nice."

Nice? "Thanks," I answer flatly, ready for her to jog off down the street.

"Which salon did you go to?"

"Anya's," I say smugly as I snap Charlotte into her car seat expertly. I'd really come a long way since those first few days. I hadn't pinched her little chubby leg in the buckle all week.

"Really?" Her eyebrows raise. "And what did John think of that?"

None of your business, lady.

"He was very pleased," I say with a wicked smile before adding, "Listen, Hil, I need to run, I'm having lunch with Casey."

"Wow, she made time in her busy schedule for you? Great!"

What was this woman's problem with me?

"As my oldest and *dearest* friend, she always makes time for me," I spit out, trying to control my anger and make a mental note to ask Rachel what discussions she was having about me with her mommy friends. Yes, I wasn't able to come to the bunko events she invited me to and it's true I'd missed Audrey's school play a few months ago, but that didn't mean I was too busy for her.

Hilary laughs, as if she knows something I don't. "Okay. I'll see you later," she says before taking off down the street.

Charlotte starts to cry in her car seat. "Yes, I know, Charlotte. I think she's a bitch, too."

Pulling up to Fig & Olive, I can see Rachel waiting for us outside. Or rather, she's signing autographs for a few tourists walking down La Cienega. I feel a pang in my stomach as I watch the fans' faces light up with joy as she chats them up, even patiently posing for multiple pictures. Still not used to seeing a version of myself, I wonder when I let my hair get so blond, going from the golden hue I'd always coveted to a harsh white. My mantra has always been you can never be too blond or too skinny. Now, as I watch my emaciated arms wrap themselves around a couple and their son, I wonder if I may have taken that mantra a bit too far. Rachel looks over and sees us, breaking away and opening the van door, pulling Charlotte out of her car seat easily. Charlotte squeals in delight. That baby can definitely see straight through us to our souls.

We're escorted to one of the best tables in the restaurant and I follow the way people watch Rachel, or the way they watch Casey Lee, walk in. They're fixated on her, some even whispering to each other. How odd to literally sit back and see the way others see you. Rachel's turned into a pro, striding confidently in her sky-high Manolo Blahniks and blowing a kiss to Randy Jackson across the room, clearly enjoying every minute. I guess stepping into my life was easier than I thought.

She's so caught up in hobnobbing that she doesn't notice my highlights until she finally sits down. "What did you do to my hair?" she asks accusingly as she leans over and tugs at a strand.

"Ow!" I cry and the couple next to us looks over. "What does it look like I did?" I whisper. "I gave it an update."

"An update?" she snorts. "Don't you need to consult me when you change *my* hair? I guess now's the time to tell you I'm chopping off all of yours tomorrow," she says with a fake laugh.

"Calm down," I say quickly. "All I meant is that you always complain that you never have time to get your hair done, so I went and did it for you."

"Okay," she says, backing down. "But just out of curiosity, when did you find time to go to the salon? How long were you there? Three, four hours? Because you also got my eyebrows done, and if I know you the way I think I do, you waxed something else too."

I smile. "Well, you said I could call Jan," I say sheepishly. I've always been a sucker for a good Brazilian wax.

"In an emergency!" she says loudly, and the man and woman turn toward us again and I see a look of recognition pass over their faces as they take in Rachel. I give her a pointed look that says, *Cool it*.

"In my mind, it was an emergency. You *needed* these highlights." I shake my head around like the woman from the L'Oréal commercial.

"Whatever," she says, but I can tell by her relaxed tone that she's forgiven me already. "What did John think?"

"W-what?" I stammer as I pick up the menu and hold it up to avoid her eyes.

She leans over and pulls the menu down. "What did John say? Did he even notice?"

"The wax?"

"No! The highlights!"

"Oh, of course." I choose my words carefully. "He said it looked nice."

"Really?" she asks, looking hurt that he complimented me. Even though he thought he was actually complimenting her. In college, I was always uncomfortable when John said something nice about how I looked in front of Rachel, even though his intentions were always seemingly innocent. The air in the room always got thick for a brief moment, me breaking the tension with some self-deprecating comment.

The waiter walks up to take our order. When he leaves, I'm about to bring up what happened with Sophie when Rachel starts talking about Charlie. How Charlie is so nice, so sweet, and so helpful. So great at his job. Why had I never mentioned him again?

"There was nothing to say," I say firmly, even though there was so much to say, too much. But I had been afraid to confide in Rachel. At the time, it just seemed easier not to talk about it.

"Destiny told me everything." She holds my gaze. "You can stop bullshitting me now."

I break eye contact and start playing with the napkin in my lap. Charlotte drops her sippy cup and we both reach over to grab it at the same time. Rachel gets it first and hands it back to her with a wide smile. Charlotte giggles and claps, dropping it once more.

"I don't know what Destiny told you, but it was nothing."

"Nothing? Really? I can't even get the nicest guy at my work to sit with me at the craft service table for five minutes."

"My work," I say quietly.

"What?" she says as she reaches over and hands Charlotte some crackers.

"I said, it's my work, not yours. That Charlie is my coworker, my bad decision. My baggage to deal with, not yours." My words come out sounding harsh and I instantly regret them. I know we're both doing the best we can in this crazy situation. I look over at the server and make eye contact, praying he'll come take our drink order. I need a glass of pinot grigio to continue this conversation.

"Oh, but giving me a hairless vajayjay and butthole is your decision to make for me?" she says and we both explode in a fit of laughter.

"Hey, I'm sorry," I say, reaching across the table and putting my hand on hers. "It's just the Charlie thing . . . it's hard for me. Can we not bring it up again?" I plead.

"Fine, but you know you can talk to me about anything. I'm here for you if you need me," she says.

"I know, but I just need you to let it go. And to stop being buddy-buddy with him at work, okay?"

"Yes, if that's what you want," she says as she points her perfectly manicured finger at me. "You know, you don't have to be afraid of nice guys, Casey."

"Not allowed to bring it up, remember? Plus, if we can't figure out how to get back into our own bodies, it's not going to matter." I frown. "What are we going to do to get our lives back?"

"I've been thinking about that a lot," Rachel says. "And I have an idea."

"What? Tell me!"

She pulls her phone out of the latest Chanel handbag and types something. "I just texted you an address. Meet me there tomorrow at 10 a.m."

CHAPTER 14

rachel

Casey pulls up in my dirty minivan and I give a short wave. She still doesn't know why she's here. I walk over to the car and run my hand over the ding on the bumper, remembering the accident I got into six months ago. Sleep deprived and jittery from too many cups of coffee, I rear-ended a Porsche at the corner of Robertson and Alden while craning my neck to catch a glimpse of Kim Kardashian at the valet stand in front of The Ivy. Thankfully, I was going less than ten miles an hour and the most damage done was to my ego as Kim and her entourage giggled as the owner of the Porsche berated me while I stood there apologizing while Charlotte screamed from the backseat, the impact jolting her from her nap.

Today, Casey jumps out of the van, glances at the offending ding, and laughs. After the accident I'd called her, sputtering and bawling, unable to take a breath to tell her what had happened until she said she was going to run out of the studio and come find me if I didn't spit it out, thinking something terrible had happened to John or the kids. When I finally calmed down enough to tell her, she was silent.

"What?" I'd asked. "Is it so horrible that you're speechless?" And that's when I heard her laughing. A deep laugh, so hard that I imagined tears running down her face like mine. I started laughing too. The hilarity of it all; "me" smashing into a ninety-thousand-dollar car with my eight-year-old minivan on one of the most famous boulevards in the country as Kim Kardashian looked on. That was part of the glue that always kept our friendship strong—we always reminded each other to laugh at ourselves.

"Don't," I warn her before she brings it up.

"Didn't say a word." She breezes past me and looks up at the sign from the sidewalk. "Why are we at a wellness center? And who is Jordan?"

I hold up my hand. "Hear me out—"

Casey cuts me off. "Did you bring me to a psychic?"

"I did," I say unapologetically. "We don't have a lot of options here, Casey."

I pull my sweater around me, trying to block the wind that seems to have kicked up in the last few minutes. "She comes highly recommended."

She looks from me to the well-dressed woman waving us inside. The chime she has over her doorway sways in the wind and I can't help but think it's some sort of sign. "Please," I plead.

"Fine," she says as she shakes her head and begins walking toward the door.

"So, I need one of you to cut this deck. Doesn't matter who."

I look at the woman named Jordan, who informed us that she was in fact a spiritual counselor, not a psychic, or one of those bottom-feeding carnival fortune-tellers. *There's a huge difference, she'd said, and laughed.* And I'd liked her instantly. Although, as I take in her designer shoes and form-fitting dress, I think that she doesn't look at all like a psychic or spiritual counselor or whatever she says she is.

I also notice a huge rock on her left hand, which is wrapped around a deck of tarot cards. She's staring at me so intently that I avert my eyes, feeling as if she'd just read my mind.

"I just got engaged," she says.

"Wow, you are really good," I say. "How did you know I was wondering about that?"

"I saw you looking at the ring," she says simply.

"It's gorgeous," Casey interjects. "When's the big day?"

"Oh, we haven't set a date yet. It's my second marriage," she says sheepishly. "We'll probably do something low key, with my son." She shuffles the tarot cards again and holds them out to us. "I'd love to tell you all about it, but I do charge by the hour." She laughs. "Cut the deck."

I turn toward Casey and she gives me a look as if to say, *you do it.*

What I didn't tell Casey earlier was that I had actually found Jordan on Yelp. Yes, she had come highly recommended, but not by anyone I *actually knew*. But after meeting her today, I felt okay about asking Casey to meet me here. What better person to help us than a well-dressed woman with a sense of humor who can see into the future? Plus, she didn't bat an eyelash when we walked in. If she recognized Casey Lee, she didn't let on. I liked that. Already craving anonymity after being famous for only a short while, I can't imagine how Casey deals with someone always watching her. Like when you inhale that sushi for lunch or you leave the house without taking the time to painstakingly blow out your hair. And dating? How is it even possible under this harsh spotlight?

But then I'm struck by another one of my panicked thoughts. What if this woman can't help us and I'm in Casey's body forever? Sure, being Casey has its perks, like having my coffee waiting for me each day when I get to work and the fabulous clothes I get to wear on air and off. And I can't forget her tight abs. But what about my family? I know John and I haven't exactly been connecting the past couple of years, but he's still the person I chose to spend the rest of my life with. And the girls . . . I can't even think about them. What if being a part of my own family isn't an option anymore?

I realize Casey's waiting for me to cut the deck. Jordan cuts it again and then instructs me to pick three cards. Trying not to think about it, I take three off the top and hand them to her. As she studies the cards I selected, I send her telepathic questions.

Do you know I'm in my best friend's body? Can you help us?

She looks up quickly, startling me, and I half expect her to answer. But she doesn't. Instead she looks at the cards again and shakes her head.

"What? What is it?" I scoot my chair closer to the table, hitting it and almost knocking over a glass of water.

"It's just as I saw last night." She pulls a sleek leather notebook out of her even sleeker leather handbag and turns the pages rapidly until she finds what she's looking for. "Yes, here it is. These cards indicate what I picked up during my meditation." Then she stops to explain. "That's what I do, meditate the night before I see a client."

I nod approvingly, not knowing what else to do, and she continues. "I got a strong feeling that you came here for my help."

Casey gives me a look that says, *duh*.

"That you two aren't what you seem," she continues. "That there's something going on here that's . . ." She pauses, trying to come up with the right word. "Magical."

Casey and I look at each other excitedly, effortlessly reading each other's mind. *She knows,* we think. *And she's going to help us.*

Please, God. And as I have so many times since becoming trapped in Casey's body, I make promises to God. *I'll be more lenient with Audrey. I'll stop checking her Facebook account! I'll be more tolerant of Sophie, I'll even let her wear something semi-revealing once in a while. Maybe even buy her a lacy bra from Victoria's Secret. I won't put Charlotte in front of Sesame Street so I can eat breakfast in peace. Shit, I'll even start having sex with John again if you switch us back, God.*

"So, then you know. You know what's going on here." Casey breaks her silence.

Jordan frowns. "Well, I only know what they want me to know."

"They?" Casey and I say in unison.

"The spirits, the angels that guide you, I get messages from them," she says matter-of-factly, as if this is totally common.

"So what are they telling you?" I ask, trying not to sound as impatient as I feel. Starting to watch the hope of switching back fade away.

"That you're not at all what you seem, that you're masquerading, that you're stuck." She looks up from her notes. "Is this making sense to you?"

"That's all true," I say.

"There was a party?" she asks.

"Our high school reunion," Casey offers.

"There was a bartender there that we think is involved in

this." I wave my hand back and forth in the space between Casey and me and start speaking quickly. "But he's disappeared . . ." I trail off, realizing we haven't yet spoken aloud about what's *really* going on here. Will it help to tell this woman or does the fact she hasn't mentioned it mean she's just a hack with tarot cards she ordered off the Internet? But then again, she did know about the party and that we're masquerading. Not exactly something you bring up in everyday conversation.

Masquerading. That word makes it sound like we're playing dress-up, like we chose to disguise ourselves. But we didn't . . . *did we*? Who would choose this for herself, let alone her worst enemy?

I look at Casey, suddenly appearing so fragile, the circles around her eyes deepening, her face pale. Each day we've been switched seems to be taking more of its toll on her emotionally. The last eight, nine—what's it been?—maybe ten days that we've been like this. You'd think I'd know the exact amount of minutes, hours, days, but I don't.

I decide to go for broke and trust Jordan. "We are masquerading. But it's a little bit more literal than you may realize." I hesitate. What do we have to lose by saying this out loud? The worst that can happen is she'll laugh at us and kick us out of here for wasting her time. It does seem like she has higher standards than maybe most. "You see, the thing is, I'm her and she's me." I exhale for maybe the first time in days. It feels good to say it.

"Can you be a little more specific?" Jordan asks in a way that tells me she cares about my answer.

Casey jumps in. "I'm in her body and she's in mine. We woke up like this the day after the reunion. We got in a fight, some jerk bartender named Brian brought us each a shot, and after we drank them, we woke up like this." She puts her arms out to her sides.

I jump in. "I'm really Rachel Cole. I have three kids. I live in the suburbs. I'm not famous unless you count my mean karaoke rendition of 'I Think We're Alone Now' by—"

"—Tiffany," Jordan finishes. "I know the song. Some high notes there. Impressive."

"Do you get what we're saying here? We've switched bodies!" Casey raises her voice impatiently.

"And?" Jordan stares at us blankly.

"And what? Aren't you the least bit fazed?"

"Look around, ladies. Think about what I do for a living. I've seen and heard it all. People talking to the dead, being married to the dead, dead people that reincarnate as their former spouse's pet . . ." She pauses and I can't help but think what if that happened to me? If I died unexpectedly and came back as John's pet. The only pet he has is a garden snake that he keeps in one of those tanks at his office. How much would that suck? I didn't consider until this moment that there could actually be a worse situation than the one I'm in now, a worse body to be in. I think of myself hissing, spitting out my long tongue, hitting it against the glass of the tank, desperately trying to let John know that I'm hungry for my next mouse. I make a sour face imagining it.

Jordan snaps me back to the moment. "The question is, what do you need from me?"

"Isn't it obvious?" Casey asks, not rudely, just more like a person who wants to make sure she gets her money's worth.

"I can't read minds. I can only get what I get when I meditate the night before I see a client. What I write down. What they—"

"We know. What they want you to know." I think of the snake again and curtly finish her sentence and then rethink my attitude. "I'm sorry, we're just frazzled here. We're looking for answers on how to switch back, get our lives back, be who we were."

Jordan frowns. "But they're telling me you weren't happy with who you were."

I think about John. Our marriage. How our relationship has been strained. When did it start? When did we stop kissing each other good-bye in the morning? Sending playful emails? Sharing a glass of wine at the end of a long day? I think of Casey. I had never stopped to ask myself if she was happy. I had always assumed that she was. The life she lived, the success she has achieved, they were all things our society considers valuable. But I realize now that she's been living an empty life for years. And I was so caught up with my own crazy world I hadn't even noticed. She never even mentioned Charlie to me, a relationship that clearly upset her. What does that say about the kind of friend I am?

Jordan looks at me. "You. You, Rachel, not you, Casey, have a lot of angst inside of you. I wrote this down last night." She consults her notebook again. "You're confused about love. And stressed. Look here, I wrote the word *stress* in all caps. It's at a higher level than I have seen in most people. I also wrote the name Jack. Does that mean anything to you?"

My eyes fill with tears. "That's John, my husband, that's his nickname. What I used to call him . . ."

Casey squeezes my hand. "Things haven't been so great between them."

For a moment I think about her and John and I'm panged. I try to erase the visual of them sleeping in the same bed, accidentally brushing up against each other. And I want to snap,

But things are going very well between you two lately, right? But I think better of it.

Jordan gives me an empathetic smile, almost as if she relates, and then she looks at Casey. "And you, Casey, I didn't get as much for you. It's almost as if you're . . ."

"Empty?" I offer without thinking, looking down to avoid the sharp look Casey throws my way.

"Yes, empty works," Jordan says and looks at Casey sympathetically. "Care to talk about it?" she probes gently. "You can't lock everything you feel down there forever," she says as she points to Casey's gut.

Casey is visibly uncomfortable but holds Jordan's stare. "I'm okay," she says simply and Jordan nods, unwilling to push the issue any further.

I change the subject back to the switch. "Well, if they're so smart, then ask them how we switch our bodies back, what exactly we should do to reverse this spell."

Jordan smiles sincerely. "I'm sorry, I know you guys want me to wave a magic wand, but I don't have that answer for you."

We both remain silent, waiting for her to reveal something, *anything*.

"There is something that might help. They are telling me that you already have the answer to switching back and it's right in front of you. You need to think about why you switched in the first place and that will lead you to how you switch back."

"Are they saying anything else? Anything? Do we have to pee in the same fountain? Do we have to drink from the same cup? There has to be something," I plead.

Jordan closes her eyes and is silent for almost a full minute before she speaks. "There is something else. They're saying the word *promotion*."

"As in a promotion at work? Or promoting something, as in publicity? What exactly do they mean?" Casey asks eagerly.

"I'm sorry, I don't know. They just keep saying it over and over. But I don't know the context. I suppose that's for you to figure out."

Casey's shoulders slump and I rub my temples.

"Doesn't anyone get that we don't know the answers here? That we're not going to figure this out?" I say to no one in particular. "Can you at least tell us, or can they tell us if we'll—"

Casey finishes my sentence, "—be able to switch back?"

Jordan closes her eyes for a moment and I hold my breath. This could be it, the moment that changes everything. When she pops them back open a few seconds later, she says apologetically, "When the universe is off balance it always wants to right itself. But whether that happens or not is up to you."

CHAPTER 15

....

I hang up the phone with the caterer and check one more thing off the list for John's party. With Destiny helping out with the venue, I've been able to handle almost everything else, including getting the invitations out on time. I've tried to keep all of our interaction confined to email. Talking to her on the phone, pretending to be Rachel, makes me worry that I'll slip up and she'll realize whom she's really talking to.

I'm both relieved and concerned that I've gotten so comfortable in Rachel's life so quickly. While it makes the day-to-day much more bearable (I'm no longer asking the kids where everything is, causing them to wonder if early dementia has set in), I worry that the longer we're in each other's bodies, the harder it will be to get back to who we were. Although I think I can safely say no matter what happens, I probably won't ever be the same after this experience.

I'd stayed up half the night trying to figure out what the word *promotion* had to do with switching our bodies back.

There wasn't a chance I'd be up for one anytime soon—not with Dean and Fiona constantly bad-mouthing and sabotaging me. And I wasn't exactly getting any younger. In fact, there was part of me that wondered if I was going to get axed when I turned forty. And Rachel didn't even have a job. Well, a paying job anyway. Rachel's kids make my job at *GossipTV* seem easy. And on top of it all, she'd been working for free for years. Bitch needs a raise!

I'm still sitting at the kitchen table, lost in thought, when Audrey bounds in the door with a huge smile on her face, Sophie stomping in behind her. Audrey's always been quiet and sometimes sullen, even as a baby. I remember coming over to John and Rachel's apartment when she was a newborn, watching Rachel struggle and silently counting the minutes until I could get back to being an irresponsible twenty-two-year-old. Now, having become a pseudo-mom to Charlotte, I feel terrible that I wasn't helpful. I had no idea what she was going through and never made an effort to understand what it was like to give up everything she'd worked for to raise a family. I see now that she made a sacrifice. My *GossipTV* life seems so far away to me, and each day I feel a little more detached and find myself caring a little bit less about how long I can stay on top of the dog pile there.

"Well, someone looks like they had a good day," I say to Audrey as she grabs a bottle of water from the fridge.

"I did." She beams. "Guess what happened?"

"What?" I ask.

"Chris McNies asked me out to the movies this weekend." She does a little twirl in the kitchen. "Mom, he's only like the most popular guy in school! And he wants to go out with *me*!" But then her smile fades. "Not that it matters."

"Why?" I'm bewildered at her change of tone. "Why doesn't it matter?"

As she has so many times in the past few days, she looks at me like I'm nuts. "*Because,* Mom, you said I can't date until I'm seventeen."

"Really?" I ask before I can stop myself. "That seems sort of harsh."

Audrey's mouth falls open. "What's going on with you lately?"

"Nothing," I say and try to think quickly. How hypocritical of Rachel and John to impose that rule on Audrey. They started dating when they were freshmen in high school and by the time they were seventeen, they had already had sex more times than they could even count. If they found love that young, why wouldn't they want the same for their daughter?

I make a snap decision. "You should go out with him," I say before I can change my mind.

Audrey squeals and runs over to give me a hug. "Really? Do you mean it?"

"Yes," I say. "I mean, you're almost seventeen, right?"

"In eight months."

"Oh well, same difference," I say lightly. "What are you waiting for? You better go call him and tell him you're available this weekend!"

She throws her arms around my neck before grabbing her phone off the counter and heading to her room to spread the news. "Thanks so much, Mom. This is the nicest thing you've ever done for me."

Although I highly doubt that's true, it feels good to have made Audrey so happy. And I'm sure Rachel won't mind too much. I know they've always been a bit overprotective of Audrey, their firstborn. Maybe they just needed a little shove in the right direction to give her a little more room to breathe.

"Dad's going to freak out when he hears what you just did." I turn and see Sophie standing in the doorway, arms crossed.

Whoops. I hadn't really thought about that. "Maybe we don't have to tell him?" I give her my sweetest smile. "It could just be our little secret?"

"The problem is, secrets always have a way of coming out, Mom," she says wisely. Then she smiles. "You are so dead."

"What are you acting so nervous about?" Rachel pulls me aside later in the kitchen. She's joined us for dinner again so she can see John and the kids. Normally I would welcome her with open arms, but all I can think of is that she's going to discover that I went behind her and John's back and gave Audrey permission to go out with Mr. Super Stud.

"Nothing," I lie as I hand her the mashed potatoes that I slaved over earlier that day. I was proud to say that my food was becoming a bit more edible. What was becoming of me?

"Sophie! Audrey! Dinner!" John calls as he joins us at the table. The girls come bounding down the stairs, Audrey, with that huge giddy smile still glued to her face and Sophie, wearing a smug one, as if she couldn't wait for the fireworks to begin.

Sophie starts in immediately. "So, Audrey, how was your day?" she asks, reaching for the salad.

I interrupt before Audrey can answer. "I was actually hoping we could hear about Aunt Casey's day first." I nod at Rachel.

But she shakes her head. "No, I'd rather hear about how the girls are doing." She smiles at Audrey.

I sink down in my seat.

Audrey can barely contain herself. "Today was the best day *ever*, Aunt Casey!"

"Wow, really? What happened?" Rachel looks over at me and I look away and scoop some corn onto my plate.

"Chris McNies asked me out!"

John, having barely uttered a word since he got home, perks up. "The star quarterback? That Chris McNies?" I can tell he's impressed.

"Yes!" Audrey exclaims.

"That's fantastic news!" Rachel interjects, and for a minute I think I might be okay. But then she adds, "It's too bad you'll have to turn him down. I know your mom and dad have a very strict policy about dating before you're seventeen." She looks over at me pointedly.

"That's the best part, Aunt Casey! Mom said I could go! We're going out this weekend!"

"What?" Rachel and John yell out at the same time. I sink even lower in my seat, trying to disappear.

"Rachel, how could you tell her that? That's a decision we made together! You can't just change the rules whenever you feel like it," John says, his face reddening.

"Yeah," Rachel chimes in. "What were you thinking?" John looks over, clearly surprised Casey would take his side.

Audrey's eyes fill with tears. "What are you saying? I can't go? Everyone at school will laugh at me if I have to say no now. *Everyone* else is dating. Why do you guys still treat me like I'm a baby?"

"Hold on a second." My voice is shaking. "That's not what we're saying."

"Yes, it is," Rachel says firmly and John gives her an annoyed look, probably wondering why Casey is taking such a vested interest in his children all of a sudden.

I look at the tears streaming down Audrey's face and my heart breaks for her. I know I have one chance to make this right. "Listen, everyone calm down. John, I'm truly sorry. I was wrong to make this decision without you."

He seems shocked by my apology. "Thank you for saying that." The frown on his face softens.

"But here's the thing," I continue. "When we made that decision Audrey was only . . ." I pause, unsure.

"Eleven." Audrey fills in the blank for me.

"Right, she was eleven. We had no idea the mature, responsible woman she would be at sixteen." I smile at her and she wipes another tear away and smiles back, a look of pride washing over her face. "So who says we can't reevaluate? She's right, all the other girls her age are dating."

"Not all of them," Rachel chimes in.

"All of them," I push back. I look over at John, surprised to see him intently listening. "What if we set some strict ground rules and give her a chance? If she breaks our trust, then we can take away the privilege." And I save my strongest argument for last. "After all, John, you and I started dating in high school."

Rachel refuses to make eye contact with me. "Yes, and look at you guys now," she says so quietly I can barely hear her. But I know I've got her thinking.

"Please, Dad!" Audrey pleads. "Any ground rules you want."

John stares me down before answering. "Okay," he says and Audrey and I cheer. Rachel's face is impassive. "But with major ground rules."

"Thank you, thank you, thank you!" Audrey jumps up from the table and hugs him tightly. I catch Sophie rolling her eyes.

"Thank you," I mouth to him when he looks over at me. Then lean in toward Rachel, lost in thought. "Sorry."

She whispers back through a clinched smile, "I'm going to kick your ass later. You know that, right?"

"I do," I say, hoping she'll go easy on me. But, no matter how angry she is at me, the look on Audrey's face tells me it was worth it.

CHAPTER 16

....

rachel

Audrey dating. Audrey in the backseat of the star quarterback's car. Audrey losing her virginity. Audrey dropping out of high school because she's pregnant.

As I lie in Casey's silky sheets, my mind is racing, one horrible thought replacing the last with an even worse one.

My eyes are heavy and I have to blink a few times to read the clock on Casey's bedside table. It's 5:30 a.m. In just an hour, I need to be sitting in hair and makeup at the studio. I've hardly slept all night thinking about last night's dinner topic; my sixteen-year-old daughter's dating life, which went from nonexistent to active in the span of five minutes.

I'm in no mood to face the makeup artist after the snide comments I overheard her make yesterday to her assistant about the dark circles under my eyes. I'd frozen behind the audio room door as I'd listened to her bitch about how she'd better win an Emmy this year after all the work she has to do to make me look pretty—especially now that we shoot the show in high definition. I haven't slept much since Casey and I switched and it's taken a serious toll on my, or should I say Casey's, face. After I'd heard her remarks, I'd wanted to punch her in the face as I stared at her in the dressing room mirror, the hot lights betraying every blotch, pimple, and line on my face. I'd felt an ache in my chest for Casey and wondered if she was always treated more like an object than a human being.

Looking around Casey's bedroom, I'm almost shocked at how impersonal it is. How, if I saw a picture of it, and didn't know any better, I could easily mistake it for a hotel room. A five-star hotel room, but a hotel room all the same. The walls are painted a shade of light gray. The furniture is expensive but not lived in. Not comfortable. It's the kind you buy and arrange exactly as you see it in a catalog. The kind you buy when you don't have to think about what the kids are going to do to it.

The pictures on her walls are of places, not people. In fact, she has hardly any photographs of friends or family anywhere. The other night, I had to search her entire apartment until I finally found a picture of her and me. It sat on a shelf toward the bottom of a bookcase in her office. It was one of us in college, our arms draped around each other's padded shoulders. Red cups in hand, we wore matching half-drunk smiles and high-waisted jeans.

I'd sunk down on her dark hardwood floor and cried, wishing more than anything we could be back there again. I missed those college girls who didn't have a care in the world, our whole lives ahead of us, our bright broadcasting futures just around the corner. But that was before an unplanned pregnancy changed everything, for the better and for the worse. And I'd made another promise to God. Once I got back into my own body, I vowed to be fun again.

I drag myself out of Casey's bed, my body aching, my heart aching, as I think again of last night. Of John and Casey. How in sync they were as they handled Audrey. How they seemed more like a married couple than John and I had been in forever. How Casey knew exactly what to say to keep Audrey calm, something I haven't been able to do in I don't even know how long. I'd watched my life playing out before me and I'd felt rage and sadness and even contentment as I'd seen how blissful my daughter looked. I couldn't remember the last time she'd been that happy.

But now I feel my anger resurfacing. How could Casey tell *my* daughter she could date? What gave her the idea that she could make that decision without consulting me? Or even John? She knows how critical that decision is, doesn't she? The worst part is I had to sit idly by and watch, unable to stop it.

And in the end, my daughter is going on a date. My husband has a better relationship with the fake me than he has with the real me. And in forty-five minutes I'm going to be verbally assaulted by a woman with a mascara wand. And there's not a damn thing I can do about any of it.

"You didn't sleep again." Destiny pushes a Starbucks coffee cup into my hand as I walk into my office.

"You sound like that horrid makeup woman." I take a long drink, the coffee burning the back of my throat.

"Fuck her. She's just pissed off at the world. I hope you didn't take it personally."

"Spoken by the twenty-nine-year-old without a single wrinkle." I smile.

I think again about Casey and how she's not only getting older, but she's doing it in front of bitchy makeup artists and in front of America. And even parts of Mexico and Canada. I almost laugh out loud as I remember the meltdown I had a few months ago on my thirty-eighth birthday when I'd discovered more wrinkles on my neck. I'd been so depressed that I'd worn turtlenecks for a week straight. It makes me wonder yet again if I was ever cut out for this business in the first place. If I would've been able to handle the incredible scrutiny.

"You want some good news?"

"I'd kill for some." I sigh.

"We beat *Access L.A.* in the ratings last night."

I stare at her blankly.

"We beat *Access L.A.*! You know that show we've *never* beat? Our nemesis? It's like Leno and Letterman. And we're finally Leno. The execs are doing a happy dance. They're saying your interview with Ryan McKnight was our Hugh Grant moment. They're saying you've *never* been better."

"Never?" I frown.

"Don't look so happy there. You'd think I just told you someone died. But it's the exact opposite. You're the It Girl of the moment. *Entertainment Weekly* even called this morning."

"Sorry, I'm just tired. That's great news." I force a smile, but am worried about what Casey will think of this.

"That's better. Now let's get you into that makeup chair before she comes looking for you."

Later, after the show is taped, I'm dragging myself back to my office, thinking I'm so tired that I might have to crash on my couch, when I hear them talking. It's Charlie and a few of the executives huddled around a computer. I stop before they see me.

"This is great. This is so great. It's all over the Internet," Charlie says excitedly. "Look, look here, ThePulse.com is predicting that we're going to stay on top in the ratings. When was the last time The Pulse even cared what we did?"

"To think, just a few weeks ago, we were wondering if we needed to put someone else in her spot. Maybe even try it with just Dean. We weren't bringing in that eighteen-to-twenty-five demo. But with last night's numbers, with us beating *Access L.A.* It's unbelievable. Casey's *it* right now." One of the execs high-fives the other.

I'm stunned. Casey was in danger of losing her job? Her worst fear might have been realized if we hadn't switched bodies? This switch might have saved her career? I might have saved her career? I can't believe that. These executives are getting ahead of themselves here. It's one night's ratings. We have to keep it up, don't we? But if we don't, then will they replace her? I close my eyes and try to breathe.

"The way she handled that interview with Ryan. Compassionate yet skeptical. She was on fire," the other exec adds excitedly.

I can't help but smile. I did nail it, I think as I remember the interview.

Even though the associate producer had given me a stack of research, I'd stayed up half the night doing my own prep work. And as I arrived at the studio hours before anyone else, reading and rereading my materials in my office, I'd felt more ready for the interview than I had about anything in my life. But a few minutes before the taping, when I'd gone to Ryan McKnight's dressing room to meet him, I'd caught him looking at a picture of his five-year-old daughter, Penelope, his eyes filled with tears. I'd left the dressing room quietly, before he could see me. And during the interview I'd used what I'd seen. I'd thought about my own daughters and I'd asked him what he'd do if someone were unfaithful to Penelope. He was instantly in tears. Then I'd gone for it. I'd asked him what he'd say to his wife now if he could. I'd told him to look into the camera, to pretend he was talking to her. And he'd started sobbing again. And I knew I'd gotten *the* interview. No one else had Ryan McKnight crying.

Long after they'd taken off my mic, removed my makeup, and fed the promos out to the stations, I sat alone on the set, staring up at the thousands of lights, letting it all sink in. Just weeks ago, the closest I ever came to a celebrity as huge as Ryan McKnight was by seeing him on the cover of a magazine while checking out at the grocery store. Now, not only had I interviewed him, I got the interview with him that no one else could.

The executives give each other another high-five and it snaps me out of my thoughts. "If Casey keeps this up, who knows what could happen. She could even be ready for her own show."

Her own show. This is her dream. To be free of Dean. To be the star. My first instinct is to call her. But then I remember. She didn't interview Ryan McKnight. I did. And I feel a pain deep inside. She's not going to like this. She's not going to like this at all. But then I can't help it. I think of dinner last night and I smile. I smile for me. Because I did this. I made a choice in her life the same way she did in mine. And who knows? Maybe we're both better for it. Suddenly I remember what the psychic said: Could this be the promotion she was talking about? She said she didn't know the context, but couldn't this be it?

"Wow. That will be an amazing opportunity for her," Charlie says sincerely and I want to hug him. After everything, he's still her biggest champion, her biggest fan. I wish she knew that.

"We're already tossing around ideas. All preliminary of course. But if things continue, if Casey can keep this up, a show will happen for her. And she's single. No kids. She'd jump at a chance to host her own show in the Big Apple, right?"

Charlie smiles, but his eyes look sad. "I don't know, you'll have to ask her. But you know Casey, she'd do just about anything for the next great thing."

And I find myself wondering. What will she say? Or, if we haven't been able to switch back and I'm still Casey Lee, what will I say?

CHAPTER 17

....

casey

"What do you think?" I twirl around and ask Charlotte, who giggles her approval.

Finding something suitable to wear to the *GossipTV* studios was, well, challenging to say the least. I finally discovered a black belted sundress hidden under a pile of bland sweaters and paired it with the boots I bought for Rachel at a sample sale a few years back. I can tell by their pristine condition that they've been sitting in the corner of her closet since the day she opened the box. I silently vow to make sure they don't end up in the back of her closet again where all fashion-forward merchandise (not to mention gifts from me!) goes to die.

Although after being in Rachel's life, I have to admit that I can't really blame her for shoving the stuff back there. This life, her life, doesn't have a lot of room for uncomfortable designer ankle boots and short sundresses. How ignorant I'd been, always on my high horse, mocking Rachel's wardrobe choices, never once thinking about why she wouldn't want to wear a two-hundred-dollar pair of leather booties. Even if I did risk my life for those boots—nearly knocking myself out as I collided with another woman, both of us grabbing for them, me winning, only to discover after paying for them that they weren't even my size—I know now that Charlotte would probably spit up all over them anyway. Or that Rachel may want to wear comfortable shoes because she never, and I mean *never*, gets to sit down. My legs had been aching more this past week than after hiking to the top of Runyon Canyon with my very hot, but merciless personal trainer.

I can handle the never-sitting-down part. I'm used to being on my feet in killer heels for hours, but just remembering that day at the studio just before we switched, when my boots were killing my toes, now seems like years ago.

It's the time to myself that I've missed the most. As much as I adore Charlotte, I'm still shocked at how all-encompassing caring for her is. Between making sure she doesn't fall down the stairs or saving her from electrocuting herself when she nearly stuck my car keys into the light socket (I'm still trying to remember not to leave my things in low places), I'm lucky if I've even run a brush through my hair by noon. I cringe now as I remember blowing off Rachel when she'd complained about never having a minute to herself. How deep down, I thought staying at home with a baby was the easy way out. That I secretly felt she had given up. I cringe, remembering my ignorant comments to her at the reunion. I always thought I was the one with the real pressure, fighting off every twenty-something bitch trying to knock me off my perch. Now I understand the truth. Caring for Charlotte was the hardest job I'd ever had, that I would ever have. And that includes that stint I had working with Tyra Banks a few years back.

I've been anxious about my trip to the *GossipTV* offices all morning, part excited, part nervous to step foot in the place that I had given most of my life to for the past three years. And I think again about the interview with Ryan McKnight. How Rachel had stepped in just two weeks ago and seemed to be playing me better than I'd been playing myself. It was more than a little disconcerting. Sure, I was relieved she hadn't gotten me fired the first day as I'd been stupidly worried she might. But did she have to be so good? With each episode I watch—rushing to the bedroom the minute after I lay Charlotte down for her nap—I start to feel more and more replaceable. And the scariest part? With each day, I care a little bit less that I may be.

I pick up Charlotte and the Gucci diaper bag I had FedExed here earlier this week (bought with the *real* Casey's credit card, of course) and head out the door with her on my hip.

I walk into the offices twenty minutes later with mixed emotions. I have to stop myself from greeting the crew members by name as they walk past, oblivious. I can't help giving Fiona the evil eye as she passes me in the hall, looking me up and down before sneering at my outfit and glaring at Charlotte like she's an alien. We don't get many babies visiting our set.

I pop my head into my dressing room and Destiny looks up from her iPad. "Rachel? What are you doing here?" she asks, looking tired. More tired than I remember. And I wonder if she's always this exhausted, but I choose not to see it because then I'd have to acknowledge that she practically has to live here to get all of her work done. Is she another person in my life whom I've failed to really see?

It's so good to see her that I run up and give her a tight hug, smashing poor Charlotte in the process, who lets out a squeal in protest. "It's really good to see you."

"Whoa," she says as she detangles herself from us and straightens her dress, one that we bought to celebrate the time I made *Entertainment Weekly's* bull's-eye after I put Spencer Pratt in his place during an interview after Heidi's plastic surgery overdose. My successes—big *and small*—were always Destiny's too: if I was ever canned she'd be out on her ass also.

"Hey, Rachel!" she calls warmly. "You here about the party?" she says as she reaches over to grab a large manila folder with "John's party" written on it.

"Actually, I'm here to see Casey."

"Hmmm . . ." she murmurs. She glances down at the iPad and taps the calendar. "Does she know you're coming?"

"Yes, she does. Or I thought she did?" I say, my face warming as I realize that Rachel may be blowing me off. "She just texted me this morning," I add.

"Okay, okay," she says and speaks into her headset. "We've got someone here for Casey. What's her ETA?" She listens for the response and nods. "Thanks," she replies, before turning back to me. "She's over at the craft service table. That's—"

"I know what it is," I say, cutting her off.

"Oh, okay," she says, confused. "Allow me to walk you over. This way please." She waves her arms toward the hallway.

"Thanks," I respond, slightly embarrassed that Rachel had clearly forgotten I was coming and that Destiny was covering for her. She was just doing her job, protecting me—or rather Rachel—from distractions. Is that how I had painted Rachel to Destiny? Had I made her think my oldest and most loyal friend was nothing more than a distraction at work that I couldn't afford?

"How's the party planning coming?" Destiny inquires as we make our way toward craft services.

"Great," I respond, before adding sincerely, "Thanks for all your help."

"It was nothing," she responds lightly. "Casey thought you could use some." Then she chuckles. "Between you and me, I think she was surprised how under control you already had things."

"Really? She didn't think I could handle planning a simple party?"

"No, I don't think that was it," Destiny backtracks. "I think she was trying to be nice."

"Yes, I'm sure that's what it was," I say quietly. Destiny glances over at me, worried she's thrown her boss under the bus. "It's fine," I say to put her mind at ease.

I hear Destiny exhale a sigh of relief as we turn the corner and almost run into Dean who tries to brush past us, but Destiny stops him. "Dean, this is Casey's best friend, Rachel."

Dean looks at me. "Casey has friends?" He laughs. "Shocking."

I can sense that Destiny is about to jump in but I cut her off. "Nice suit," I say, using my free hand to finger the sleeve. Then I look down at his shoes. "You seem taller than you do on TV. Wait, are those heels on your shoes?"

His face turns crimson.

I pat his shoulder and continue. "It's okay. I hear Tom Cruise needs them too."

Destiny snorts and Dean walks off in a huff. She shakes her head. "I didn't know you had it in you, Rachel."

I smile. "There's a lot of things you don't know about me."

"I bet," she says, still smiling. "Hey, did you hear the good news?"

"What?" I ask, even though I know full well what she's about to say.

"Casey's interview with Ryan McKnight killed. We beat *Access L.A.* for the first time!"

I feel dizzy and grab on to the railing as we walk down the stairs toward the craft service table. It was one thing reading about it online in Rachel's bathroom after everyone went to bed, where I was still somewhat removed from it and could talk myself out of feeling jealous, nervous, helpless, or all of the above. But now, standing here in the studio, the lights hanging from the rafters above us, the set looking smaller than I remember it, *my* assistant's eyes lighting up and her voice raising several octaves in excitement, I feel the impact in a way I hadn't before. This was huge for me. The only problem was that I hadn't actually done it. My best friend, who hadn't been in front of a camera since boxy T-shirts and brown-braided belts were in style, had done it. "Congrats," I say weakly. "That's great."

"The executives are flipping out over it, and of course Dean is totally pissed. We're leaving Tuesday to go to New York for the follow-up."

"What?" I stammer. *New York? Follow-up interview?*

"Yep, I can't wait to hit the Big Apple!" she says as we spot Rachel. "There she is!" She points over to the table in the corner, where Rachel is sitting close with Charlie, sharing a huge plate of pasta with him.

What was she doing feeding my body refined carbs? And why was she sitting with Charlie and sharing those carbs with him?

I walk up to the table gripping Charlotte a little too tightly. "Hey there," I say through clenched teeth. Taking them in, a plate of greasy pasta between them, their knees touching, Rachel talking a mile a minute about some typo in the Prompter, Charlie's eyes fixed on her.

They look up in unison. "Oh, hey," Rachel says slowly, acting surprised to see me. She immediately pulls Charlotte from my arms and coats her cheeks with kisses. Charlotte squeals in delight and nestles her head into Rachel's shoulder. I catch Destiny and Charlie sharing a look and I suppress a smile. The Casey they know would *never* have picked up a drooling baby after undergoing two hours of hair and makeup. Or ever, for that matter.

"Watch the drool," Destiny reminds Rachel.

"It's fine," Rachel says firmly and Destiny looks over at Charlie again. He shakes his head. I think he stopped trying to figure me out a long time ago.

"Want to hold her?" Rachel asks Destiny. "Isn't she adorable?"

"Um, thanks but no thanks," she says as she takes a step back, clearly not wanting to catch whatever baby-loving bug is going around.

"Nice lunch," I say pointedly, nodding my head at the offensive fettuccini Alfredo Rachel had been shoveling into my body when I walked up.

"Carbs provide energy," she says unapologetically. "Who wants a life without bread and butter?"

Destiny laughs and touches Rachel's forehead. "Are you feeling okay?"

"Casey," I say, thinking about all the times I'd gone without, the desserts I'd skipped, the baskets of warm bread and butter I'd sent away. Realizing now how silly it all was. How I shouldn't have obsessed. Wanting to tell her, *it's okay, eat what you want.* But I can't. It's still my body, which is my livelihood. "You know what happens when you don't watch what you eat. You wouldn't want to ruin all the hard work you've put into your body, now, would you?"

Rachel gives me a warning look. "Don't worry about me so much." She reaches out to touch the Gucci diaper bag. "I see you've been making some changes too. Does John know about this?"

"It was a gift from a very stylish, generous benefactor."

"And what was wrong with the JujuBee one you already had?"

"Everything," I say, and we both laugh while Charlie and Destiny eye us warily.

"Listen," Charlie interrupts and puts his hand on Rachel's back, and my stomach drops. "We've got to get Casey to set." Then looks at me. "Are you guys staying for the taping?"

I nod, even though a part of me wants to leave.

"Destiny, can you get Rachel set up in the control room so she can watch?"

"Sure, I'll take you guys there." Destiny points her finger toward the hallway I'd walked a million times. "This way."

"Thanks," I say and try to ignore the pang in my heart. Watching Rachel and Charlie together hurts more than it should.

Later, after Destiny has introduced me to the people I've worked with for years, I can tell they are trying to put on a happy face despite having to share such a tight space with a babbling baby.

As Rachel throws to a tape of an interview she did with Jennifer Garner, I watch her carefully, trying to figure out what she's doing differently than me. And I decide that there's a warmness to her that I've never had. In the clip, she's playing with Jennifer's kids, something I wouldn't have thought to do. When I interviewed Rebecca Romijn last year I made sure her twins were nowhere in sight—I didn't want her to be distracted. But as I hold Charlotte tight, I wonder if in my scramble to the top, I'd failed to see what's most important to the people I'm interviewing. Which is what should be most important to me.

Destiny arrives at the control room promptly at the end of the show and escorts me down to the set. "What'd you think?" Rachel asks brightly as I walk up, but she already knows the answer. She was awesome.

"You were fantastic," I say, and mean it.

"Thanks." She tilts her head self-consciously and I find myself thinking how odd it is to watch myself do it. It's always been a quirk of Rachel's. In high school, after each football game, she'd bound up to me, breathless, tilting her head and asking what I'd thought of her halftime performance.

"So, New York, huh?" I ask, pulling her aside. "When were you planning on telling me?"

"We just found out, I was going to tell you today, promise," she answers sheepishly and looks away.

"Right."

"I was, I swear. Are you pissed?"

"No, of course not," I answer too quickly, not wanting her to know that I am in fact a little pissed. Because if I admit it, I'll just end up looking petty. I lean in and whisper, "I'd just like fair warning if my body is leaving the state, thank you very much."

She smiles at my attempt at a joke. "Are you at least happy for me?"

"Yes!" I answer with more enthusiasm than I feel. "And more important, I'm happy for me. This could mean big things."

"Yes it could," she answers simply, leaving me wondering if she knows more than she's letting on.

"But you have to do me one favor. And it's a big one."

"What?"

I touch her lips with my finger. "Promise me fettuccini Alfredo will never pass through these ever again."

CHAPTER 18

....

rachel

I white-knuckle the armrests as our plane lifts away from Los Angeles, the girls, John—my life.

The panic I'm feeling now is worse than any I've experienced this past couple of weeks, which means I'm very close to hyperventilating. If this plane crashes, no one will ever know what happened, will ever know that I died in Casey's body. God, that sounds so terrible. I squeeze my eyes shut, trying to block it out. Sure, Casey will try to convince John that we switched bodies, she'd swear on our friendship, on my grave, on anything, but he'd just give her a sympathetic look, chalking up her behavior to that of a grieving best friend, never knowing that his real wife went down with the rest of Flight 2525.

"You're gripping those armrests so tightly it looks painful." Charlie's voice jars me out of my panic. I've noticed Charlie has that way about him, always knowing what to do or say to make me feel better, even if he doesn't realize I need to feel better. It can be as simple as paying me a compliment after, unbeknownst to him, the makeup girl has given me a total complex earlier that morning. Has Casey noticed that he has this quality? It's one I've craved from John for as long as I can remember. The feeling that I'm supported no matter what.

"Sorry, slight fear of flying," I lie, wishing that I could confide in him. That I could tell him everything. That I'm not Casey. That I'm an ordinary girl with love handles, three daughters, a husband, even a book club. Yes, in that order.

"Let's get you a drink," he says, and smiles.

As he motions to the flight attendant, I watch him. He's only grown better looking since I met him. He's not handsome in a George Clooney kind of way, but in a construction-worker-meets-fraternity-boy kind of way. His thick dirty-blond hair is always slightly messy, his face always a day past needing to be shaved, but his shirt is always tucked in, his shoes always matching his belt. And his brown eyes literally melting you. But none of this is upon first glance. You might pass him on the street and not even notice him because he's not particularly tall, his features not particularly distinct. But when you look at him, really look at him, you can see it.

He couldn't be any more different looking from John if he tried. John is almost six foot four, his dark hair not nearly as thick, his face more angular, his features more sharp. And I can't remember the last time his blue eyes melted me.

"Yes, let's get me that drink," I say with a smile. And decide that for at least right now, I have no choice but to embrace this life. I push thoughts of my girls from my mind and focus on the present. Isn't that what we're supposed to be doing these days? Living in the present? Focusing on the here and now?

The hours fly by as each drink goes down a little smoother than the last. We talk about everything. Well, *he* talks about everything because I'm basically interviewing him and not letting him ask me any questions. Because I have no idea what he's told Casey and what he hasn't, I play it safe and ask him to tell me stories about himself that I don't already know. He tells me about his older brother, the lawyer, the one he thinks his parents are more proud of. His dad is a lawyer too and wanted both of his boys to follow in his footsteps and run his firm when he retired. But Charlie said he didn't have it in him. He fought it until he couldn't fight it. And then he dropped out of law school because he could no longer lie to himself that it felt right.

I want to tell him that I dropped out too. That I never admitted to anyone that when I became pregnant I didn't feel conflicted. There was never a "what do I do?" moment. John, on the other hand, was completely thrown. He was excited, but also scared shitless. He said it was too soon and worried if we'd make it. He loved me, but said he hadn't planned to propose to me until we were both established in our careers. But as he'd paced back and forth in front of his futon couch, his hands flailing wildly, I was calm. I knew in my heart having the baby was the right thing, whether John married me right away or not. I easily chose the baby over the career, which surprised me more than I think it surprised Casey or John, although I never told either of them that. I always thought I'd go back.

I'd been so career driven. Always the one who chose studying over barhopping. Casey and my other roommate would roll their eyes at me when they stumbled home drunk and I was still burning the midnight oil. The photo I found in Casey's apartment brought me to tears because I remembered that night so clearly. It was taken on a rare night when I let Casey talk me into going out. And I recalled thinking how good it felt to be out getting hammered and wondered why I always took things so seriously. Why couldn't I just wing it like Casey always did? Things always seemed to come so easy for her.

When I found out I was pregnant it was almost a relief because I wasn't going to have to try and potentially fail. That's what I was always so scared of—failing. I was fantastic in the college studio, but what would happen when I was in front of the *real* cameras?

I think of my interview with Ryan McKnight. Turns out, I would've been great. Really great.

"What about you? Tell me something personal about you. You're always deflecting." Charlie tries again to get something out of me.

"Deflecting, huh? Where'd you learn that one? Dr. Phil?" I laugh.

"Still deflecting."

I take a long drink of my champagne. Somewhere over Kansas we'd decided it was time to celebrate our success—that we were on our way to the Big Apple to bring *GossipTV* and "our" careers to the next level.

"I'm happy. Right now, in this moment. I am very happy," I say without hesitation.

"Well, I'm happy to hear you say that." He puts his hand over mine and I let it rest there, let myself feel the heat of his palm, the electricity flowing between our hands. And I wonder for a moment what it would feel like to kiss him.

"Excuse me, I'm so sorry to bother you, but aren't you Casey Lee?" a young, petite blonde stammers then covers her mouth. Charlie quickly removes his hand from mine like he's been caught doing something he shouldn't. "I'm sorry, I'm just a little nervous. I never approach anyone. And I live in L.A.; well, you know how it is. I see people all the time, but you, I look up to you. I hope to have a career like yours one day."

I smile, thinking she reminds me of Casey at that age. So pretty, so ambitious. She would've approached Mary Hart back then. I wouldn't have had the balls.

"It's okay, what's your name?"

"Darlene, but I'm thinking of changing it."

"Don't," I say too quickly and she gives me a confused look.

"Just stay true to who you are," I say, thinking of the makeup artist, of Dean, of Fiona. Any of them would stab Casey in the back for a buck.

"That's great advice, thank you. I just have to tell you, your interview with Ryan McKnight, oh my God, it had me in tears. And I think he's a total douche bag to cheat on his wife like that. But I still bawled."

We all laugh.

"Could I bother you for an autograph? I know, how lame of me to ask, right? You're trying to enjoy your flight with your boy-friend and I'm interrupting."

I don't correct her but grab the pen and paper she's thrust in front of me.

I decide Charlie can be my boyfriend, if only for this mo-ment, while I sign the autograph. I'm already pretending to be someone I'm not. Why can't I pretend that too?

CHAPTER 19

....

casey

"What about this?" Audrey steps out of the dressing room in a low-cut shimmering top and a pair of skintight Rock and Republic jeans.

I think of Sophie in the barely there miniskirt. Why do these young girls feel they need to show so much skin to feel pretty? Are women like me to blame? I'd never wanted to see myself as a role model, but it's becoming harder to deny. "Let's keep looking," I say as I grab a shirt off the rack that will cover more of her. "Why don't you try this top with these?" I say, handing her a looser pair of jeans.

"Okay," she says as she disappears back behind the curtain and I start fingering through the sweaters neatly stacked on the table. Audrey's date with Chris is tonight and I promised to help her find the perfect outfit. I may not change a diaper very well, but one thing I do excel at is shopping.

Audrey saunters back out and I can tell by the look on her face that we have a winner. It's a long striped T-shirt paired with a belt, and it looks perfect with the jeans I picked. Skinny, but not painted on. I grab a short faux leather jacket I'd been eyeing earlier. "Try this with it. And maybe we could find you some black flats to tie the whole outfit together. I think Tory Burch has a new pair out."

"Oh my God, Mom! It's perfect!" she squeals and turns to hug me. "Since when did you get all fashionable? Did you ask Aunt Casey for advice or something?"

I poke her playfully. "Something like that."

Audrey twirls around and I can't help but smile. In a strange way, I'm slightly jealous. I struggle to think of the last time I'd been on a proper date. Probably when Charlie and I drove up the coast to have dinner, because I insisted we go somewhere where no one from work could see us. He'd picked me up and we'd driven to Santa Barbara, having dinner at an Italian restaurant off State Street. We'd talked for hours, only stopping when we realized we were the last patrons. He took my hand and led me back to the car, leaning me against the passenger-side door, kissing me there, passionately. I could still remember the faint taste of garlic, wondering if it was from him or me, and then letting myself go and enjoying the moment. But that was before everything changed between us. And now, I'll probably live my whole life attempting to live up to the perfection of that date. Which is most likely why I've given up trying.

Bursting through the door an hour later, Audrey is still brimming with excitement. "I'm going to jump in the shower now so I have plenty of time to get ready." Audrey drops the bags onto the table and starts up the stairs. "Will you help me straighten my hair later, Mom?"

"Of course," I reply, excited that she wants me to be part of her special night. I was hoping she would, but didn't want to push it. The one thing I've learned since being her mom is that having a teenager is a bit like dating a new guy; you can't let them know how bad you want it.

She races past Sophie at the top of the stairs, who is standing sullen with her arms crossed. "Did you get me anything?" she asks. "Or was today all about Audrey?"

I shake the bag I'm holding. "Maybe. But you'll need to wipe that look off your face." I smile and pull out a pair of black sequined boots.

"Mom!" She runs over and grabs them out of my hands and starts pulling them on her feet. She looks up at me. "How did you know?"

"I have my ways." I'd seen her staring longingly at her friend Sarah's pair last week and had made a mental note. I know Rachel would probably kill me later for spoiling them, but it made me feel so good to see Sophie smile that it would be worth her wrath.

"Dad! Check these out!" she calls out to John as he passes by on his way to the kitchen, Charlotte in his arms. I smile. He looks good holding that baby.

"Nice," he replies as he raises his eyebrow at me. "Mom sure has been doing a lot of shopping lately." He eyes the Gucci bag on my shoulder.

"This was a gift from Casey," I remind him.

"Ah yes, that's right," he says. "What was the damage today?"

"Not too bad," I say defensively, not wanting to have this discussion in front of Sophie. I wasn't used to being questioned about how I spend my money. "Sophie, why don't you take these up to Audrey's room?" I take the bags off the table and hand them to her. After she's gone, I turn back to John. "You only get one first date. I thought it would be nice to make it special for her."

"She has a huge closet full of clothes! Did she really need something new?"

"Jesus, it's just one outfit."

"And the boots for Sophie."

"Yes," I sigh. "Those too. It's not a big deal."

"You know I don't like to micromanage your spending. But you know our situation. You can't just buy whatever you want, whenever you want."

Their situation? Rachel and I never talked money and I had always assumed that they lived comfortably.

"I'm sorry," I say. "I just wanted to make them happy. Did you see the smile on Sophie's face?"

He softens and hugs me. "I know. Putting a smile on her face is a very difficult thing to do these days! We just need to make sure we live within our means. The pharmaceutical industry is so unstable right now that we can't go crazy."

Unstable? Don't people always need drugs? Rachel never mentioned anything about John's job and that it might be in jeopardy. He's been at the same company for over a decade and I had always thought of him as untouchable.

Despite my better instincts, I relax into his arms, feeling his chiseled chest press against mine, breathing in the faint smell of his aftershave. Guilt sweeps over me immediately, but I tell myself I'm just playing the role of loving wife.

The doorbell rings later that evening and I think I may be even more excited than Audrey. I rush to the door, my fingers shaking, and open it to discover a ridiculously good-looking seventeen-year-old wearing a letterman jacket. I peer past him to see a shiny black Land Rover in the driveway. *Wow, go, Audrey. Didn't know you had it in you, girl!* I try my best to squelch my cougar instincts.

"Mrs. Cole?" he asks. "I'm Chris McNies and I'm here to see Audrey. Is she available?"

Manners too.

"Yes, come in," I stammer as John walks up behind me.

"You must be Mr. Cole," he says as he holds out his hand for John to shake.

"Have a seat." John attempts to sound gruff but I can tell he's crushing on this guy too. "I want to have a quick chat with you."

Ah, yes, *the chat* was basically John's premeditated speech he'd warned me he'd be giving Chris about not speeding, drinking, or having sex with our daughter tonight. I stay back in the kitchen with Charlotte to avoid the awkward moment.

They walk out a few minutes later, Chris with a slight smirk on his face and John clearly relieved. John nods at me as a sign that Chris agreed to all his ground rules. "Audrey!" John calls. "Chris is here!"

Audrey appears at the top of the stairs looking stunning. Her hair, usually wavy, now hanging straight, her skin dewy and eyes sparkling with first-date anticipation. I quickly pull out my phone and snap a picture for Rachel. As I gaze at the photo, I wonder, when did Audrey become a woman? I'm sad that the real Rachel is missing this moment. I get a lump in my throat as I think of her, on location, in New York with Charlie, no doubt eating at all my favorite New York haunts, living my life. But as Audrey hugs me tightly before waltzing out the door with Mr. Perfect, I wonder if it's the life I want anymore.

John shuts the door and peers through the window to

watch them leave. "Nice guy," he says. "He better not break her heart."

"I know," I say, and try not to think about the smug look on his face I caught earlier. I sit down on Rachel and John's worn couch, admiring its comfort and making a vow to myself to get rid of my own uncomfortable furniture the moment I get back home. "Thanks for letting her go. Potential broken heart or not, it's time to let her grow up."

He sinks into the couch next to me. "True. It's just so hard. I had to stop myself from jumping in the car and following them." He laughs, but I know he's serious.

I touch his arm. "She's a smart girl, she'll be fine."

For the second time today, he pulls me in for an embrace and I bury my head in his shoulder. "It seems unfair that Audrey is the only one dating," he says. "Can I take you out this week?"

I pull back, surprised. It's one thing to slip into your best friend's body and live with her husband who doesn't seem to give a shit anymore. It's a whole other thing to start going on romantic dates with him. But how can I say no? John really seems to be coming around and the last thing I want to do is send him back to being that detached jerk I moved in with a few weeks ago. I tell myself I'd be doing this for Rachel, that she'll come back to a husband that's ready to plug back in. "Sure, I'd love that," before I can stop myself.

CHAPTER 20

....

rachel

"You know we actually need to get some work done at some point," I say as Charlie twirls me and I start to lose my balance as my ice skate catches. He grabs the sleeve of my coat and pulls me upright before I fall. Charlie to the rescue. *Yet again.* If he only knew how in the span of just a few days he'd made me feel sexy and self-confident for the first time in years.

"We're doing research." Charlie flashes me a boyish grin and I can't help but laugh, despite my anxiety that we're not in the office working alongside the producers and associate producers trying to secure interviews with the key players in the Ryan McKnight scandal.

"Remind me. How is ice skating in Central Park research again?" I gaze up at the sun reflecting against the skyscrapers and grab Charlie's hand to steady myself.

"I think Ryan McKnight skated here once."

We've been having so much fun since arriving in New York last night, grabbing hot dogs from a street vendor, sitting on the steps of the Metropolitan Museum of Art people watching and talking until we couldn't stand the cold a minute longer, then ducking into a Starbucks for hot cocoa. I don't want to bring us back to reality and remind Charlie that we still don't have the exclusive interview with Ryan McKnight's estranged wife, Daisy. That even though a crafty production assistant tracked down her cell phone number and I called and gave her my best sell for why she should come on, she'd told me she'd need to think about it and call me back. But that might never happen. Then what?

I try to relax and enjoy the moment. Why am I always so high strung? Why do I force Audrey to do her homework the second she walks in the door from school? *Why don't I ask her about her day first? About boys?* Maybe if I did, we'd be closer. And I'd know her the way Casey seems to in just a few short weeks. Maybe I'd even agree that she was mature enough to date. And maybe the photos Casey texted me of Audrey getting ready for her first date wouldn't have caused me to fall into a heaping mess on the marble floor of my hotel bathroom. I was conflicted that she's dating at all, while feeling guilty and regretful that I wasn't there.

Suddenly, a man with a long-lens camera is skating in our direction. Is he taking pictures of us? Just as I turn to ask Charlie what's going on, another man with a camera appears and begins snapping photos, and I realize, they're the paparazzi. I pull my arm up to protect my face, as if that's going to help. They're obviously taking pictures of Casey and who they think must be her flavor of the month.

Since the interview with Ryan McKnight, Casey Lee has become a household name—this week even gracing the cover of *People* magazine (well, a square on the bottom right, but still!).

Suddenly Casey's love life is news. Should I have been more careful today? Was it a rookie mistake on my part to go to such a public place with Charlie? Were they taking pictures of us last night too? And how will Casey feel when she sees pictures of herself and Charlie in the tabloids? Ice skating, no less! Especially after she warned me I needed to keep things with him professional. I sigh, already knowing the answer.

"We'd better get going," I say, feeling defeated.

"Says who? They already got their picture, let's continue our fun." Charlie skates circles around me, literally.

I hesitate as I watch the paparazzi skate away, snow beginning to fall around us, thinking of Casey, knowing we should go, but wanting to stay with Charlie, here in this moment. "You're right. They can't stop us!" I skate past him awkwardly but he quickly catches up and I feel his arms wrap around my waist. For a moment, I let his hands rest there and lean my head back against his chest. Just as I begin to wonder what John would think if he saw me like this, another man with a camera ice skates past us and takes our picture. And I know instantly that he got *the* shot; the picture all the gossip sites will salivate over. I can write the headline for them, *Casey Lee Heats Up the Ice as She Melts into Her New Man*.

"Let's go," I say, this time not taking no for an answer.

"What the fuck were you thinking?" Casey launches into a tirade the moment I answer my cell phone the next day.

"I wasn't," I answer quietly, backstage at the studio we've rented. I hear footsteps behind me, spin around quickly, and nearly knock over a young girl who looks more like a super-model than a production assistant. She tries to hand me a stack of blue cards for my exclusive sit-down interview with Daisy McKnight. The past twenty-four hours had been a whirlwind. From the time Charlie and I left the ice rink to just a few hours later when the picture showed up on TMZ, to last night when I spent two hours on the phone successfully convincing Daisy to tell her story.

She'd cried throughout our phone conversation, revealing to me why she was choosing to stand by her husband. How she knew what the press was going to say, especially now that as many as four women had come forward, each making an allegation that he'd slept with them. So far, Ryan had only admitted to the one in the hot tub, but Daisy knew in her gut they were all telling the truth and suspected there were even more. That's off the record, she'd warned, momentarily remembering who she was talking to. *I have to do it for our five-year-old daughter,* she'd said, her voice small, sounding more like she was trying to convince herself than me.

I'd told her I understood why she'd want to keep her family together at all costs, thinking again of the photos Casey texted me of Audrey before she went on her first date, looking so beautiful and grown up (and stylish!). Thinking for a moment of my own potential indiscretion with Charlie and how if I did cross the line, where would that leave my marriage, my family, and me? Daisy had been surprised that I was so insightful about her situation because I wasn't married and didn't have any kids, did I? "I'm very close to my nieces," was all I could offer her. I hadn't worked that hard since I tried to convince the PTA to sell wrapping paper instead of flavored popcorn for the annual fund-raiser (as I'm sure Casey now knows, those PTA moms aren't a walk in the park either!).

"Casey, we need you over here for a lighting check." The

stage manager came around the corner and motioned for me to sit in an oversized cream chair while an audio guy put a mic pack on me.

Fiona glares at me from an identical chair across from mine. She's doing the lighting check for Daisy because they're both blond and about the same height. But that's where the similarities end. Unlike Fiona, Daisy is natural. No plastic surgery. Nothing fake about her. In fact she seems genuinely sweet, a former schoolteacher from the Midwest who met Ryan early in his career when he came to the Mall of America to perform "Baby It's You," the song that would catapult him into ridiculous boy-band fame. She was working in one of the clothing stores there and he'd noticed her and asked one of his "people" to inquire if she'd like to meet him. Not having a clue who he was, but incredibly curious, she'd agreed. "And we've been together ever since, twelve years just this month, you know, the night he was with her . . ." Daisy had trailed off and I didn't push her to talk about the fact that he cheated on her on their wedding anniversary. I just promised myself I'd handle the interview well for her sake. She trusted me now.

"I don't know what I'm more upset about," Casey snaps, "that you went ice skating with Charlie and got all lovey dovey with him—which by the way you're going to have to explain in a minute—or that you were wearing that god-awful coat. Wait, I'm zooming in now. Jesus, is that my old pea coat from college?"

I slouch down in my seat and close my eyes, not prepared to have this conversation even though I know I owe it to Casey to have it.

"Sorry to interrupt you, Casey, but can you please sit up a little taller while we check this lighting? We're almost done."

The stage manager is hovering nearby and I know he's anxious to get this done with only an hour until we roll tape. "I told her," the stage manager says into his headset to the director in the control room.

"Yeah, sorry." I sit up.

"Yeah, sorry? That's all I get?" Casey spits.

"Not you, I was talking to the stage manager."

"Can you focus on this please? It's only my life we're talking about here."

It's not just your life anymore, I think, and despite it all, I can't help but smile as I remember Charlie's arms around my waist. How safe I felt. How sexy I felt, even in Casey's old pea coat.

"Are you even listening to me?" Casey snaps.

"Yes, I am. Sorry, but I can't really talk about this *here*," I say as the roving cameraman positions his camera in front of me. I stay sitting tall even though I want to jolt backward, still not feeling completely comfortable with a camera so close to my crow's-feet.

"Oh, is that so? You certainly didn't have any problem gallivanting around town with Charlie and suddenly you want to be discreet? Everyone knows you were out canoodling with him, even if they're pretending they don't. They've all seen the picture. This is my professional reputation at stake here. Don't you realize that? Are you trying to ruin my career?"

I shuffle the blue cards in my hand, reading over the questions Destiny typed up from the notes I carefully wrote out after my conversation with Daisy last night. I look around the New York studio rented just for this interview. I did this. I made Ryan McKnight cry. I got Daisy to agree to an interview. I'm the reason Casey Lee is on the cover of *People* magazine.

"Last time I checked, I revived it," I say, raising my voice, causing the stage manager and the supermodel PA to spin around and look my way. Fiona's eyes widen and her signature scowl crosses her face, and Destiny, who was walking toward me with a stack of research I'd asked for, stops dead in her tracks and gives me a look as if to ask, *are you okay?* I nod my head yes, even though I'm not. Not by a long shot.

There's a long pause on the other end of the line and for a moment I wonder if Casey has hung up. I wouldn't blame her if she did. I was that mad.

Casey finally speaks, this time her voice more controlled but still icy. "I don't know what the hell you think you're doing, Rachel, but you're married. You have children. If I didn't know any better, I'd think this whole Hollywood thing has really gone to your head and you are on your way to following in your new BFF's, Ryan McKnight's, footsteps. And P.S., you're not the one Charlie's falling for here. Don't forget he thinks you're me."

CHAPTER 21

....

casey

I hang up on Rachel and throw the phone onto the bed. "Damn it!"

Charlotte looks up from her blocks in surprise at my angry tone. "Your mommy is really effing things up." I pick her up and squeeze her, trying to get the images of Rachel and Charlie doing their best *Skating with the Stars* impression out of my head.

Charlie. I got an instant migraine when I pulled up PerezHilton.com this morning, shocked to discover my own face staring back at me. In another circumstance, I might have been thrilled to grace the gossip giant's Web page, as long as it didn't involve a sex tape. But this was different. Rachel was cavorting with a man I had cared about. Probably the only man I'd ever cared about. I'd never told anyone what had happened between us, and even now, thinking about it made my heart hurt. And here comes Rachel, having no clue the Pandora's box that she's opening, showing me (and the rest of the country!) the play-by-play of what Charlie and I could have had, even after I asked her to stay away from him. It doesn't escape me that not only is she eclipsing my career in just a few short weeks, she's also trumping me in the love department as well.

And that's pretty ironic, considering her love life seemed DOA when I got here. John barely even looked at me the first week, and I had to practically force any details about his day out of him at the dinner table, making me wonder how long they had been eating in silence. And she wasn't kidding when she said he wouldn't try to have sex with me. It almost felt as if Rachel and John had been living separate lives in the same house, something that both surprised and saddened me. I'd always put their relationship on a pedestal, so finding out it was far from perfect, that it was downright lousy, was beyond disappointing. Why hadn't she confided in me? Had I really become so caught up in my own life that I didn't even know my best friend anymore? I glance again at the picture of her beaming and leaning against Charlie's chest and wonder how long she's been unhappy in her real life.

"Mom?" Audrey interrupts my thoughts. "Does this look okay?" She does a small, insecure twirl, her dress spinning like a top around her long legs.

"You look beautiful." Since her first date with Chris, I've suddenly become her fashion guru and we're becoming closer than ever. At the end of their date she'd bounded in the front door, on time and sober (I'd done one too many segments on binge-drinking celebrity teens), and bursting with excitement that he'd asked her to the formal dance. Her happiness was contagious, and soon John and I found ourselves jumping up and down, holding hands and celebrating with her. I did my very best to brush away the inner voice inside my head that made me wonder if Chris was all that he appeared.

"Oh my *God,* is that Aunt Casey?" She points to the computer screen.

"Yes," I say flatly.

"What is she doing?"

"Something she shouldn't be," I answer and close the laptop. "She's acting like an idiot!"

"Why do you say that? She looks like she's having fun with that guy. She looks . . . happy, happier than I've ever seen her look."

I pop the laptop back open and peer at the picture again. Is that what I look like when I'm with Charlie? Not Rachel as me, but the real me? I sigh and think back to how my heart would skip a beat when he walked into the studio. That he was the only person there who seemed to get me. How much it hurt when he wouldn't even make eye contact for months after I melted down and told him never to call me again. And how I wish I could tell him that I still question if I made the right decision that day. "Yes, she does look happy. But she works with him. You can't just go around ice skating with your producer."

"Why not?" Audrey asked. "If you find love, why should it matter where you find it?" She scrolls down the page and clicks on the other photos. "Don't you want Aunt Casey to be happy?"

"More than anything," I say quietly. "But life isn't always that simple."

• • •

Three hours later, I hang up the phone and mark yet another hotel off my list. I've called half the hotels in the city trying to locate Brian, our body-switching bartender, to no avail. Even if there was a Brian on staff, no one fits his description. But I've refused to give up, calling at least ten hotels a day, hoping once I track him down, he'll finally tell us how to get our lives back. I know both he and that psychic told us there's a lesson to be learned here and that it has to do with a "promotion," but so far the only thing I've learned is how to steam carrots and why Spanx are critical after having three kids. And with each day I'm here, I start to wonder even if we do make it back to our own lives, will I still fit into mine?

As I walk down the hall to Charlotte's room and pull the blanket over her as she sleeps soundly, I want to figure out what the word *promotion* means in all of this, but I'm also scared of what it could mean. If it's the key to switching back, leaving here might not be as easy as I want it to be. As much as I've always loved these girls, I'd always thought of motherhood as a burden, something I vowed to never be a part of. Something I thought I didn't deserve. Now, as I stroke Charlotte's sweet face, I'm not so sure anymore.

"Hey," I hear John whisper from the doorway.

I put a finger to my lips and tiptoe into the hall. "Hey." I glance at my watch and shut Charlotte's door behind me. "You're home early."

"I am," he says, a sly smile on his face as he tries to hide a box behind his back

"Um, what's going on?" I reach behind him and grab the box. "What's this?"

"That," he says pointing to it, "is what you're wearing tonight. Audrey's going to watch the kids. Get dressed, I'm taking you out!"

"Are you serious?" I squeal. I hadn't been out, well, since I was Casey. The thought of a Belvedere and soda makes my mouth water.

"You deserve a night out. Now go put this on," he says, pushing me toward the bedroom.

I shut the door behind me, hoping he doesn't follow. I have no idea what I'd do if he picked this moment to want to watch me undress. Even though it's not my own body, it would just be awkward. I glance nervously at the door as I shake the box, equally scared to discover what might be inside. John always dressed well, but he wasn't exactly someone I would want choosing my outfit, especially when I hadn't had a proper night out in weeks. I pull away the paper apprehensively and find an exquisite black silk dress and oversized hoop earrings. It's simple and sexy all at the same time. *Well done, John!* I set the box down on the bed and stare at Rachel's reflection in the mirror, touched by John's sweet gesture. He'd always been thoughtful; it was one of the things I'd always loved about him. Getting up early and running out to get coffee when we all woke up hungover in college, and after Rachel found out she was pregnant with Audrey, making late-night trips to satisfy her every craving, never complaining when he gained ten pounds himself from indulging in all the late night snacks she demanded. That was the John I knew and loved.

I take my time getting ready, cherishing this rare time alone. I used to take time for granted, and now I realize Rachel doesn't get much of it to herself. As I slip on the black dress, I also can't help but wonder how Rachel will feel about her husband taking me on a date. And was John expecting some kind of gift in return? He may have given me my space while I was getting dressed (thankfully!), but would he later tonight when I was undressing?

I wondered if Rachel and Charlie were sharing a suite in New York. I've never taken her for the cheating type, but these weren't exactly normal circumstances. Was it still cheating if she did it as me? And would the betrayal sting as much?

I smooth my dress one more time before heading downstairs where John is giving Audrey strict instructions for tonight. "Mom!" Audrey's eyes widen. "You look amazing!"

"Thank you," I say, hugging her tightly. "Your dad bought it for me."

She fingers the soft fabric then high-fives her dad. "Nice job."

John blushes and I'm struck by how cute he looks.

"I do manage to get a few things right here and there," he says as he grabs my hand. My heart skips a beat, involuntarily. "Are you ready for some fun?" he asks.

I think of Charlie and Rachel, imagining them drinking champagne somewhere in New York. "You have no idea!"

CHAPTER 22

....

rachel

As I pull the down comforter around me, I'm surprised by how good it feels to be back in Casey's bed. To not wish even for a second that I was in my own with John. Charlie and I returned from New York earlier this afternoon, and although we shared a car service from the airport and he'd not so subtly hinted at wanting to come over (his hand planted firmly on my upper thigh the entire ride home), I'd feigned exhaustion and promised to call him later.

As the driver pulled my bags out of the trunk and Charlie stood awkwardly on the curb, I'd wanted more than anything to invite him in, but that damn little voice inside my head warned me that it would be a very bad idea. That annoying little voice that has been constantly reminding me that I'm not the real Casey Lee. That I'm not, as the real Casey had so harshly pointed out, the one Charlie's falling for. But what if the voice is wrong? If Casey's wrong? What if I am the one he's falling for?

Sure, it's not my body, but it's my personality, my mind, and my humor. Isn't it?

We'd had an amazing time in New York—professionally and personally. The interview with Daisy McKnight was even better than the one with her husband. Even though there were five cameras and a dozen staff and crew surrounding us, it felt like we were just two girlfriends talking. I abandoned my blue cards midway through and she'd opened up about everything—even things she'd said originally would have to be off the record, like her suspicion there were several other women. And in the last few minutes of the interview, I took a risk. I asked her to call Ryan on camera. And if he answered, to tell him how she felt. And she'd agreed without hesitation, pulling out her bedazzled iPhone. I held my breath as the phone rang and looked at the staff and crew, all leaning in, looking like vultures circling a carcass as they waited to get the shot, the sound bite, whatever was needed to make this interview a hit. Of course we'd needed to handle some technical housekeeping before we could roll tape on the call. An audio guy had to hook Daisy's cell to a microphone so we could hear Ryan's end of the conversation. And Ryan had to give a verbal release for his interview to be used on camera after he'd answered. To our surprise, he did. But even after all that, the conversation between them was emotional and heartbreaking and raw.

I'd scanned the room for Charlie, as Ryan and Daisy cried together and Ryan apologized. When I'd found him, our eyes locked and I knew he was thinking what I was thinking. This was it. The career-changing moment that would open more doors than I ever thought possible. But I could also tell that he was looking not at the Casey Lee everyone else saw, the one whose face was plastered with foundation and eyes were heavy with multiple layers of false eyelashes, but the Casey who couldn't wait to wash her face, throw on a pair of sweats, and knock back a couple of cocktails and scream to the rooftops, *I've arrived! I may be pushing forty, but dammit, I've arrived!* But then there was that little detail about not really being Casey Lee, and unless I wanted to stay in Casey's body permanently (was that even an option?) this was not *my* career-changing moment, this was not *my* unspoken moment with a cute and sweet man across the room, this was not *my* life.

When the interview was over, Daisy whispered to me off camera that she and Ryan would give me the exclusive on their first sit-down interview together. I was intoxicated with pride after everyone—even Dean through his gritted veneers—complimented me. Well, if *you didn't suck* counts as praise.

But the best accolades came from Charlie. He'd pulled me aside and told me that I'd never been better and should be very proud. Then he'd kissed me on the cheek and I felt my knees start to buckle under me, wondering if a kiss on the cheek could do that, what could a kiss on the lips do? Then he whisked me off to dinner and drinks and before I knew it, it was time to fly home. He stood in the hall outside my hotel room and I knew he wanted to come inside. But I'd made an excuse then just like I had today. I'd told him I still had to pack before the flight. He'd simply taken his finger and ran it down the length of my arm and said, "Rain check, then." When I got inside my room and stared at the suitcase I knew Destiny had already packed for me, I hated that I'd told a lie. But he'd never understand the truth: that I was married; that I had three daughters; that I was living someone else's life.

The sound of the doorbell pulls me out of my reverie. I put

on a silk robe from a chair beside Casey's bed and head toward the front door. When I peer out the peephole, Charlie is standing there with a cat-who-ate-the-canary look on his face. I pull the door open only far enough to see him through the chain.

"Hey."

"Hey," he mimics. "So you gonna let me in or what? I have big, make that huge, news."

I debate asking him to tell me through the chain, but think better of it. If he's making a house call, it must be important. I pull the tie around my silk robe tighter.

"Give me a second."

"Um, okay, you know where to find me," he says and laughs as I close the door on him.

I hurry into the bedroom, throw on a sweat suit, run into the bathroom and rub toothpaste across my teeth, and fling the front door open. "Sorry about that. The place was a mess," I say, thinking Casey's housekeeper comes so often I barely have time to mess it up.

"You missed a spot." He runs his finger over the dust-free table.

I grab a pillow off the couch and swat him with it. "Whatever, just give me the news already."

"Sure you don't want to organize your closets first or clean out the refrigerator or something?"

"Tell me!"

"Are you sitting down?" he says with a chuckle.

I look down at my feet planted firmly on the floor. "Should I be?"

"Uh, yes, for sure."

I lower myself onto the couch slowly, starting to have a pretty good idea where this conversation is going, but suddenly

I'm not at all sure I want to hear the news. Not because it won't be good, but because it won't be mine.

Charlie watches my face change. "It's good, you know."

"I know." I force a smile. "Okay, lay it on me."

"The New York executives are so excited about the buzz the show is getting from the promo clips of the Daisy and Ryan phone call we fed out last night that they're coming to L.A. to meet with you."

I consider the news. So it's happening. They're going to offer me, well, Casey Lee her own show in New York. The only question is, what am I going to say?

"Casey. Hello?" Charlie waves his hand in front of my face. "You know what this means, right?"

"I think so . . ." I bite my lower lip, fighting back the tears. Suddenly remembering, of all things, my college graduation. I was so pregnant that I could barely walk, but I'd insisted on going to the ceremony. I needed to see Casey accept her diploma. To see John get his. I needed the fact that I didn't graduate to be real. As I'd watched Casey fling her graduation cap in the air and hug John tightly, I'd rubbed my stomach, feeling incredibly sad and jealous and also incredibly happy all at the same time. It was exactly how I felt now.

"I thought you'd be excited. I thought this is what you wanted."

"This is what I wanted." *I just didn't realize it until it was twenty years too late.*

"Then why don't I believe you?"

"It's complicated."

"Try me."

"I can't. You don't know how badly I wish I could explain it to you . . . all of it. But you'd never understand. Never in a million years."

"Come on." He sits on the couch next to me, so close that I can smell his scent, which has driven me crazy the past few days. It makes me want to grab him and bury my nose in his neck and inhale deeply.

If he only knew how much I'd love to tell him everything, how the woman he's been falling for is really an exhausted stay-at-home mom; that if I lean in like I want to right now and kiss him passionately, that it will be the first time I've kissed a man besides John in over twenty years; that it scares me how strongly I'm considering doing just that. "It's nothing," I finally answer and pull myself up off the couch, away from temptation. "I'm just in shock, that's all." I walk over to the mirror and look at Casey's reflection. "It feels like it's not really happening to me."

Charlie walks up behind me and wraps his arms around my waist. "Casey Lee, you better get used to this. Because this is just the beginning of the biggest damn thing that's ever happened to you."

CHAPTER 23

. . . .

casey

I freeze when I see the black convertible Bentley sitting in the driveway. "What the . . ."

"Don't get too excited." John laughs as he tosses the key in the air. "It's just a loaner from a friend."

"It's gorgeous," I say and walk around to inspect it before hopping in.

"Bet you never thought you'd be sitting in one of these, huh?"

"Right," I say, not mentioning that I almost bought one just like it last month. I was at the dealership, ready to sign the papers for my dream car when I spied a couple in the showroom, kissing gently. I imagined them driving around town, top down, a slight breeze flowing through their perfectly coiffed hair. I tried to think of the person I could have my own convertible adventure with but the image of Destiny and me driving down Wilshire Boulevard kept popping into my head. Buying the Bentley suddenly seemed like a childish, silly thing to do—just another way to amuse myself. I grabbed my purse and hurried out past the lovey-dovey couple, ignoring the calls from the confused salesman.

"This is great," I say sincerely. "What a gorgeous day." It had been unseasonably warm for the past week, even for Los Angeles. I lean back and close my eyes to breathe in the sunshine. And even though I'm still pissed at her, I wish Rachel could be here to enjoy it. Rachel, who drives an old minivan with crushed Cheez-Its mashed into the seats and discarded juice boxes crowding the floor, would appreciate this. "Where are we going?"

"Down the coast," he replies vaguely as he backs the Bentley out of the driveway gingerly, as if he's afraid he might break it.

"If you're going to drive like that the whole way, we may never get there!" I tease.

"Oh yeah? How's this?" He guns the engine as he pulls out onto Washington Boulevard.

"Much better! How far down the coast are we going?"

"Far enough to get away from it all," he says and puts his hand on my exposed leg. I resist the urge to flinch and try to settle back into my seat. The warmth of his hand is so comforting, wrapped tightly around my thigh. Is this how it feels to be someone's someone? I plug in the iTouch and select Pearl Jam, our favorite band from college, and am rewarded with a huge smile from John. "You remembered."

"Of course. It wasn't that long ago."

He sighs. "It sure feels like it sometimes."

We chat the entire way down. Me, asking questions about his work; John, surprised that I asked. *Doesn't Rachel want to know what he does all day? Who he interacts with? What's in his head?* He opens up about his company's top drug going generic next year and the possible layoffs that will likely come along with it, how although he's not too fearful for his own job right now, he worries about all the sales reps and district managers who work with him. He tells me that he's been losing sleep about the future of pharmaceuticals in general. He's been there so many years. Where would he go?

"It's never too late to reinvent yourself," I say, trying to make him feel better although it's not something I'm sure I believe. If I had to switch industries, I would be devastated. But it's clearly weighing heavily on his mind and he's gone to so much trouble to make me, or rather Rachel, happy. I feel strangely desperate to make him feel happy too.

We pull up to our destination, a charming hotel in Laguna Beach. My heart starts to pound as I imagine being trapped in a hotel room with him all night. I'm definitely going to have to throw down the period card. "We aren't staying here tonight, right?" I ask briskly, and then not wanting to sound ungrateful, quickly add, "I'm just not sure that Audrey can handle the baby overnight."

He hands the keys to the valet and comes around to help me out of the car. "Don't worry. There's an amazing bar on the roof. I thought you might like to watch the sunset with me."

I exhale deeply and smile. "I would love that," I answer as he grabs my hand and takes me into the lobby and up the winding staircase that leads us to a beautiful rooftop patio. John gives them our names and the server shows us to the best table and removes the RESERVED sign. "Wow," is all I can say as I take in the panoramic view of the Pacific Ocean and the palm trees swaying in the slight breeze, the sun sparkling on the water below us. "This is gorgeous!" Something about getting out of L.A., down to the more easygoing pace of Orange County, is so refreshing. Sure, I had been to a ton of beautiful places in Malibu and Santa Monica, but I still had to be "on." Whether at a party or a shoot for *Gossip TV,* I always had to work my ass off at those things, schmoozing and kissing the asses of people I could barely stand to be around. All, except of course, Destiny and Charlie. But I don't want to think about Charlie right now. I grab John's hand. "Thanks. This is perfect."

The server sets our drinks down and we toast the wonderful view. John asks me if I'd ever consider living down here and I tell him I'm not sure. The thought of having Rachel and the kids this far away from me makes me uncomfortable. I sip my drink slowly as Rachel would. John had looked at me funny when I ordered a Belvedere and soda, probably remembering the reunion and how belligerent Rachel got. It was obvious that night that she usually didn't drink that much. But now, after living her life, I understood why. So much effort went into making sure the kids were taken care of that I almost didn't blame her if she was too tired to go out, too tired to devote much energy to anything, even John.

I think back to the John and Rachel I knew in high school and in college, the way they lit up when the other was around. The three of us were inseparable, except for the temporary boyfriends that would flit in and out of my life. I was so picky, Rachel would constantly tell me. But the truth was that I wanted what they had and wasn't willing to compromise until I found it. As I look at John smooth-talking the pretty blond server into moving the heater closer to our table, I realize that I'm still looking for it. And I can't quite understand why Rachel and John just let it slip out of their fingers so easily.

"So, Audrey's really been on cloud nine all week," he says when he turns back to me.

"I know, right? It's like she's a completely different person," I say, smiling to myself and for a split second considering that maybe she's switched bodies with one of her happier, nicer friends. "What do you think of Chris?" I ask, still feeling a nagging bad vibe.

"He's a great catch," John says with a twinkle in his eye. "They say he's going to make the All-CIF team this year. And that he's being scouted by USC and Michigan."

"I know!" I feign excitement before carefully adding, "I just hope Audrey's not so awestruck by him that she makes bad decisions." I look at him hard, trying to snap him out of his man crush.

He holds my gaze. "I thought you were the one who was pushing this whole dating thing. Now you're against it all of a sudden?"

"No! Not at all," I backtrack. "I still agree that Audrey should be dating. But I'm just questioning whether Chris is the guy she should be dating," I say, thinking back to the queasy feeling I had in my stomach when he smirked at me, hoping I'm just being paranoid.

"He gave me his word as a man that he would treat her with respect. And I believe him."

I had forgotten how seriously John considered someone's promise. Never one for contracts, he was always a *let's shake on it* kind of guy. Not exactly popular in today's overly litigious society, he believed that a person's word was the most important promise he could give. It was something that had always infuriated Rachel but that I found endearing, and I caught myself smiling at his faith in Chris. Maybe I should have some too.

"Okay," I concede. "I'm just excited to take her shopping for her formal dress!"

John frowns. "Just promise me you'll stay off Robertson Boulevard this time?" he asks, referring to the area famous for its designer brands and ridiculous prices.

Even though he'd explained his concerns, it still felt odd to have to answer to anyone about how I spent money. I'd done well for myself, especially since getting my hosting gig on *Gossip TV,* and I made sure to put enough away so I could live comfortably when they decided I was too old to be in front of the camera.

"Casey offered to pay for it when I told her Audrey was going," I say, deciding that's easier than dealing with John's rage when I bring home a thousand-dollar dress. Because you only get one first formal dance, and I am determined to be the fairy godmother to Audrey's Cinderella.

"Where has Little C been anyway? Out of town?" John asks.

"She's been in New York," I say, not wanting to talk about Rachel. Not wanting to think about our fight, the harsh words we both said. How this body-swapping thing has only driven us further apart. Wondering again what the point of it all has been. And if we ever switch back, will we be able to stay friends?

"New York! Wow, that girl, she really gets to live the life."

"I don't think her life is all it's cracked up to be," I respond lightly and turn to stare at the view.

"Hey, are you feeling jealous again? Is this because she finally beat *Access L.A.*?" He laughs sheepishly, and then catching the confused expression on my face, adding, "I do read the entertainment section occasionally."

Jealous? Again? Was Rachel jealous of me?

"I'm not jealous," I say defensively. "Why in the world would I be jealous? I've got a husband, a family. I've never even had to hold down a real job!" I regret the words the minute they leave my mouth. I know now that being home with three kids is probably the hardest job I'll ever have.

"Hold on." John puts his hands up. "Don't be like that. We're having such a nice time." He reaches over and strokes my arm. "It just seems like Casey's really hitting her stride at work lately, that's all."

"Yeah, I've noticed," I say quietly and lean into the curve of his arm despite myself.

"Hey," John says gently. "It's not too late for you to live out your dreams too. I know you've been dead set against going back to work, but if Casey's success is getting to you, then maybe it's time for you to get back out there. Didn't you just say it's never too late to reinvent yourself?"

"I don't know," I say, wondering what the real Rachel would do. Most people in TV are over the hill at forty, not just getting their feet wet. And what else is she qualified for?

"It's just that, there's definitely something different about you ever since we went to the reunion."

I take a huge gulp of my drink. "I can explain . . ." I start to mumble.

"Shhh . . ." He puts a finger to my lips and I'm terrified he's going to kiss me. "I don't really care what happened. I just thought you wanting to go back to work might be the reason behind it. All I know is that the woman I fell in love with is back. *We're* back." He signals the server for another round. "I was starting to think we might have lost us forever."

I gaze back at him, humbled by his kind words. This was the John I had known for years, the one who would walk over hot coals for Rachel. The one who would borrow a hundred-thousand-dollar car from God-knows-who and drive over an hour to have a drink and watch the sunset with her. I only wish *she* was here to see it instead of gallivanting all over New York with the one man I've ever cared about. "I thought we had too. It's nice to see *us* again."

John leans in to kiss me and I turn my cheek at the last second. "What?" he says, looking hurt, and I'm worried I've ruined the moment.

I point to my throat. "I think I'm getting sick. I don't want you to catch it."

He looks relieved. "Well, we can do other things later that don't require kissing."

I put what I hope looks like a smile on my face and whisper in his ear, "I've got my period, honey. Sorry."

CHAPTER 24

....

rachel

I hit delete, erasing the email to Casey I spent the last hour writing and rewriting. It doesn't matter how I arrange the words, when I read them back, they sound hollow and fake. And maybe they are. Maybe I'm trying too hard. We haven't spoken since our fight a few days ago (the longest I can remember being mad at each other since I talked her into that spiral perm in junior high). And even though we've literally never been closer—I'm inside her body!—we've never been further apart. Of all the times to be in an argument. My phone beeps and I grab it.

Downstairs. Can't wait to see you.

A text message from Charlie. Here to take me to the black-tie party for *GossipTV's* five-hundredth episode. Since the McKnight interview aired, it's become Hollywood's hottest ticket (the McKnights are even rumored to be dropping in). I take a last look in the full-length mirror, amazed at how beautiful Casey Lee looks in the short, sassy strapless gown picked out by Rachel Zoe, *celebrity stylist.* The one whose show I used to watch late at night on Bravo while wearing John's sweat pants and breast-feeding Charlotte. The same one who hand-selected this gorgeous silk dress I'm wearing.

"Wow." Charlie kisses me on the cheek and helps me into the limo.

"You clean up nice too," I say with a laugh, instantly relaxing. "And you shaved." I touch my hand to his smooth cheek.

He gives me a shy smile. "You like?"

I imagine kissing him. "Very much."

"So about the other night . . ." I start to explain that I'm sorry for rushing him out of the apartment, for not opening up to him about what was wrong.

He puts his finger up to my lips. "Let's just enjoy this evening."

Relieved, I take his hand in mine. As we ride in silence to the party, I think about how great it was to see Audrey, Sophie, and Charlotte yesterday—even though they didn't see me.

To say I stalked them is fair. I'd swiped a pair of Jackie O—like sunglasses from the wardrobe department and headed down to my house, hoping to catch a glimpse of the girls as they arrived home from school. Sure, it probably would've been easier to swallow my pride and just face Casey. But I wasn't ready. And I also wasn't sure I was prepared to be so close to my own life again. Spying on my family from a production assistant's car I borrowed, parked slightly down the block, was as close as I was willing to get. Even though I missed them terribly, I had compartmentalized those feelings, finding them as hard to face as Casey. I wasn't sure what was happening with Charlie, but I was having feelings for him that a wife shouldn't be having for a man other than her husband. That much I knew for sure.

What I didn't bank on was also seeing John and Casey.

I'd done a double take when John stepped out of the car and grabbed Charlotte from her car seat. It was only four o'clock. What was he doing home? I couldn't remember the last time he'd left work that early. Audrey and Sophie pulled up behind them with Casey. I watched as the family united and John handed Casey the baby—my baby. As they walked into the house, John put his hand on her ass (well, *my* ass) and Casey put her hand over it for a few seconds before flirtatiously swatting it away as John kissed her head. What was going on? I didn't want to think about it. Casey would never betray me like that, would she? If you'd asked me a few weeks ago, I would have said, *Never*. Now, especially after the way I had acted in New York, I wasn't so sure.

What I did know for sure was that after seeing that public display of affection between my best friend and my husband, it would be easier to hold Charlie's hand. Who cares if John didn't actually know that Casey wasn't his real wife? Casey sure as hell did.

But I push the image of John's hand on Casey's ass out of my head as Charlie and I pull up to the party. If there was ever a time I needed a game face, it was now. The entrance to the building is lined with photographers and camera crews and I feel my heart start to beat faster. I exit the limo very carefully, having seen way too many inappropriate pictures of Britney Spears' hoo-ha in the tabloids.

The night is a whirlwind of ass kissing and painful small talk. At least there are some major celebrity sightings. Everyone from Heidi Klum to Victoria Beckham is there. Finally, Charlie and I steal away for some fresh air. As we head out onto the patio, I inhale deeply and take a drink of my champagne.

"Socializing is hard work." I rest my head on his shoulder and look up at the lights scattered across the Hollywood hills.

"I'd think you'd be used to it by now." Charlie laughs, loosening his bow tie.

"I'll never be used to it." I sigh, thinking again of how much work Casey's seemingly all-glamorous life is turning out to be. The hours spent in hair and makeup, the endless production meetings, the pettiness.

"Well, if you keep kicking butt at work, I think there might only be more of this kind of thing, not less." He turns serious for a moment. "Thought any more about what you're going to say to the executives?"

"About New York?"

"No, about your hair—of course, New York."

"I think I'm just going to wait and see what they say. I'm trying to live in the moment."

"Like this moment?" Charlie brushes my hair away from my face. Is this it? Is he going to kiss me? Am I going to stop him?

He leans in and I don't feel myself moving away. I don't want to move away.

"There you are!" I spin around and nearly run into a woman with fiery red hair coming at me like a rocket. She's followed by two men I recognize from New York.

"Speak of the devil!" Charlie says a little too loudly, nervously tightening his bow tie, getting back to business. "We were just talking about you."

"Oh, you were, were you?" The redhead extends her hand and I notice that her nail polish is the exact same color as her hair. "I'm Ava Greenwood, president of programming for Gossip Network. And you already know Mark and Jenson."

I nod accordingly and air kisses circulate. I want to gag, but quickly pull it together.

"So we'd planned to talk to you tomorrow, Casey Lee, but this party is just *buzzing* about you." She puts her hand on my arm, leans in a little too close, nearly spilling her champagne on me. "And did you see the McKnights? They just arrived and I heard they were asking for you. And we realized we'd better remind you that you're very valued here. And we wouldn't want to see you go."

"Go?"

"Don't play coy, my dear." I think I smell garlic shrimp on her breath. "There have to be people calling trying to lure you away. I could name three people right now that I'm sure have contacted you." She and the execs exchange a look.

Destiny had passed me several messages and forwarded emails saying as much, but I honestly hadn't had the time to read them.

"And you may have heard rumblings about this." She gives Charlie a look before continuing. "But we officially want to not only offer you your own show in New York City, but—and we can discuss this more later—we're also prepared to give you a generous raise."

"Very generous," Jenson—or was that Mark?—chimes in.

"And if I didn't want to relocate?" It's not until all three executives stare at me like I have three heads that I remember I'm not Rachel Cole. I'm Casey Lee. And she would've never asked that question because she's been killing herself for years to get an opportunity like this.

Ava leans in even closer. "Then I'd have to remind you about your contract. The one you signed that clearly states you're will-ing to relocate at any time."

"Of course." I recover. "I'm fully aware of the details of my contract." Ava and her minions breathe a collective sigh of re-lief. But I know I need to buy myself some time. Because as great an opportunity as this is for Casey, there is no way I could leave my family. "I'd just like to talk it over with my agent and have my attorney review the contract. Can I have two weeks?" I feel Charlie's hand squeeze my arm and I hope I've said the right thing since I have no idea what I'm talking about.

The executives share a quick look before Ava gives a small nod. "Oh, yes, that should be fine." She reaches her hand out to mine again. "But just two weeks, Casey. We need to strike while the iron's hot."

I take her hand and hope she doesn't feel mine shaking. "Two weeks," I repeat, realizing that the deadline is the same night as John's surprise birthday party. And it looks like the surprise will be that his wife will be moving to New York City in her best friend's body.

Ava starts back toward the party, but spins around. "Oh, and Casey dear?"

"Yeah?"

Ava walks closer to me and whispers, "I know you've obvi-ously gotten pretty comfortable in your job." She looks me up and down, her eyes resting on my middle section. "But we'll need you back to your fighting weight when we head to the Big Apple." She smiles tightly and I crumple into a chair the minute she's gone.

Did she just call me fat? I mean, sure, Rachel Zoe seemed a bit surprised when she'd taken my measurements last week. And yes, I had to fight with the zipper on a pair of Casey's jeans the other day, but still! I run my hand over Casey's still very flat stomach despite all of my emotional eating. Sure, maybe I'd put on a couple of pounds, but she was still rail thin—too thin if you ask me. Is this what she goes through? A size zero told to shrink even more?

Charlie sits next to me, unaware of Ava's comments, which I decide to keep to myself. "Isn't this what you've been working for? Your own show?"

"Yes and no, but it's complicated."

"I'm hearing that a lot from you lately, but I don't get it. Since when is this so complicated for you? Since I've known you, this is the kind of opportunity you've always wanted. But now that it's actually here, you look about as excited as someone who's about to get a root canal."

I can't meet his eyes. He's right. Sitting through a time-share presentation sounds more appealing to me right now. I look back toward the party and notice Fiona watching us, having no doubt she took in the entire scene with the executives and put two and two together. If I'm not careful, she'll pounce on this opportunity and try to sabotage it for Casey. "I shouldn't be out here. I should be inside mingling—doing my job." I start to make my way toward the door but Charlie steps in front of me.

"Hold it. You're not going anywhere. Not until I do this." Charlie leans in, presumably to kiss me just as flashbulbs go off, momentarily blinding me as I turn to my right and see a long-lens camera sticking out of the bushes. Still seeing spots, I grab Charlie's arm. "C'mon, let's go."

"What's the rush? Looks like you two were about to share something special out there. Maybe continue what you started on the ice," Fiona says bitingly as she slinks over from behind the archway, where she must have been watching us.

I roll my eyes at Charlie. "Want a drink?"

"Are you sure that's the best idea?" Fiona cackles. "This is an important juncture in your career. I'd hate to see you screw it up by being drunk."

"*Juncture:* that's a big word for you, Fiona. Are you sure you even know what it means?"

Charlie stifles a laugh. "C'mon, Case, let's get that drink."

"Make it a double!" I laugh. "I want to be extra wasted when I talk to the McKnights. Heard they were asking for me."

Fiona ignores my dig. "Whatever, Casey. Everyone knows the executives are offering you your own show. The question is, when are they going to realize you have the shelf life of a carton of cottage cheese?"

"Speaking of cottage cheese, you should really hit the gym, Fiona. Your dress is so short, I can see yours on the back of your legs. So sad for such a *young* girl," Destiny says as she grabs my arm and steers me away, leaving Fiona self-consciously tugging at her dress.

"Thanks." I hug Destiny. "I've never been so happy to see you."

"You know I've always got your back." She leans in. "So, people are talking. Is it true? They officially offered it to you?"

"Yes."

Destiny lets out a squeal. "Oh my God, this is it. Finally. We're getting what we've always wanted!" She throws her hand over her mouth. "Sorry, I forgot where we were for a minute."

We're *getting what* we've *always wanted*. It hadn't occurred to me until now that this decision would affect more than just me, or Casey. Of course this is huge for Destiny. She's been Casey's assistant for over a decade. Just another reason I can't screw this up.

She studies my face. "What's wrong? Why don't you seem excited?"

"I'm going to grab those drinks. Destiny, you want something?" Charlie asks.

"No, I'm good. I'm high on adrenaline right now!"

"I'm just taking it all in," I say before Destiny can press further.

"Uh-huh. I know you. You're never this quiet unless something is wrong. Does this have something to do with Charlie? I heard they are thinking about offering him the executive producer job."

I try to hide my surprise. Why hadn't he told me such huge news? "No, it's not that." I spot Fiona across the room glaring at me and whispering something to Dean. "It's just Fiona. She gets to me when she makes comments about my age. What if she's right? What if they realize I'm too old for this?"

Destiny crosses her arms over her chest.

"What?" I ask.

"I'm waiting for you to stop bullshitting and to start telling me what's really going on here."

CHAPTER 25

....

casey

They say it takes twenty-one days to create a habit. But as I bounce Charlotte on my hip outside the Santa Monica hotel we've chosen for John's surprise party, I think it's far less than that. In the time I've been Rachel, I've created so many new habits that I'm not quite sure how I'll shake them if I ever get back to being myself. Like the way I've learned to feed Charlotte and make the girls' lunches and John's coffee all at the same time each morning. Or how my favorite part of the day is when Charlotte and I curl up on the couch and watch *Yo Gabba Gabba* together. Or how I sit on Audrey's bed each evening while she models outfits for me. During these moments I wonder if I'll ever be the same Casey Lee again.

I glance at my watch. Rachel texted me that she wanted to meet, but we still haven't spoken since I hung up on her in New York. I wasn't angry anymore, but for some reason, I couldn't bring myself to call her. Maybe I couldn't bear to hear about all the success she was having, how incredible she was when she interviewed Daisy McKnight, how I couldn't silence the little voice inside me that said I wouldn't have been as good. There's also the fact that being part of her *real* life and her *real* family has made me long for one of my own.

A town car pulls up and Rachel steps out wearing oversized sunglasses and holding her cell phone. She eyes me cautiously before pulling a small plastic bag from inside the latest Gucci satchel. The wardrobe department must have just gotten it in, I think as I adjust Charlotte's diaper bag on my shoulder. "Peace offering," she says as we make an exchange, the baby for the bag.

Tears fill her eyes as Charlotte grabs her face and laughs, clearly recognizing her mother, even though she has my face. "I've missed you so much, baby girl." She squeezes her tighter.

I open the bag and discover my favorite facial cream and mask. "And I've missed you so much, my love," I say as I caress the jar.

"I know how close you and your La Mer are. I thought you might be in withdrawal."

"I was," I say as I rub my cheek. "And no offense, but you could really use it!"

"Bitch," Rachel replies playfully before turning serious. "Are we okay?"

"Yes," I reply. "But can we not talk about it?" I plead. "Can we just chalk it up to body-switching stress?"

"Agreed!" Rachel looks relieved. "I'm sorry, Casey. I shouldn't have been so careless with your life in New York."

"Hey! We're *not* talking about it!" I tease.

"Right, sorry. I just had to get that out. Moving on."

"Hey, Casey, where's your boyfriend?" A man wearing worn jeans and holding a long-lens camera aimed at us jumps out from behind the valet stand.

I glance at Rachel, who's pursing her lips. *What will she say?*

"I don't have a boyfriend!" she shouts defiantly.

"Easy, killer. I was just asking." The photographer puts his hands up in front of him.

"Look, buddy, we're just trying to have some girl time. Can you give us a little space please?" I say with a smile.

"Whatever. I heard Snooki and JWoww are just around the corner, which is a bigger story anyway," he says between gritted teeth, but still snaps a bunch of photos of us before he scurries off.

"Bottom feeders!" I huff.

"Thanks for getting rid of him. I don't know how you deal with that all the time," Rachel says as we walk into the lobby of the hotel.

"No problem. I'm used to it. C'mon, I want to show you what we've got planned for John's party." Inside the elevator, I push the button for the top floor. "I think he's going to love it!"

"I bet he'll be very appreciative." She looks skeptical.

"What?" I ask.

"Nothing!" she responds and I decide not to push it.

The elevator doors open to reveal a beautiful ballroom. "It's gorgeous!" Rachel exclaims as she steps over to the window to take in the view of the beach below. "This space is perfect." She sets Charlotte down and we both watch her crawl over to a chair and pull herself up easily. "She'll be walking soon," Rachel says quietly, turning back toward the windows, the waves crashing into the sand.

"You'll be back by then," I say with more confidence than I feel.

"How's Audrey?"

"Good. She's getting so excited about the winter formal. You should see how poised she's becoming! Are you going to come dress shopping with us?"

"Yes, just as long as something doesn't come up at work," Rachel says as she checks her email and for a minute I'm shocked at how much she sounds like me. Or rather who I used to be.

"I'd think you'd move mountains to be there," I say lightly. "She really wants you to come, you know."

"Of course I don't want to miss it. But let's be honest here; she wants her fabulous *Aunt Casey* with her, not me. And you, of all people, know how it is. I can't control when the next celebrity is going to fuck up and cause a huge scandal." She waves down a passing waiter and asks him for a Diet Coke with lime. A flash of irritation passes his chiseled features before he realizes it's Casey Lee asking and quickly replaces it with a wide smile full of blinding white teeth. "Right away," he says before returning in record time with her drink.

"Yes, you're right. I see exactly how it is," I say pointedly.

She rolls her eyes at me. "Come on. You know what I mean. Don't be like that."

"Like what?"

"Like you don't understand what I'm going through right now. How much pressure I'm under! The decisions I have to make."

"Decisions? What decisions?" I ask.

"Nothing," Rachel says, backtracking.

I'm about to push her more on this when I see someone out of the corner of my eye. It's *Brian*. The bartender.

I grab Charlotte off the floor. "Come on!" I say to Rachel as I start to run toward the door.

"What?"

"I just saw Brian!" I call back to her as I pick up speed and see him turn a corner toward the stairs. "Wait!" I scream. "Brian!" I reach the stairs and start climbing, heaving as I struggle to carry Charlotte, remembering Rachel's words from early on, that I'd feel out of shape in her body. But as I attempt to take the steps two at a time, feeling the strain of muscles I didn't even know I had, I think of my trainer, Hans, who sculpted Jennifer Aniston's killer abs and trained Jennie Garth for *Dancing with the Stars*. I push myself to go faster and I can see the back of Brian's head as he's racing up the stairwell in front of me, heading out the door at the top. I look back. *Where is Rachel?*

I burst through the door and find myself on the roof of the hotel. Brian is standing to the side, casually smoking a cigarette. "You!" I call out as I walk toward him.

"Hi, Casey," he says and winks.

"Don't wink at me, asshole."

"So harsh! I thought Rachel's life was chilling you out a bit." He takes a drag and exhales, blowing a smoke ring that disintegrates inches from my face, and I move my body to shield Charlotte from the smoke.

"Please," I gasp, out of breath from chasing him. "Please tell us how to change back. We've learned our lesson."

"Have you?" He laughs. "It didn't sound like it just now in the ballroom."

"Seriously, what kind of magic is this? Is it a curse? Tell me how to make it right. Please," I plead, choking back tears. "I just want my life back."

"Do you? Do you really want it back?" He throws the cigarette down and stubs it out with his Vans tennis shoe. "Was it really so great? Were you really so happy?"

"It wasn't perfect. But it was my life."

"You're right," he says. " But . . ."

"But, what?"

"I guess I'm just wondering why there's only one of you standing up here right now."

I look back toward the door, wondering again where Rachel is. And when I turn back, Brian's gone.

As I walk carefully back down the stairs holding Charlotte tightly, wiping the tears from my face, I hear my own voice carrying up the stairwell. "Fantastic! No, no, that's great news." I walk into the ballroom and see Rachel, phone to her ear. "Okay. I can't wait to see you either."

I freeze. *Is she talking to Charlie?*

She hangs up and turns to face me. "Hey, sorry about that."

"Sorry about what? The fact that you didn't move a muscle while I hauled Charlotte up two flights of stairs chasing the one person who can help us switch back? Or sorry I just heard you talking to Charlie like you're some lovesick teenager? How many times do I have to tell you not to get involved with him?"

"Calm down. It's not what you think."

"Then please, enlighten me." I move Charlotte to my left hip.

"You just tore out of here, I wasn't sure who or what you were chasing. And then I had to take a work-related call."

"Do you want to switch back?"

"What?"

"You heard me. Do you even want to switch back? Do you want your old life back or have you decided that mine suits you better?"

"What kind of question is that? Of course I want my life back!"

"Do you?" I ask again. "Because you seem to be getting quite comfortable in Casey Lee's life." I sit down at the nearest table, pull out a bottle for Charlotte, and hand it to her.

Rachel takes the empty seat next to me. "Do I really have a choice? Would you rather be out of a job right now?" She shakes her head. "And please, let's not forget that you seem to be pretty comfortable playing house with John and the kids." She points to Charlotte, half asleep on my lap. "Don't you think that's hard on me too? Even Charlotte seems to like you better than me."

"Stop," I say.

"Come on, I'm not stupid. Audrey's never been happier since you've been there." She sighs. "John, too."

"How would you even know? You haven't been around. If you really wanted your life back you wouldn't have let a silly fight with me keep you away from your family. Just be careful. You know how much I've given up to be where I am. I'd hate to see you make the same mistakes."

Rachel starts to say something, but stops.

"Speechless, huh? That's what I thought. And for what it's worth, it's not better without you around, it's just different. And if it makes you feel better, Sophie still seems as wildly unhappy as she did before."

"Now, that I believe." Rachel laughs and puts her hand on mine and squeezes it lightly. "Tell me. What did Brian say?"

"He thought it was pretty interesting that I was the only one who chased him down like her life depended on it."

Rachel doesn't answer. "Did he say anything else? Anything helpful?"

"No. Nothing," I say and run my hands through Charlotte's hair. "We're in deep shit, aren't we?"

"Yep."

CHAPTER 26

·············

rachel

I lean into the plush leather seat in the back of the limo and take a drink from the bottle of Fiji Water the driver left for me, next to a copy of *USA Today*. These perks used to make me feel uncomfortable, but I've started to look forward to them. I curl my legs underneath me and watch the ocean slowly disappear from view as we turn onto the freeway and head toward the studio. I wonder: *Why didn't I chase Brian too?*

Casey's question has been gnawing at me since the moment she asked it. I grab the newspaper and bypass the front page, and go straight to the Life section. Sandwiched between a quote from Jennifer Lopez about her divorce from Marc Anthony and the latest fashion faux pas made by Rihanna, there's a short blurb about *Gossip TV*'s five-hundredth-episode party next to a small picture of me posing with the McKnights.

That night at the party, I'd searched the crowd for Ryan and Daisy, finally locating Daisy, trapped next to a table covered with picked-over platters of food, being held prisoner by the creepy audio guy. Her eyes pleaded with me to save her and just as he was launching into a story about the inappropriate things that happen when people forget they're wearing a microphone, I whisked her away. I led her into the restroom where we both exploded into a fit of giggles as the door shut behind us. As she reapplied her lipstick to her perfect collagen-free lips, she'd confessed that she'd never gotten used to the Hollywood parties, the movie premieres, the press junkets, and that she always felt like a fish out of water, dressed in millions of dollars' worth of diamonds. I stared at Casey's reflection in the mirror, and I'd wanted to confess that I knew exactly how she felt, that I was someone completely different on the inside too.

If Casey's life was really my own, Daisy and I would no doubt forge a fast friendship. I felt with her just like I had when I first met Casey. I sat beside her in English class and she'd whispered that she had a major crush on Bruce Patman from the *Sweet Valley High* series. And two years later, it was Casey who introduced me to John, who'd recently transferred to our high school. She'd talked a lot about him before I'd met him, but she'd never mentioned how gorgeous he was. He'd jabbed Casey in the ribs playfully and asked where she'd been hiding me. We'd stood in the same spot for what seemed like hours— so long I hadn't noticed when Casey slipped away. I didn't see her again until she came back to tell me we'd miss curfew if we didn't leave soon. In those last moments before leaving, I'd memorized his face—his slightly crooked smile, his strong jaw, and those navy-blue eyes. And as I'd drifted off to sleep that night, I'd hoped that he'd memorized mine.

More than twenty years later, I didn't expect us to still get butterflies when we saw each other, but when exactly did the light in his eyes go out? The one that used to burn bright when he'd first see me after a long day at the office. The one I'd see when he gave me a foot rub as we watched TV, his hand working up my leg, his eyes eventually inviting me to the bedroom. Is that why I didn't chase Brian? Because there's someone in my life now who has that light in his eyes when he sees me?

Destiny intercepts me as I arrive at the studio. "Change of plans for today," she says, squinting as she scrolls through her iPad. "The Santa Barbara shoot has been moved up. We need to head up there this afternoon . . ."

I toss my bag into one of the rigid white wing chairs on the opposite side of my desk and turn on my computer. "What happened?" I ask, releasing my feet from my four-inch heels, my toes thanking me.

"Melissa McCarthy has to be on the red-eye to New York tonight. So you'll only have about thirty minutes with her before she needs to leave for LAX. Her publicist was adamant that she has a hard out at 4:30 p.m. Oh, and she reminded us again, no questions about her weight. She wants to keep the focus on her career." Destiny rolls her eyes.

Already used to these standard requests from publicists, I don't respond. Plus, as a woman who has her own body issues, I don't care what Melissa McCarthy eats for dinner and I don't think any other women watching will care either. "Did her publicist send a rider?" I ask, referring to the list of a celebrity's requests for his or her dressing room, which can be everything from "needing" the room to be at a certain temperature, only bottled water with electrolytes, to red roses—not yellow, not white, not any other color.

"Nope. Says Melissa doesn't care what's in there."

"I had a feeling she wouldn't." I smile, thinking about her well-deserved Oscar nomination. It's nice to see a woman who doesn't have supermodel looks and a size negative zero body get some credit for her talent. "Is it still at the Four Seasons?" I click through my emails and notice one from Ava marked urgent, the subject line: *still waiting.* I don't have to open it to know what it says; she wants to know if I'm moving to New York.

It's only been a few days. You told me I had two weeks.

"Another message from Ava?" Destiny asks, noticing my strained expression as I stare at the email, neither opening it nor deleting it, like the others.

I nod, then start my normal routine of checking the gossip sites.

"What's up with that anyway—why haven't you answered her?" Destiny closes her iPad, signaling me that she needs my attention. Even in just a few weeks, Destiny and I have developed our own shorthand.

Nothing new on Perez Hilton, nothing on D-lister. TMZ has the first mug shot of Lacey Lane, the CW actress who was arrested yesterday for shoplifting.

"Hmm?" I look up.

"You heard me."

"Can we talk about this later? I need to prep for this Melissa McCarthy interview and then we have the sit-down with Beyoncé later this week. I wonder if she'll bring Blue Ivy? Hey, we'll have to get a picture of the two of you together since you're practically identical twins."

"Don't change the subject. I want to know why you're not jumping at this New York thing. Is there a chance we're not going?"

"Destiny, I promise, we'll talk later, okay? When does our car leave?"

Destiny relents and reopens her iPad.

I grab the latest issue of *Us Weekly* from the corner of my desk and start casually flipping through it as I think about what I want to ask Melissa during the interview. There's a spread about the outfits Julia Roberts' niece, Emma, wore while promoting her latest movie; an article about Giuliana Rancic's baby news; and a *Who Wore It Best?* that I almost bypass until I see that the woman being compared to Blake Lively is *Casey*. It's the cranberry minidress she wore to the high school reunion. Seeing twenty-something Blake Lively wearing it makes me cringe for Casey. She looks great, but the dress is clearly meant for someone younger. I think of Fiona clawing for her job and can't blame Casey for trying to compete with women almost half her age.

Charlie appears in the doorway and gives me an easy smile. "You ready for me to brief you?" He holds up a stack of blue cards and a binder of research and I notice he's let his stubble return. *Yes, you can brief me. You can brief me right on this desk.*

Destiny gives me a pointed look, not missing Charlie's flirtatious tone. "We'll need to leave by noon to get up there and have enough time to get you into hair and makeup before we roll tape at four."

I look at Charlie. "Is the crew already up there setting up?"

He nods. "They just arrived. It's going to be a multicamera shoot and I told them I'm tired of the interviews we do in hotel rooms looking like interviews in hotel rooms, so we're going to do this one out by the pool."

"That'll be tricky with audio, won't it?" One of the many things I've learned in the past few weeks is that shooting outside is easily complicated by unpredictable things like planes flying overhead and cars driving by; things I wouldn't have ever noticed until I tried to interviewing Mariska Hargitay after she got her star on Hollywood's Walk of Fame.

"The pool area is quiet and removed from the street—you know that. We interviewed Rob Lowe there, remember?"

"Oh yeah, of course. Ready to go over the questions for Melissa?" I change the subject quickly.

"At the end of the day, I'm just a mom who likes to enjoy a cheeseburger and a beer. I'll never get used to all this Hollywood stuff," Melissa McCarthy says with a laugh a few hours later.

I know exactly what you mean.

Melissa's publicist hovers nearby and whispers something to Destiny. The camera is recording the time so I can see that it's 4:29. I know I need to wrap this up.

"Thanks so much, Melissa, for taking the time to talk with me. And congratulations again on your Oscar nomination," I say with a smile before reaching out to shake her hand.

"You did it again," Charlie says as the crew packs up the equipment.

"Thanks. I'm glad you're happy with it."

"You were great. That cheeseburger and beer line is golden. You really have a knack for getting celebrities to talk to you like they're everyday people."

Because I'm *an everyday person.*

"Hey, so can I talk to you for a sec?" Charlie lowers his voice.

"Of course. Everything okay?"

Charlie motions for me to follow him into the suite Melissa McCarthy and her entourage abandoned twenty minutes ago.

We walk in and I smile as I look around the room. No bowls

full of all-green M&M's, no vases filled with only white tulips, no humidifier that blows only cold air. Charlie sits on the arm of the couch. "So, I know it might be a risk asking you this because we haven't been back here since right before . . ."

Before what?

Charlie takes off his baseball cap and runs his fingers through his hair before continuing. "I was wondering if you'll let me take you to dinner at our place up here?"

"Of course!" I answer brightly.

"Great," he says, looking both shocked and relieved as he inhales deeply.

What happened between them that night?

Charlie walks over to me and grabs my hand. "Because I think we need to talk about everything. And this time, I'm not going to let you dodge me."

CHAPTER 27

....

casey

"Rachel, wake up." John is beside me, his hand gently shaking me awake. I glance at the clock. It's 3 a.m. "What is it?" I ask, alarmed. "Is it the kids?"

"No, they're fine. I think you were having a bad dream. You were whimpering."

"Oh," I say, as the dream comes flooding back to me. I was chasing Brian up the stairs at the hotel again, but this time, my feet felt like cement blocks, each step a monumental effort. I kept calling out for Rachel to help me, but she was nowhere to be found. I finally just gave up and lay down on the cold, un-yielding floor.

"It was odd, you kept calling your own name," John says before getting up and heading to the bathroom. I reach over and grab a glass of water off the dresser, still trying to understand what happened at the hotel yesterday. Why Rachel chose to take a call from Charlie instead of chasing down the one person who could help us get our respective lives back. Why she's barely been over here to see the kids. Rachel is the last person I would have pegged to get caught up in the celebrity lifestyle I lead. In fact, she has always been the one person who saved me from completely succumbing to it, her house always feeling like a sanctuary from the craziness of it all. But what bothers me most is that she's obviously falling for Charlie.

Charlie, always hoping he'd see that softer side of me again, and Rachel, feeling unappreciated by her own husband and family, being totally vulnerable to someone as caring as him. It's the perfect storm. It's ironic how it wasn't until I found myself neck-deep in Rachel's life that I could finally see my own clearly. I squeeze my eyes shut, feeling despondent that I might never get the chance to tell Charlie how wrong I was the night we broke up. That it's taken going to hell and back in my best friend's body to realize that I haven't really been living at all.

I feel the mattress rise and fall as John turns over. I begin to move over to make room but feel his strong arms circle around my waist and pull me against the fold of his body. I lean my head down but don't pull away, craving the comfort. "You okay?" he whispers, his breath tickling my ear and giving me goose bumps.

"Yes," I answer quietly and rub my arm to make them disappear, as if they're betraying me, betraying Rachel. Whatever's going on with her and Charlie, I still have no business getting goose bumps from her husband, even if I can't remember the last time I've let someone hold me like this. Either way, I let the rhythm of his warm breath on the back of my neck coax me into a dreamless sleep.

"Is that Tori Spelling?" Audrey cranes her neck to get a better view of the lithe blonde standing at the valet stand, wearing a beautiful canary maxidress, holding a baby in one arm and grasping a small child's hand in the other.

"No," I lie.

"Are you sure, Mom?" She narrows her eyes and pulls out her phone to take a picture. "I think that's her."

"It's not," I say as I put my hand over the phone, thinking about how Tori Spelling deserves her privacy. In this moment she's just a mother trying to balance her purchases, a cup of coffee, and four small children all at once. Even though I've made a living exposing these little nuances in order to prove celebrities are human, just like us, it made me uneasy. "Don't."

"Fine," she relents before glancing around the room again. "Do you see anyone else? I thought you said we'd definitely see some celebrities here."

I look around the Joan's on Third dining room, recognizing a few industry faces, but no one that a sixteen-year-old would get excited about. "Sorry."

"I wish Aunt Casey were here. She would know who everyone is!"

"Well, she couldn't make it. I'll have to do," I snip, but quickly force a smile when I see Audrey's confused expression as if asking, *Why would Mom be upset that Aunt Casey couldn't make it?* "Something very important came up at work."

When Rachel called a few hours ago to cancel, I was livid. Something about Melissa McCarthy and being in Santa Barbara. Charlie and I had some of the best moments of our short relationship there, and the thought of him being there with Rachel breaks my heart. "Audrey's counting on you," I told her as I paced the living room, trying to console a teething Charlotte, whose normal easygoing, cheerful disposition had been replaced by a tantrum-throwing, drooling devil baby for the past forty-eight hours.

"I'm sorry, there's nothing I can do," she answered plainly, closing the door on any further discussion. I could hear her fingers typing on her keyboard in the background, and I wondered if she was even listening.

I was counting on you too, I thought as I hung up the phone and grabbed another teether from the freezer.

Our apathetic server, most likely killing time in between auditions, slaps the bill down on the table and I hand her two twenties before she can escape again. "Ready?" I ask Audrey as I stand up and begin digging through my purse for my valet ticket.

"Need some help?" I hear a familiar voice and look up. "Destiny!" I'm so happy to see her that I throw my arms around her, getting her long curls caught in the strap of my canvas tote bag.

"Nice to see you too, Rachel," she says, laughing as she detangles herself from my bag. She turns to Audrey. "And you must be the lovely Audrey. I've heard so much about you from your aunt."

"Nice to meet you." Audrey blushes and looks around Destiny. "Is Aunt Casey here too?"

"No," she says quickly. "But I've been given strict instructions to make sure you find the most fabulous dress ever." She reaches into her purse and pulls out my American Express Black Card. "It's all on your Aunt Casey."

Audrey jumps up and down, squealing. I put my arm around her shoulder and lead her toward the door. I look back at Destiny. "Where to?" I ask, already knowing the answer.

"Where else? Saks!"

• • •

Once the personal shopper has been given explicit instructions on what Audrey's allowed to wear (no plunging neckline or superminis), Destiny and I settle in and wait for Audrey to model her favorites. "So how's Casey doing?" I try to sound breezy. Destiny was always too intuitive for her own good.

"Good," she says casually and I realize I'm going to have to do better than that.

"She's been talking about a guy at work a lot lately, what's his name again? Chuck?" I ask innocently, trying to play it cool. I had never mentioned Charlie to Rachel when I was dating him and Destiny only knew because, well, it was almost impossible to hide things from the person who practically ran your life. In fact, I went out of my way to act like it was business as usual for me, murmuring my agreement when Rachel would make a joke about the latest twenty-something I had probably hooked up with. My relationship with Charlie both intrigued and terrified me, and I had been determined to handle it as if it were a fragile, irreplaceable keepsake, until I freaked out that night, throwing it on the ground and stomping it into a million pieces.

"Charlie?" She looks up from her BlackBerry.

"That's right! Charlie. How are things going with them?"

"Fine, I guess," she says, her voice steady and guarded, and I fight the urge to hug her for being so loyal. She knew that I hadn't confided in Rachel about Charlie and even though she didn't say it, I could always tell by the disapproving look in her eyes that she thought that was a mistake. And now, looking back, I wonder if she was right. Rachel knew me better than I knew myself. She knew everything—every quirk, every secret, and especially every lie I told myself. She would've known just the right combination of words to keep me in the relationship. To talk me off the ledge that night I melted down and destroyed everything. But maybe that's what frightened me. And maybe that's exactly why I didn't call her.

"It's okay. She finally told me about him . . ." I hesitate, looking for the right word. Are they just flirting? Or could it be more, could they be falling for each other? I look down at Rachel's wedding ring on my finger and remember Charlie's words. *I would marry you.*

"Where'd you go?" Destiny snaps her fingers in front of me, her acrylic nails catching the light.

"Sorry. I was going to say Casey told me all about their relationship, that they're getting close." I decide I can handle it if they're physical. It's the emotional part that I'm not sure I can stomach. "Do you like him?" I add, desperately wanting Destiny's perspective.

Destiny sets her phone on her purse and I finally have her attention. "I love Charlie. He's the nicest guy ever. I just don't know if Casey realizes what she's getting herself into."

"What do you mean?"

"Well, she already screwed it up once. And up until a few weeks ago, I would have bet you a million dollars that she'd never date him again. She was just so closed about the whole thing. Almost traumatized."

"Traumatized?" I repeat, thinking back to that night. Destiny was right, I had been. I had stumbled home, crawling into a ball with my favorite chenille blanket wrapped around me, and I'd bawled until my eyes were swollen. I'd cried, not just about Charlie, but about where I was in my life—wondering again if I'd made different decisions twenty years ago, what my life would look like. Would it have been better? And when Destiny showed up at my door I wouldn't tell her what had really happened, just that things with Charlie and me were over for good.

I think that even then, I knew I had messed up the best thing that had ever happened to me.

"And now it's on her Facebook page." Destiny sighs and I know it's because she feels protective of me. "Have you seen it?" she asks.

"I haven't been on Facebook," I say, lying. In truth, I'd been stalking my own Facebook and Twitter pages to the point of obsession, getting up at all hours of the night to find out what people were saying about me and what *Rachel* was saying about me. But I'd finally forced myself to stop after John caught me in the middle of the night hunched over my cell phone on the edge of the bathtub scrutinizing yet another TwitPic of Charlie and Rachel together.

"Her fans are going crazy over her relationship with Charlie. There's even a poll, and people are voting on whether or not they should be dating."

"Oh? And what is the poll showing?" I try to sound nonchalant as I lean in closer and breathe in Destiny's signature Chanel scent, strong and sultry at the same time, just like her.

"It's neck and neck," Destiny replies casually.

"What would your vote be?" I ask quietly, Destiny's opinion suddenly meaning more to me than I realized.

"The jury's still out for me because of how things ended last time. But I will say that there's something different about her lately. She seems so open and warm and relaxed, not only with Charlie, but with all the celebrities she's been interviewing. You should've seen her with Melissa McCarthy."

I feel a twinge in my stomach. Maybe it's time I face the fact that Rachel is a better version of me. "You don't think she was any of those things before?" I brace myself for her answer, knowing that she has every right to say I wasn't putting in my best work in the last several months, phoning in many of my interviews, asking predictable, boilerplate questions, especially right after Charlie and I broke up.

"Of course she was," she says slowly, like she's talking to a child, and I feel the tension in my shoulders release, surprised by how much I still need that validation. "You of all people saw that side of her. But I used to think that you and I were the only ones who would ever see how warm and caring she really is, and now she's showing that real side of herself to everyone."

"I understand," I say, remembering the night after Charlie and I first kissed, how he'd pulled back and seen the frightened expression on my face. He'd brushed a strand of hair away from my eyes and as if he'd read my mind, he'd told me not to worry, that this would be our little secret and that no one at work would have to know. I'd hated that I didn't correct him, that I didn't say, "It's okay, I'm falling for you and I don't care who knows." But I couldn't say that because I did care. I cared too much.

"And that's why all the doors are opening for her now."

"What?" I say as I grab her arm. "What doors?"

Destiny's eyes dart back and forth and she knows she's said too much. "Nothing," she backtracks. "It was just a figure of speech." But the right side of her mouth tilts up to the side, a sure sign she's lying. "Look!" she points to the doorway and Audrey floats out in a black organza halter dress with soft flowing ruffles that cascade toward the floor. She twirls around to reveal an open back and I mentally calculate how much of Audrey's exposed skin John will be able to tolerate. I think of Chris Mc-Nies setting his hand on the small of her naked back and get a sick feeling that I try to push away.

"What do you think?" she asks, beaming from ear to ear.

"It's gorgeous," I say. "And so are you."

Destiny holds her phone up to snap a picture. "Fabulous!" she cries as she hits a few buttons. "Just sending it off to your aunt."

"Where is she?" Audrey sighs, her tear-filled eyes meeting mine in the mirror. I'm suddenly struck by how hard it must be for Rachel to watch her daughter wanting someone else to be there for her more than her own mother.

I glance at the text message from Rachel saying again how sorry she is that she isn't here. As I watch Audrey turning in front of the three-way mirror observing her body from all angles, a shy smile forming on her lips as she falls in love with the Michael Kors dress, I wonder why Rachel doesn't seem to realize what she's missing. I know she and Audrey have struggled this past year, but it's missed moments like these that Rachel won't be able to get back. Doesn't she understand that a blurry picture on a BlackBerry isn't going to properly capture the dress, let alone the moment? I shake my head, wondering how many of these moments in my own life I've missed.

"Is this the one?" I ask, already knowing the answer.

"Yes!" Audrey grabs the sides of the dress and twirls around.

The personal shopper steps in disapprovingly, her pale pink Chanel suit looking muted against the sea of vibrant designer gowns on the rack next to her. "She has several more to try on. And you might want to consider buying two—that's what many girls are doing now, changing midway through the dance." She hungrily eyes the Stella McCartney, Marc Jacobs, and Marchesa gowns next to her and I can almost see her mentally calculating her commission if she can get us to buy another.

"We'll take *this one*," I say as I stand and walk over to hug Audrey, who flinches slightly then releases into my arms.

"You can't do that!" the personal shopper says indignantly. "It's the first one. You never go with the first one!"

Destiny steps between the personal shopper and me, waving the American Express card in her face. "When you know, you know," she says firmly. "Now wrap this up and show us some shoes."

The personal shopper perks up at the sound of the possibility of a bigger commission and scurries off, no doubt planning to bring us several pairs of Christian Louboutins. I watch Audrey sitting on the velvet bench outside her dressing room, her long legs bent inward, her knobby knees touching, her thumbs flying across the keys of her phone as she texts her friends about her new dress, and I'm struck by how young and innocent she suddenly looks. I start to worry about what might happen when Chris McNies sees her in this dress. Is this what Rachel goes through? This roller coaster of emotions, one minute feeling like you're on top of the world having just pleased your child, the next worrying that you've made a huge mistake? Obsessing that she'll make the same mistakes you did?

"Thank you," I say to Destiny, squeezing her hand. Something about the way she handled that prissy salesperson made me miss her more than ever. I wanted to scream, *it's me! Casey! I'm right here!* But instead I just raise my hand and give her a high-five.

She smacks my hand with hers. "And that, Rachel, is how it's done."

I watch as Audrey slips on a pair of three-inch stilettos that elongate her long legs even more, and I hope that Destiny's right.

CHAPTER 28

....

rachel

I wipe the bead of sweat trickling down my hairline with my left hand while frantically typing an email to Destiny with the thumb of my right. Rushing down the hallway, I try to ignore the pain of my throbbing toes wedged into a pair of heels that after twelve hours feel at least two sizes too small. I push open the auditorium door with my hip and when I see the red velvet curtain on the stage still closed, I release the breath I didn't realize I was holding. The performance hasn't started; I'm not too late.

The house is packed and I search for Casey, John, and Audrey in a sea of familiar faces. Faces of my friends I haven't seen in weeks, even though it feels like years. Standing in the back of the Adams Middle School Performing Arts Theatre—the pale gray carpeting still worn, the walls still painted a shade of orange just slightly too bright, the brand-new blue velvet seats (a recent purchase from years of fund-raising money—quite a

coup!) still a stark contrast against the rest of the outdated auditorium—it all looks familiar. So why do I feel like a stranger?

What would I say to my friends now, after living in this
other world? Would we fall into easy conversation about carpool
schedules and travel soccer uniforms? Or would I stammer, trying to find something to talk about while I attempted to ignore
the buzzing of my BlackBerry, feeling like a woman who's not a
mother awkwardly bobbing her head up and down like she un-
derstands (or cares about!) the frustration of being up all night
with a baby who's spiking a fever or the challenges of finding
something (anything!) to talk to a teenager about that won't
result in a yes-or-no answer. As I look down at my size-two suit
and the Gucci handbag hanging from my wrist that costs more
than our mortgage payment, I realize how Casey must have felt
in these situations before she became like me—an outsider.

Finally I spot the back of my own head—Casey is sitting
next to John. John's arm is slung over the back of her chair and
he's leaning in, flanking her on one side, Audrey on the other.
I can see the side of Audrey's face and she's smiling. And my
throat becomes dry. Are he and Casey playing *our* game?

We used to compete to see who could think of the conversation topic that would get Audrey to look up from her cell phone
for more than ten seconds. And bonus points if you could get
her to talk, smile, or even laugh. John usually won, not surprisingly. I'm convinced he could engage Audrey by talking about
anything—global warming, the national budget deficit, or even
the latest episode of *NCIS*. Audrey had always looked at John
differently than she did me. Her face was usually somewhere
between a blank stare and a scowl depending on her level of
irritation when I spoke. But when she looked at John, her eyes

almost always lit up and she still reminded me of her five-year-old self, when she'd jump into his arms, wrap her arms tightly around his neck, and giggle wildly as she leaned back, her pigtails swinging in the air over her head.

I tried to tell myself this was a typical mother-daughter dynamic, but I wasn't so sure. I think of my own mom who was always so kind, never impatient, always supportive rather than critical, even when I called to break the news that I was dropping out of college just a few credits shy of graduation to have a baby. Why couldn't I be more like her?

A tougher nut to crack for both John and me has always been Sophie. She was performing tonight. And for the first time, I'm on the audience side of the curtain before the show starts. For the past two years, I've been a part of the group of moms that volunteer in the theater. Ever since Sophie showed an interest, I'd jumped in to support her, relieved to see her finally care about something. It was after Sophie's first play two years ago when she was the lead in *Alice in Wonderland* that John and I had seen that she could break out of her shell. And from opening night until the play closed two days later, she'd been on a high. She'd even talked to us about her friends and school, and we'd hoped this was signaling a change in her that would remain permanent. But as soon as the play ended, Sophie went back into hiding like a snail ducking the rain.

I meet Hilary's eyes and wave. She half smiles and her brow furrows the way it does when she's trying to figure something out and I remember I'm not Rachel. I think about how much Casey has come to dislike Hilary in the past few weeks and smile. It's true, I can't imagine the two of them ever being friends under normal circumstances. They both thrive on being the center of attention. Since dropping out of college, I had told myself that I was meant to lie low in the background and support the most important people in my life: John, the kids, and even Casey. I'd completely let go of the Rachel who used to thrive every Friday night as I cheered for John and the rest of our high school football team, climbing to the top of the human pyramid at halftime, basking in the applause that followed. I forgot how much I came alive in front of the camera at the college broadcasting studio each week. Until now. Leading Casey's life was reminding me of that part of myself, and like a sleeping bear that's been awakened after a long hibernation, I was hungry for more.

As I approach Casey and John, I notice Casey has her hand on John's knee and I flinch. Is Casey playing the part or is there a real attraction?

"Aunt Casey! I saved you a seat!" Audrey beams and stands up so I can sit next to her. Rachel looks up and quickly pulls her hand off John's leg.

"Hey, little C." John smiles and stands to give me a hug. I breathe in the smell of a cologne I don't recognize (a gift from Casey?). I pull away, scanning his face for recognition. Don't you realize *I'm* your wife? Shouldn't you know that something's off? That the woman next to you—the one who just had her hand planted firmly on your thigh—isn't the one you've loved for over twenty years?

Casey's eyes meet mine and without speaking a word, I know she's asking me if I'm okay after seeing her hand. *Um, yeah, I saw it, bitch. And you'd better be acting!* I nod and bite back the tears burning in my throat as Audrey excitedly recounts every detail of the shopping trip for her formal dress. The trip I missed because I chose to stay with Charlie in Santa Barbara. But watching Casey now reminds me that I've also been playing a part. Did I really have to miss it because I was working? Or was I using that as an excuse?

My heart ached when I got the picture of Audrey in the floor-length gown. I'd been out to dinner with Charlie. I couldn't stop staring at the screen on my phone for so long that Charlie finally asked me to show him what was so important.

"Is that your best friend's daughter? She's going to break some hearts in that dress." Charlie grabbed my phone from me to take a closer look and I'd forced a smile, but all I could think about was John's reaction to Audrey looking so grown up. He was going to hate that dress and would no doubt be mad at me that I'd bought it for her. I pulled the phone back from Charlie and analyzed Audrey from head to toe, taking in her confident posture, her self-assured smile, her sparkling eyes, wondering not just if I was making a huge mistake by not being there but trying to recall a time I'd seen her looking that way. Was that Casey's influence? Not wanting to consider the answer, I'd turned off the phone and wondered why I didn't go. Why I'd lied about needing extra footage of Melissa McCarthy so I could stay here with Charlie instead.

We were out to dinner at "our place," which turned out to be a quaint Italian restaurant tucked away in a corner off State Street in downtown Santa Barbara. It was packed full of wood picnic-style tables draped with red-and-white–checkered cloths, with carafes of house wine and baskets of warm bread that we drowned in a sweet olive oil. Charlie teased me about my love-hate relationship with carbohydrates (apparently Casey had once called them the Antichrist) and I poked fun at his love-hate relationship with Dean. The waiter began to refill our glasses without asking, and the flirting continued. And I'd hoped Charlie wouldn't put me on the spot about his relationship with Casey, that he'd just enjoy the night. But I wasn't so lucky.

"So, I've got a couple of glasses of wine in you and that's all it used to take. What did you used to call it—your truth serum?" Charlie smiled.

I'd nodded yes. That's what Casey had called alcohol for as long as I could remember. But even before we shared our first drink, Casey was like an open book. It wasn't long after we'd met in that English class that she'd told me her entire life story, down to her mom's odd obsession with creepy porcelain dolls and the inappropriate crush she harbored for her second cousin, Shane. I'd been in awe, wishing I could be so open, having always been much more guarded with my feelings. Hoping all those years later in that Italian restaurant with Charlie that I wouldn't let my guard down then either, that he wouldn't see right through me.

"So I'm just going to cut right to it. What's going on? Why are you spending time with me after everything that happened? After you said it was over—all of it—even our friendship. And please, Casey, I'm begging you not to try to dodge this. I think at this point, I deserve some honesty." He was looking at me in such a way that I expected him to add, "admit that it's not really you inside that body."

As I stared at him, searching for the right words, but knowing any I chose would be wrong because they'd be lies, I tried my best to tell as much of the truth as I could.

"I think you're one of the best men I've ever met. You're

kind. You're smart. You're talented. You treat me with such respect and . . ." I trailed off, not knowing if I should add the word on the tip of my tongue.

"Love." Charlie supplied the word for me and I'd been unable to say anything else. I'd held the gaze of his brown eyes, looking lighter, almost hazel in the candlelight. "I still do, you know." Charlie broke our silence.

"Even after what I did?" I asked slowly, wondering if he'd supply the story, if I'd finally find out what happened between them. I'd felt like such an imposter in that moment, trying to get intimate details from him that, for whatever reason, Casey had never shared with me.

"It wasn't just you, I know that now. It was me too. I pushed you too hard, came on too strong. It wasn't something you wanted, I knew that, but I wouldn't relent. Of course you freaked out on me."

What didn't Casey want? What would have made her freak out?

And then maybe it was something I saw in Charlie's eyes, maybe it was simply knowing Casey for so many years, but something just clicked and I knew what had happened. And moments later, Charlie confirmed my suspicions.

Still in a daze, when we were leaving the restaurant, all I wanted to do was sleep. Charlie slung his arm around my waist and I'd laid my head on his shoulder, absorbing his warmth, the cool air slicing through my light sweater. While we waited for the valet to get our car, two men appeared, one with a Beta Camera on his shoulder and the other who was shoving a microphone in my face. The man with the mic announced triumphantly that he was from TMZ and wanted to know when we were going public with our "engagement." He'd nodded toward the ring on my left hand. I'd glanced down at the costume ring and laughed. "This isn't an engagement ring."

"You two seem pretty cozy, but also like you're trying to hide something, going out to dinner off the beaten path. What's the truth?"

"The truth is you need to go to hell. Turn that thing off." Charlie shoved the cameraman, who stumbled backward.

"Jackpot," the guy with the mic said with a laugh. "Thanks for giving us our lead story for tomorrow night."

"Get out of here, you punk," Charlie yelled after him.

I'd prayed that they'd find a bigger story by the next night, but of course they didn't. The footage ran on the TMZ show, on their Web site, and was even picked up by our competitor, *Access L.A.* I'd hoped Casey hadn't seen it.

My BlackBerry buzzes, jolting me back to the auditorium, back to where I should be. I fight the urge to check my email, knowing it's the script for tomorrow's interview with Jennifer Lopez and her take on balancing single motherhood and life in the spotlight.

Tears well up in my eyes as I watch Sophie shine on stage, trying not to notice that John grabs Casey's hand during Sophie's solo, his face perplexed when Casey pulls away quickly and glances in my direction with an apologetic look. I finally try to stare straight ahead, ignoring the movement out of the corner of my eye, instead focusing on Sophie's standout performance.

Exactly ninety minutes later, the crowd is on its feet and Sophie and the cast come out for an encore bow. She's smiling from ear to ear and I look over at John to share a moment of pride for our daughter's victory. But he's not looking my way, he's beaming at Casey, who's grinning back at him with tears in her eyes. My BlackBerry buzzes again and I finally give in and grab it, tired of feeling like a third wheel in my own life. I scroll down the list of emails and scan the subject lines, finding one from each executive "checking in" about New York City and five from Destiny. I start to open the one that says "Dean Rumor" when I hear Sophie's voice. She has one arm wrapped around John, the other around Casey. I watch them and wish I knew why I'd never tried harder to be more affectionate with my girls. Am I to blame for their bad attitudes toward me? Sophie spots me and breaks away from John and Casey. I watch Casey's face fall and my stomach turns in recognition.

"Aunt Casey, you came!" She hugs me tightly and I cling to her, not wanting to let go. Trying not to think about the fact that she thinks I'm her aunt, not her mother.

"How was I? Tell me everything." Sophie looks up at me with wide eyes, waiting for my expert opinion.

I try not to focus on what Aunt Casey would say because if I say anything as her mom, I won't be able to hold back my tears. "You're a star, honey. You're a star!" The tears come anyway.

CHAPTER 29

....

casey

The clock ticks past 2 p.m. and I glance at my phone again. As if on cue, it buzzes and I reach down and anxiously read Rachel's text. *Sorry! I'll be there in ten minutes!* I sigh deeply.

"What is it, Mom?" Audrey calls over from the chair she's sitting in before Jose, her stylist, snorts his disapproval and firmly moves her head back into place.

"Just like this," he says in his thick, accented English to her for the third time in the last twenty minutes, an accent I happen to know is not quite as thick after a few mojitos. He locks eyes with his assistant and rolls them as if to say, *amateurs*. "Jose cannot get your hair perfecto if you're shaking your head around like you're in some sort of Whitesnake video." The assistant chuckles.

"Calm down, Jose," I say and get a sharp look in return, forgetting that Rachel, suburban stay-at-home mom, can't say the things to him that Casey, important celebrity client and long-time friend, can. He shakes his head at my gall and continues to work Audrey's long, dark hair into a sweeping updo fit for an A-list celebrity.

"I thought you said Casey was coming?" Jose asks pointedly, as if we didn't belong in his salon without her.

"She'll be here," I say simply, a little taken aback by the way Jose's been acting. I'd come here for years and was always treated like a long-lost friend, met at the door with a flute of Veuve Clicquot and chocolate-covered strawberries. Swept through the waiting area to an available chair and the latest issue of *Entertainment Weekly*. Jose fawning over whatever I was wearing or what celebrity I had profiled on the show the night before. Sometimes we'd even go for drinks afterward at his favorite gay bar, him parading me around to all his friends. Me, dancing the night away with a bunch of incredibly handsome men with six-pack abs. I'd loved every minute of it.

But now, standing here as Rachel, things look a lot different. We waited stiffly for over a half hour in a tiny room in uncomfortable black modern chairs without as much as a tattered copy of *InTouch* to glance at. Not that Audrey noticed or cared; she was so excited about the winter formal tonight that nothing could bring her down. Finally, a sour-faced assistant escorted us over to Jose, who looked us up and down and shook his head slightly before pulling Audrey's hair out of a ponytail while rapidly speaking Spanish to his assistant. "Sit," he ordered before disappearing for another ten minutes, finally returning as if he were doing us a favor by coming back at all. I sat in disbelief at the way he would treat my best friend when I wasn't around and mentally planned the scathing email I'd write to him once I was back in my own body.

Finally, I hear Casey before I see her. She's led in like royalty, Jose practically shedding tears of joy upon her arrival.

Champagne suddenly appears on a gleaming silver tray and Jose painstakingly explains exactly what he has in mind for Audrey's hair, even though when I'd asked him the same question earlier he'd waved me off and instructed me to sit down and let him "make the magic."

"Hi, all," Rachel says, giving Audrey a tight hug before sitting down next to me. She adjusts her skirt, one of my favorites, a pencil skirt with soft gray pinstripes, and fidgets in her seat as she tries to get comfortable.

"What?" she asks, catching me watching her. Her hand flies up before I can answer. "Oh, I know what you're thinking, I'm sorry." She inches closer to me. "I've gained five pounds."

"Where?" I scrutinize my thin frame, not able to detect exactly where the extra weight is. Maybe in my face? Maybe it does look a little fuller?

"This skirt is a little tight," she says and frowns, running her hand over her stomach.

"I think you look great. I needed some meat on my bones; I know that I was too skinny." I thought about this that morning as I put on Rachel's jeans and studied her figure in the mirror. She has hips. She has soft curves in all the right places. She's feminine. The way I wish I was allowed to look. But I can't have both a career and a healthy body.

"Sorry I was late," Rachel says, changing the subject.

I nod toward the firm grip she has on her BlackBerry.

"Work?" I ask.

"Something like that," she says vaguely, as if I wouldn't understand. Is that how I used to talk to her? Like my job at *GossipTV* was so complicated that she wouldn't understand even the slightest detail? I think back to how I would grasp my cell phone tightly at all times, one time choosing to drop an entire plate of food when I slipped at a party rather than unclasp my grip on what I thought was my lifeline to the rest of the world. The old me would probably die if she knew that my phone lay buried in the bottom of my purse on silent most days now, the people needing my attention most always right in front of me.

Rachel had been vague with me about everything in her life (my life!) since returning from Santa Barbara. I had tried several times to get more information out of her about that trip, both dreading and dying to know what really happened. When I asked where they had dinner, I fought back tears as she told me they went to *our spot*. Rachel seemed to sense that information would hurt and quickly changed the subject to John's upcoming surprise party. I didn't press and assured her that we were all set, the RSVPs were trickling in and aside from a few minor details I was pretty much done planning. I knew she was trying to spare my feelings by not gushing about her time with Charlie, but it still felt like she was hiding something. I prayed she hadn't figured out what had really happened between us, although I can't imagine how it wouldn't have come up at dinner. I didn't want her pity. Or her disapproval for not coming to her in the first place, although I think she'd be able to understand why. And why, now, I realized how incredibly wrong I had been.

"You're hanging out with us the rest of the day, right?" I ask.

"Yes," she says and glances over at Audrey. "You'd think I'd miss this?" she says loudly so Audrey can hear, and in return gets a beaming smile from her.

"Of course not," I say sarcastically and Rachel gives me a sharp look that I hold until she's forced to look away.

"Sophie's play was awesome," she finally says, breaking the silence a few minutes later.

"Yes," I agree. "John couldn't stop talking about it for days!"

Rachel's face clouds over at the mention of John, and I know it bothered her that his hand seemed to be permanently glued to my knee that night. I had felt so guilty that later, after John was asleep, I had snuck downstairs and called Rachel to make sure she was okay. She swore she was, but her declarations felt hollow. *I'm just playing a role,* I insisted. *You of all people should understand,* I added, thinking of her frolicking in Santa Barbara with Charlie.

"Voilà!" Jose calls out as he spins the chair around to reveal Audrey's hair swept into a beautiful cluster on top of her head, a few expert pieces hanging over her cheekbones, highlighting the fake eyelashes and smoky eyes the makeup artist had already applied.

"Gorgeous!" I cry, both excited and nervous that Audrey looks ready for the red carpet, not a high school dance. "Do you love it?" I check in with her and she nods, smiling broadly.

Rachel walks over and hugs her tightly as Jose makes a warning noise to watch the hair. "You look incredible," she says as she wipes a tear from her eye. In that moment, I know I've been too hard on her; of course these kids are still the most important people in her life. Hell, I've only been here a few weeks and they're the most important people in mine. I grab her arm to let her know that I understand. She smiles before whipping her buzzing BlackBerry from behind her back and I realize she never let go of it.

"What can I say? She wants the big reveal!" I say to Sophie through the cracked door, unwilling to let her into Rachel's bedroom, which has turned into an impromptu dressing room since we returned home from the salon. "You'll understand one day when it's your turn."

"Whatever," she retorts, crossing her arms over her chest tightly, as if she's literally closing herself off to us. "You guys are acting like she's heading to the Golden Globes."

"This is an important night for her." I reach over and uncross her arms and she smiles shyly. "Let her have her moment," I plead. "Everyone deserves one. Right?"

"Okay," she concedes and I'm relieved. "But how much longer?"

"Ten minutes, I promise!" I say as the doorbell rings, announcing Chris McNies' arrival. Sophie bounds down the stairs to answer the door.

"You handled that well," Rachel says as I close the door.

"Thanks," I respond lightly. "Audrey, Chris is here."

She squeals and I'm reminded that she's just a sixteen-year-old girl, not the twenty-something sophisticated woman she appears to be in her dress and makeup. John hasn't seen her yet, although he'd begrudgingly approved the dress last week. "Doesn't the back seem a bit low?" he'd said as he walked around her, inspecting every angle.

"You just said no cleavage and no minis," I argued. "We didn't discuss the back."

"I didn't think we had to," he said with a laugh, and I knew he was going to be okay with it. He reached over and fingered the price tag. "Casey paid for this?" he asked.

"Yes, and the shoes and bag too." I spoke quickly, before he saw the price on the sparkling sling-back Jimmy Choos sitting on the couch.

"She's been pretty damn generous lately." He furrowed his brow. "Does she think we're some charity case or something?"

"No!" I exclaimed. "Not at all. It's just that, well, you know, she doesn't have kids of her own. And let's face it, she probably never will. So being a part of their lives is important to her." I said the last part quietly, saddened by the thought of never having a family of my own.

"So buying Audrey a dress that costs as much as our last family vacation makes her feel better?"

"It does," I said and smiled, thinking about how much I'd loved being a part of Audrey's special day. How I don't think I could go a day without seeing Charlotte's smiling face. How I've come to love Sophie's quick wit, even when she's using it against me.

"And I love it so much, Dad," Audrey interjected. "Please, can I wear it? I feel like a princess."

John pulled her in for a hug and kissed the top of her head. "Just make sure your date treats you like one. That's all I ask."

I squirmed in my seat a bit at his comment and tried not to think about the conversation I'd accidentally overheard a few days ago. I had just put Charlotte to bed when I was walking past Audrey's room. I glanced in through the crack of the door and smiled to myself at the sight of her, lying on the bed, chatting with her girlfriend as she twirled her hair around her finger. *Oh, to be sixteen again!* I'd thought as I stood there and watched.

"I don't know how far we'll go," she said quietly, but I could hear the smile in her voice. I froze as I realized she was talking about Chris McNies and the formal. *Shit. This is what I was afraid of.*

"No!" she giggled. "I wouldn't let him do that!" I sent a silent prayer that she was talking about kissing her or something else first base like that. I had never really thought of Audrey as sexual, something that Rachel seemed to be constantly worried about with her. My heartbeat quickened and sweat began to trickle down my forehead, because after listening to just a snippet of the conversation, I could now understand why. I tried to slow my breath and stand as quietly as possible as I leaned in to hear the conversation more clearly. "I've heard that about him," she said, before quickly adding, "but I'm sure it's just a rumor. I'll be fine."

What has she heard? That he moves quickly? That he dumps girls who don't give him a blow job? That he expects sex if he buys you dinner? My mind raced and I ran my hand through my hair in an attempt to calm down. *Don't freak out. This is Audrey. Not you.* I flash back to my high school prom. *It's not the same thing, Casey. Get a grip.* And suddenly all my suspicions break free.

"Mom, is that you?" I heard Audrey call out and realized that I must have made a noise. I quickly swept down the hall, trying to forget what I'd heard and the reason it had affected me so much.

A knock on the bedroom door jars me out of my thoughts and I walk over and open it gently, careful not to reveal Audrey. "She'll be down in a minute," I say to John, who's been nervous all day. "Get the camera ready!"

Audrey glides to the top of the staircase a few minutes later and my heart swells with pride as she maneuvers expertly in her stilettos. Rachel wraps her arm around mine and I squeeze it to let her know I realize how hard this must be for her. To watch her little girl grow up, and all the things that go along with it. That she's probably terrified that Audrey might make the same mistakes she did. Maybe she's even questioning settling down with the first real boyfriend she had and hopes Audrey won't tether herself the same way. I know she's also thinking of what happened to me on my prom night.

I look down and catch John's eyes filling with tears. Even Sophie is smiling brightly as she bounces Charlotte on her hip, in complete awe of Audrey's transformation from shy girl to gorgeous young woman. I motion to John to take pictures as she floats down the stairs, her eyes on her handsome date standing at the bottom of the stairs, a ruby-red wrist corsage in his hand and that smirk on his face. I shoot a look at Rachel—did she see it too? Or was I just being overly paranoid because of my own experience? Rachel seems oblivious; she's focused solely on Audrey.

"You look incredible," Chris murmurs, his eyes hungry, his hand confidently wrapped around her tiny waist as they pose for pictures. My stomach begins to ache and I fight the urge to wedge myself in between them.

A few minutes later, they're ready to leave, and I pull Audrey aside to the kitchen, Rachel giving me a knowing look. I'd promised her that I'd talk to her before they left. Not as if she had to ask me twice; I'd been a mess since Chris walked in. "What, Mom?" Audrey asks, annoyed that I'd tear her away from her Prince Charming.

"I just wanted to tell you to be careful tonight."

She rolls her eyes. "I know, Mom, we've had this talk, like, a thousand times this week. I get it. No drinking, no drugs, no sex."

"Listen, honey," I say, desperate to get through to her after seeing Chris undress her with his eyes. "I trust you. Just listen to your gut. If something doesn't feel right, it probably isn't. Okay?" I plead with her. "I just don't want anything to happen that you'll regret for the rest of your life," I add under my breath, wishing that someone had said the same words to the teenage me.

"Okay. I promise," she says as she begins to walk away, before turning back around and giving me one last hug. "I love you," she whispers in my ear.

"I love you too," I whisper back, blinking back tears.

We wave good-bye from the door and watch through the window as Chris helps her into the waiting limousine and I squeeze John's hand tightly as they disappear from view.

Later, I can't sleep, still thinking about Chris McNies. I click off *Letterman* and stare at the black television screen, the static sound a low hum. He's just a normal teenage boy, right? I feel a chill run through me and pull the chenille throw tighter around my shoulders, although I know the blanket isn't going to warm me. John was worried about Audrey too, but he's in bed snoring right now. He was a boy with raging hormones once too, so he should know what Chris is capable of. But he wasn't that type of boy—he wasn't the type that would push it if you said no. Not the type I fear Audrey could be out with now. The type I convinced John she should go out with. The type I had had to deal with all those years ago. I push the thought from my mind and check my phone again. No texts, no calls. That's got to be a good sign, right? When Audrey left, I fought the urge to run after her and ask her to check in with me later. But I couldn't let Chris overhear that her mother treated her like a baby. And I couldn't make Audrey feel like I didn't trust her, not after everything I'd done over the past several weeks to rebuild that trust for Rachel.

But now with this nagging feeling in my stomach, I think I may have let the fact that I wanted to be cool put Audrey at risk. Should I call Rachel? I don't want to worry her. After all, this is her daughter we're talking about. If I'm this worried, I can't imagine what she would go through.

The sound of my cell phone ringing startles me out of a ragged sleep I didn't realize I had given into. I fumble through the couch cushions and the blanket to find it. "Hello?" I answer tightly. Please don't let it be her.

"Case, it's me." I hear the sound of my own voice and breathe in sharply.

"Thank God. I thought you were Audrey."

I'm met with silence on the other end of the phone. "Rachel? Are you okay? Are you crying?"

"You need to get over here right now. I'm with Audrey. I don't know what to say to her," she whispers.

I race out of the house, not wanting to acknowledge what may have happened, but already knowing. My adrenaline is pumping at a speed I didn't even know possible. I try to push the memories of my prom night out of my mind but I can't. I still remember the smell of my Anais Anais perfume, the feel of my taffeta dress, the look in Mark's eyes when I walked down our spiral staircase, my mom taking pictures with the same aggressiveness as the paparazzi do now. As I descended, I had mistaken the look in Mark's blue eyes as one of admiration, which was really hunger. But how could I have known that? I didn't know him at all. He was a popular upperclassman, who had never given me the time of day. I'd been so shocked when he'd leaned against my locker and asked me, a sophomore with braces, to be his date. I should have understood it was impossible that he wanted to go with me because he actually *liked* me. I'd gripped my Trapper Keeper tightly, covering his initials, which I'd doodled, with my hand; I'd had a secret crush on him for over a year, and the only person who knew was Rachel. I barely remember saying yes, and the week before the dance was a whirlwind as I frantically searched the combed-over stores in the mall for a dress.

We hadn't stayed at the dance long. Just long enough for him to make an appearance and for us to share a flask of something in the parking lot with his friends and their dates, none of whom spoke more than two words to me. But I didn't care. I remember looking at him with wide eyes, hanging on his every word, caught up in the fantasy of it all. I hated myself later for not having a sixth sense to know that something was off, to not understand what the winks and nods of his buddies in the parking lot had meant.

It took only about three minutes, but it felt like hours. He rolled off of me and I'd cried silently in the dark of the backseat of his car. He zipped up his pants and jumped into the front seat, leaving me in the back still pulling up my underwear. He drove me home like he was my chauffeur, as tears rolled down my cheeks. He never once looked at me in the rearview mirror.

When the pregnancy test came back positive, I told my mom even before I told Rachel. This very well may have been the worst decision I ever made.

I pull up to my high-rise and toss my keys to the valet, ignoring his confusion. I run toward the elevators and take the longest ride of my life. I feel like I'm running toward my younger self, trying to save her. But I worry that I'm too late to help Audrey too. I throw open the front door of my apartment and Audrey looks up, her eyes swollen from crying, looking like a shell of the girl she was just a few hours earlier. I run toward her and she throws her arms around me and weeps.

Rachel looks at me, her eyes rimmed with red. I can tell she's trying to hold it together now, the tears daring to leap over her eyelashes. Is she hurt because Audrey went to my house instead of her own? "She called me just a little while ago. I picked her up. She wasn't far from where the formal took place. At a hotel . . ." Her voice trails off.

"Audrey, what happened?" I brace myself. Please tell me he didn't strip her of who she is. That he didn't take everything from her. Mark's face is clear in my mind and I'm shocked by how much detail I can remember about that night. The feel of his stubble on my cheek, the smell of his cheap cologne. The taste of the whiskey on his breath. Now I hold my own breath and wait for her to answer.

CHAPTER 30

....

rachel

Audrey grips the edge of the sofa, her body trembling. I put my hand over hers, shocked by how cold it still feels. Slumped down in the sofa, wearing one of Casey's oversized sorority sweatshirts from college, her face stripped of the heavy makeup she'd been wearing, she looks like my little girl again. My eye strays to the backless dress heaped in a pile in the corner where I threw it earlier. I would've burned it if I could.

After Audrey's frantic call earlier, I'd rushed to the hotel in Beverly Hills, pulling up to find a disheveled Audrey crying on a bench next to the valet stand. We rode in silence all the way to Casey's apartment. She'd told me she wasn't ready to talk about it and I'd fought my motherly instincts to push her. As soon as the front door closed behind us, she'd become hysterical and cried for me to find her something—anything else—to put on. That she hated the stupid dress. I'd obeyed, gritting my teeth, trying hard not to burst into tears, helping her out of the dress and throwing it over my shoulder while Audrey scrubbed the makeup off her face, her tears and the water mixing to-gether.

I kneel down in front of her now and stroke her cheek, try-ing to wipe the tears away faster than they fall. I notice the Jimmy Choos by the front door and I'm flooded with so many feelings of regret. What had I been thinking all these weeks? I cringe, remembering how I missed the shopping trip to pick out the dress; maybe if I had been there this wouldn't have hap-pened. I never should have let that all fall on Casey.

I meet Casey's eyes and know she's thinking about what happened to her on her prom night, a night we haven't spoken about since her mom took her to the clinic a few weeks later. Watching Casey now, as she sits beside Audrey on the couch consoling her, her eyes hollow, in a pair of John's sweatpants, I wish I'd consoled her when she needed me, that I'd been more understanding of what she'd gone through. Instead, I was furious with her and didn't speak to her for weeks. I said awful things about people who terminated their pregnancies. At the time, I thought I was being a good friend, ignoring the terrified look in her eyes as I stood over her slumped silhouette and gave her the speech I had memorized on the way over about why adoption was the answer. And when she confessed she was going to terminate her pregnancy anyway, I refused to go with her, telling her I couldn't support her decision. I've wondered countless times if Casey's life would have turned out differently had her best friend comforted rather than chastised her. If only I could've known then that you don't have to agree with your friends' choices to still be there for them.

The fact that she chose to forgive me at all still amazes me. I think she was just ready to pretend the whole thing had never happened and forgiving me was the fastest way to do that. She let me off the hook too easily and I selfishly took the cowardly way out, also pretending as if the whole thing had never happened. I start to cry harder thinking of how I had abandoned her then and how I'd abandoned my own daughter all these years later. How could I still be making the same mistakes?

"I'm just stupid. So stupid." Audrey pulls back from Casey's grip, tears still spilling down her face. "I know I should've called you first, Mom, but I, I don't know, I thought you'd be mad that I went to the hotel with him."

I start to tell her I wouldn't have been mad, but remember I'm not her mom right now, Casey is. But then I wonder, is she right? Would the old me have been fixated on the fact that she disobeyed me? I shudder, knowing the answer.

Casey glances at me and begins to stroke Audrey's hair, an errant bobby pin the only sign of her earlier updo. "I'm sorry I made you feel that way. Of course I'm not mad that you called Aunt Casey. I'm just glad you're with both of us now. If you're ready to tell us what happened, we're here for you. Just remember it's okay and we know it wasn't your fault . . ." Casey's voice trails off. Did she think her experience on prom night was her fault?

I inhale sharply, part of me not wanting to know what happened to Audrey, but knowing that I won't sleep until I do. I grab Audrey's hand again and hold it tightly. "I love you," I say, then put my other hand over Casey's. "We love you. You can tell us anything." Casey forces a smile and squeezes my hand in return.

"He was awful. Cruel. And I feel like such an idiot." Her words are nearly buried through her sobs. For a moment, Casey and I sit in silence, tears streaming down our faces, afraid to ask Audrey what she means by *awful*.

"It's okay, go on," Casey finally says, her voice almost a whisper.

"It was fine at first, we kissed for a little while, but when I pulled back, he pushed his face harder against mine. He told me I was beautiful and sexy and that it was going to feel good. But I didn't want to do it . . ."

Casey grimaces, biting her lower lip. I know we both want to ask her, "But did you?"

"It's okay, honey, take a breath and try drinking some water." She runs to the refrigerator and grabs a bottle.

Audrey takes a sip. "I told him no. I kept telling him no. But he wasn't listening. He kept telling me to stop talking, to just enjoy the moment. He wouldn't listen."

My anger starts to mount as I picture Chris McNies taking advantage of my daughter. Had I properly prepared her for this? Had we talked about sex enough? I couldn't remember the last time we'd had a conversation about it. Please, God, let her be okay. "Audrey, did he . . ." I can't finish my sentence and Casey jumps in.

"Did he hurt you—did he harm you in any way?"

Audrey's eyes grow wide and suddenly she reminds me of when she was six, going off to kindergarten for the first time. I could see in her eyes that she was so scared and could feel her shaking as she laced her fingers tightly through mine but she was trying to stay strong, probably for me. I'd been crying all morning, make that all weekend, knowing she'd be leaving me for the first time that day.

"I told him I had to go to the bathroom, then when he tried to follow me, I kicked him hard in the nuts. Then I grabbed my shoes and purse and ran. He was still doubled over on the floor when I shut the door and ran down the hall to the elevator."

Her mouth turns up a fraction at the visual of Chris writhing in pain. "Then I called Aunt Casey."

Casey and I exchange a look and say *thank God* with our eyes. I wrap my arms tightly around Audrey and thank God again.

"I could kill that kid," Casey mutters under her breath.

"You did the right thing, Audrey." I squeeze her tightly, not wanting to let go. Not ever wanting to let go. "I'm proud of you for standing your ground."

"I hope he has permanent damage to his balls," Casey says sharply.

"If I'd been wearing my shoes when I kicked him, he might." Audrey smiles and I'm so relieved; I know she's going to be okay. She's stronger, more grown up and mature than I've given her credit for, something that's been so easy for Casey to see since she stepped into my role; something I guess I couldn't see until I had stepped out of it.

"I'm tired, Mom. Can we stay here tonight?" Audrey looks at Casey.

"Of course," Casey says. "Let me just call your dad. Don't worry," Casey says quickly when she sees the panicked look on her face. "I'll just tell him we're having a girls' sleepover."

She catches my eye and I nod in agreement. We'll have to decide how to handle John later. "Yes, of course you can stay here, Aud. Go lay down in my bed," I say. She walks to Casey's bedroom and climbs into bed, curling up into a ball. Casey grabs her phone to call John and I crawl into the bed and play with Audrey's hair until I can hear her snoring slightly, her breath deep and heavy.

"Wine?" I look up and see Casey standing in the doorway holding two wineglasses.

"Yes, please," I whisper as I climb out of the bed and close the door behind me. "So, how did that go?" I motion toward the cell phone on the kitchen counter.

"He was a little confused about why we were having an impromptu sleepover so late at night, but he was glad to hear everyone is okay."

"Are you okay?" I ask after Casey pours me a large glass of the J. Lohr Merlot she found in the kitchen.

"Yeah, you?" Her eyes flicker and I know she must be thinking of her teen self.

"I will be eventually, when I can breathe normally again. Jesus! What a night," I say as I sink onto the couch beside Casey.

"I could kill that little fucker," Casey says again. "You know, I had a bad feeling about him from the second I met him, but I thought I was being overly sensitive because of what happened to me. I wish I had trusted my gut." She looks over at me. "I'm sorry."

"Casey, there's no way you could have known things were going to turn out like this. It's not your fault." I hold her gaze. "Now or then." Her eyes fill with tears but she blinks them back. "I'm so sorry," I continue. "I'm sorry about what happened to you in high school, and even more sorry I turned my back on you." I curl my knees under me on the sofa. "If I could go back in time . . ."

"We were kids, Rachel. How were you supposed to know how to deal with date rape and a pregnancy you didn't ask for?" She sighs loudly.

"But I was your best friend." Tears start to stream down my face again. "And now, to think that could have been Audrey . . ."

Casey grabs my hand. "But it wasn't. Audrey's okay. And

back then, you didn't understand what I was going through. Shit, I didn't even understand . . ." Casey finally lets the tears drop from her eyes. "I just wanted to go back to who I was be- fore . . . everything."

"Do you want to talk about it now?" I ask gently.

Casey's chest heaves. "The whole situation was just surreal. My mom—I still don't understand it—she was so adamant, never asked me what I wanted. Which I guess may have been best. I was so numb and she wanted to sweep it under the rug. I never really thought about what it would mean . . ." Casey trails off and looks out her window toward the twinkling city lights. "You know that's why I always said I never wanted kids, right?"

"I figured." I say softly, thinking back to my conversation with Charlie in Santa Barbara. The real reason he and Casey broke up. "Case, I'm so sorry. It must have been awful. I was awful."

"You were sixteen. And very self-righteous!" She smiles through her tears.

"That's no excuse. And tonight, when Audrey was so upset, I was so scared that the same thing had happened to her . . ."

Casey leans over to pick up the bottle of wine and refills our glasses. "But it didn't. Thank God it didn't. Her mom raised her right."

I think about Casey's own mom, a no-nonsense woman who ran her household like it was a Fortune 500 company and she was the CEO. She had handled Casey's date rape and preg- nancy like she would any company crisis, by getting rid of the problem quickly and efficiently. "I'm sorry your mom didn't give you a choice. If she had—"

"Who knows, Rachel," Casey says before I can finish my sentence. "I don't know," she says again and looks toward her closed bedroom door.

"It's okay, you don't have to know," I offer.

"I've thought about it a lot lately," Casey says. "Being with Charlotte and the kids has made me realize that maybe I do want some of my own. That I can't let some asshole from twenty years ago ruin the rest of my life, my relationships . . ." Casey trails off before adding, "And there's something I need you to know. Something I should have told you a long time ago. About me and Charlie."

I lean back against the pillows and drain my glass, already knowing what she's about to say. "Tell me," I say.

"I know you're probably wondering what happened between us, why I've been so adamant about you not rekindling things with him."

"Why you never even mentioned the cutest guy at your work to me?" I add, and poke her in the arm.

"Yeah." She smiles. "I never mentioned him because I really liked him. He was so different from any guy I had ever been with. He made me laugh, but also never let me get away with my usual shit. He made me feel like he would love me no matter what happened with my career. And that scared the living bejesus out of me."

He would, I think. Charlie was the real deal. I think back to our romantic dinner. The way he looked into my eyes, Casey's eyes, like nothing else mattered. And I feel a little sick thinking about how I'd been playing around the last few weeks with someone she felt so strongly about, even if he did think I was her. Because inside, it had been me, Rachel, who had been falling for him. Again, I had failed Casey as a friend.

"Things were going really well," she continued. "In fact, I was getting ready to tell you about it, maybe even introduce him to you and John."

"So what happened?" I ask, even though I already know the answer.

"My period came late," Casey whispered. "I thought I was pregnant. I flipped out, Rachel. I said awful things to him. That he was trying to trap me. That it would ruin my career. That I would get rid of it and there was nothing he could do." I grab Casey's shaking hand. "I ruined it. And all over nothing. My period came three days later. I tried to apologize but the damage had been done. He wouldn't even look me in the eye the next week at work. And the worst part? I cried when I got my period. There was a part of me that desperately wanted that baby."

"Did you ever tell him what happened to you in high school? Help him understand?" I ask gently.

"No." Casey shakes her head. "That's not exactly something that comes up on your third date at Mastro's over butter cake."

"Mmm, butter cake." I smile before adding, "I guess I just was thinking if he had known, he might have understood why you went a bit crazy." I stand up and walk toward the fireplace, glancing at a picture of Casey and me from New Year's Eve four years ago that I'd dug out of her closet last week. We're drunk and hanging on to each other for dear life. I smile to myself. When had we stopped leaning on each other?

"What's done is done," Casey says flatly.

"Not necessarily," I answer. "These past few weeks, he's really opened his heart back up."

"Yeah, to you! He seems to like the Rachel-ized version of me much better than the real Casey." She laughs nervously and we both know she's not kidding.

"Well, yes, but it's you he's in love with." As I say it, I realize how foolish I've been to think that what Charlie and I have is real. For him, it will always be Casey. And that's the way it should be. "The only thing I did was let him back in. The question is, can you do the same when you get back into your body?"

"I think I can." She rubs her temples. "If we ever figure out how to do that."

"We will, I promise," I say, and mean it. Then I put my arms around her and try to be there for her the way I wasn't so many years ago, the way I have really never been.

CHAPTER 31

....

casey

"How many more?" Audrey groans as she slaps another personalized label on the mini Moët & Chandon champagne bottles we're giving as party favors for John's surprise party this weekend. *Let's toast to the birthday boy!* printed on the side of each one. Rachel and I thought it would be cute to give the guests something to toast with, since that's what got us into this whole body-switching mess in the first place. It was our own little inside joke.

I check my list. "About twenty," I answer and glance at her out of the corner of my eye. It had been a few days since the dance and she seemed to be bouncing back well. I thought that kicking Chris' ass in the hotel room had even given her a quiet strength I hadn't seen before. Or maybe I was just looking at her differently now. Either way, her main concern had been about what Chris would say to her at school the next week, what he would tell his friends, or worse yet, what he would post on Facebook. But to her surprise, he walked up on Monday morning and apologized, and begged her to forgive him; she reluctantly agreed to just so he would leave her alone. "It was crazy, Mom!" she said breathlessly after bursting through the door after school as I was giving Charlotte a bath. "It was as if he was scared of me!" She held up her arm and flexed her muscles. "I guess I'm tougher than I thought," she murmured proudly.

I tickled Charlotte's naked tummy and she giggled in delight. "You certainly are," I said to Audrey as I wrapped Charlotte in a hooded ducky towel.

"It's just so weird. What could have changed his attitude so much?" Audrey took Charlotte out of my hands and carried her expertly to her room to dress her.

"I have no idea," I called out as she pranced down the hall. I pulled out my phone from my pocket and sent a quick text to Rachel: *The eagle has landed.*

My phone vibrated a moment later: *Good work. I owe you one.*

I smiled to myself before responding: *The pleasure was all mine.*

I grab my notebook with the RSVPs for John's party and flip back a few pages to read the word we wrote down when we met Jordan, the psychic. *Promotion.* What did it mean? Rachel and I had a major breakthrough the other night. But was it enough? And what does a promotion have to do with it? I shake my head and put the notebook back on the table as my phone vibrates again. Another text from Rachel: *Hey, tough girl, I'm coming to dinner tonight.*

I laugh and think back to Sunday afternoon. I told John and the girls that I was heading to the store, but as soon as I was in the car, I pulled out the crumpled piece of paper with Chris McNies' address on it. After a long discussion, Rachel and I decided to let Audrey tell John what had happened, when she was ready. In the meantime, she simply told him that Mr. Popular was really a jerk and that she had decided not to date him, or even be friends with him. Maybe the fact that my own mother never breathed a word to my Dad about what happened to me made me adamant that John should know. Back then, I'd felt relief that my own father didn't know, but now, looking back, I wish he had; perhaps then he would have been able to comfort me instead of being perplexed by my sudden withdrawal and inexplicable sullenness.

So even though I was relieved when Audrey agreed it was important for her father to know, that she'd confide in him when she felt he'd be receptive to handling it, that wasn't enough for me. Of course I was proud of Audrey and I respected her wishes—but I knew I had to take an action of my own.

The next day, I pulled up to Chris' house. Even though there was a chill in the morning air, the fog from the beach still blanketing the sky, he was standing shirtless in the driveway washing his shiny black Land Rover. It was a scene out of a bad movie, him soaping up, his tan arms reaching up over the hood in circular motions. Usually, the cougar in me would have loved every minute of the show, but now all I saw was an asshole who had tried to hurt someone I loved dearly. And I was here to make sure he never did it again. To anyone.

Chris eyed me walking up the driveway, set the hose down, and smiled his most charming smile. "Hi, Mrs. Cole. Can I help you?" His smile made my anger boil and I tried to remain calm.

"How was the dance, Chris?"

He smiled smugly. "Just lovely. I think Audrey had a great time."

I clenched my fists. *Keep calm, Casey.* "Oh, really? Is that what you think? Do you consider date rape a great time?"

"Whoa." He put his hand up in the air. "I have no idea what you're talking about." But I caught a flash of fear behind his piercing blue eyes and wondered if anyone had ever called this kid on his shit before.

"I think you do." I took a step closer to him, causing him to back up against the soapy vehicle.

"I don't know what Audrey told you, but she's a liar. And a tease," he added under his breath.

"Oh, is that what you're going to tell all your friends next week at school?" I said, moving even closer.

"Maybe," he said defiantly.

I leaned in and whispered in his ear, ignoring the water from the hose drenching my sandals. It was all I could do not to punch him in the face. "Listen here, you spoiled brat. You're going to go to school tomorrow and tell everyone that Audrey doesn't like you because you are a douche bag and she is too good to be around you."

"And if I don't?" He tried to inch away but I grabbed his arm and he winced as I dug my nails in. I prayed that his parents didn't come out while I was accosting their son.

"Then I'm going to call Audrey's Aunt Casey. You know, Casey Lee, the celebrity? She has over four hundred thousand Twitter followers. Did you know that?"

Chris shakes his head and glances around, desperately looking for a way out.

"If you don't apologize to my daughter first thing Monday morning, Casey is going to let the whole world know what you did." I look over at his mailbox. "Oh, and she'll be sure to in-

clude your phone number and home address so everyone can
let you know how they feel about it too."

Chris laughed nervously. "You wouldn't do that."

I grasped my hand tighter on his arm and he flinched. "Do
you want to bet life as you know it on that? Tomorrow. Apology.
Or else. Got it?"

"Got it," he whispered.

I drove away, tears streaming down my face, my hands shaking on the wheel. Telling Chris off was liberating, like I had
finally exorcised the demon of my own past. But the real reason
for my tears was joy. I finally knew the feeling of loving someone
more than I loved myself.

"Earth to Mom," Audrey calls to me as she holds out another
tiny champagne bottle.

"Sorry," I say, smiling as I take it from her and put it into the
box that I'll take over to the venue later today. Charlotte crawls
over and climbs into my lap. "Want to help Mommy make
presents for Daddy's party?" I ask, and she gives me the same
amused smile she does whenever I call myself Mommy.

John, it seems, has no idea about his surprise party. He is
under the impression we're going to have dinner as a family at
the restaurant in the hotel. Little does he know that one hundred of his friends will be there. I wonder if Rachel thought
that throwing this party would be a way to bring them closer together, or maybe she hoped a grand gesture might wake John up
from the fog he had been in. I thought about my own time with
him, watching the John I once knew emerge from underneath
the uninterested, aloof man who was here when I first arrived.
I couldn't wait to hand him back over to Rachel; I was out of
excuses, in terms of dodging his advances.

It was time to get back to my own life, and Rachel and I

had made a pact to make figuring out how to switch back our number-one priority after the party. For the first time since this all happened, I actually felt like she was ready to come back to her own life, and despite the fact that I would miss the little things, like Charlotte's sweet kisses and Audrey and Sophie's witty banter at breakfast each morning, I needed to reclaim my own body so I could make some major changes to my life. First up? Telling Charlie how very wrong I was that night and beg for his forgiveness.

The slam of the front door jolts me from my thoughts as I turn to see Rachel walk in with a bottle of my favorite cabernet. "Aunt Casey!" the girls cry and run over to give her a hug. She grabs two glasses from the cabinet and fills them high before handing one to me. "To taking care of business," she toasts me with a sly smile and glances over at Audrey. "Thank you," she adds quietly.

"Anytime," I say before clinking her glass one more time. "To friendship," I add.

Rachel takes a huge swig of her wine. "I'll drink to that!"

CHAPTER 32

. . . .

rachel

Promotion.

Why hadn't I told Casey that I might have figured out what the psychic meant? Maybe it's because I know the gravity of what the word means—that I hold Casey's career and our fates in my hands. But there's no turning back now, I think as I push open the heavy oak conference room door and walk in, the network executives' eyes fixed on me.

"Casey." Ava rises and stretches her long fingers my way. Her acrylic nails are a bright shade of red, like Charlotte's lips after she eats a handful of strawberries. Charlotte. I push the image of her chubby cheeks and big blue eyes out of my mind and take Ava's hand in mine, giving her a firm shake, hoping she doesn't notice I'm trembling. The other two execs stand and we exchange pleasantries.

"Coffee?" Ava's assistant asks me, a look of fear in her eyes, the dark circles under them betraying the cost of working for Ava. I think of her boss's persistence these past few weeks; the phone calls, the emails, the demands that I give her a decision.

Am I easy to work for? I wonder, watching Destiny as she taps away on her iPad with one hand and reads an email on her BlackBerry with the other, my Starbucks coffee nestled between her knees. I'm not sure what Destiny thinks of me here, but I know I'm not easy at home. I've been way too hard on the girls, especially Audrey, holding on to her so tightly that I've failed to notice she's no longer a girl, but a young woman. And John. I'd disappeared so far into myself since Charlotte was born that he couldn't even see me anymore.

I force a smile and shake my head no, motioning toward Destiny and my coffee.

"So, Casey, here we are." Ava taps her pen on the sleek mahogany tabletop.

"Yes, here we are," I repeat, thinking again that I can change my mind. I can get up right now and leave and never look back. For some reason, the exterior of my house flashes in my mind. I see the white shutters, the front door we painted red because it was good feng shui, the ivy-covered lattice, the flower beds blooming with tulips. It's an adorable home. But why hadn't I seen it that way before? I used to look at it and see only the chipped paint, the dent on the garage door, the weeds that needed to be pulled. But now I feel a deep hole forming inside me as I think I might lose it forever.

"I'm just going to cut to the chase here. You going or not?" Ava gives me a cold stare and I sit up a little straighter, suddenly remembering my eighth-grade English teacher who would wait forever for you to answer a question if she called on you. Once, one of my poor classmates, a painfully shy redhead who spoke about three words to me in all the time I knew her, was called on to answer a question about something we were supposed to have read the night before. We all watched her shift uncomfortably in her seat until she finally started crying and admitted she hadn't done her homework. I felt like her now, like Ava wouldn't so much as blink until I gave her an answer—any answer.

"Yes, I'm going," I finally say. My heart is beating so hard in my chest that I inhale sharply through my nose to try to steady it.

"I'm—well, we—we are so pleased." Ava claps her hands together like a hungry seal and the two other execs start typing away feverishly on their smartphones. No doubt telling their lawyers to draw up the contract immediately before I change my mind.

Suddenly Ava's assistant appears with a bottle of Moët & Chandon and pops it, the cork flying across the room, everyone erupting in a fit of nervous laughter. I bite back my tears and decide what's done is done.

I reach for a paper cup full of champagne as I watch the room bustling with activity. Ava's on the phone chirping away about logistics. Destiny and Ava's assistant are chatting excitedly. I can't help but smile at Destiny, knowing this is part of her dream too. She has ambitions beyond being an assistant and she's talented enough to realize them. She helped Casey get to this place and she deserves to bask in this moment. This New York move will be huge for her.

This is for you, Casey, I think as I hold up the cup. This is for the baby you never got to have, for the family you never started. For all the hard work you put into your career to get to this place. For putting up with Dean and Fiona and all this TV bullshit. And I will sacrifice whatever I must to give you what you deserve. I wasn't there during a time in your life when you really needed me, but I can be your champion now. I drain my cup and eagerly accept a refill from a round-faced woman who appeared after hearing there was alcohol at 10 a.m. She winks at me and takes off down the hall with the champagne bottle before anyone else notices.

Back at the office, I know there's something else I have to do. I need to talk to Charlie about where we left things about where our relationship is going. I've been avoiding him since Santa Barbara. As I make my way to his office, I have the panicked thought again: What if we can't switch back? I stop and lean against the wall and close my eyes. It's all going to work out. I believe it's all going to work out. I repeat it over and over until I convince myself.

"Knock-knock." I tap my knuckles on Charlie's office door. It's not lost on me how tiny it is compared to mine. It's so small his desk takes up almost the entire space. The windowless walls are white and bare. His desk is devoid of any photos. A worn gym bag haphazardly thrown in the corner is the only thing that gives you any idea about the type of man Charlie is. For a moment I'm struck by how lonely he must be. No family. Married to his job. Possibly craving a future with Casey but being shut down by her—again.

I was lucky finding the right person so young, having three great kids with him. Why have I taken it all for granted?

Charlie doesn't look up from the email he's typing and I don't blame him. I haven't given him the time of day since Santa Barbara, why should he give me his attention now?

Still typing away, he says in a voice I don't recognize as his, "I heard you're going."

"And you too, right?"

Charlie laughs. "Oh, Ava didn't tell you? I'm shocked. She's such a stand-up gal."

I lower myself into a black pleather chair. "What?"

"She has *other plans for me,* as she put it."

My heart starts racing. "What do you mean?"

Charlie, still not looking up, clicks his mouse, his attention focused on something he's reading on his computer screen. "Charlie, can you look at me please?" I plead.

"Oh, I'm sorry. Now you want me to look at you. Why don't you just send me a list of instructions for when and how I can communicate with you and I'll be sure to review it." His cold eyes meet mine.

"Look, I'm sorry. I just, it's so hard to explain, I wish I could."

"Casey, I'm so tired of your excuses. For all your reasons why you can't talk about things. I'm just exhausted by it all. It shouldn't be this hard." He exhales sharply. "And then I had to hear about it from Ava. Ava, of all people. You know how much I cannot stand that woman! You couldn't even be bothered to tell me your decision to move before you told her? You didn't even think about me, did you?"

"Charlie . . . I'm sorry. I really am. I promise you it's complicated. And I don't expect you to understand. I just wish you could trust me that I *do* care about you. And my decision to move, you're right, I should've talked to you about it. But it was a choice that was so much bigger than me, than you, than us."

"A choice about your big career?" It's a question, not a statement. "How could I forget that it's all about you?"

Looking at Charlie now, his eyes burning with anger, I wonder if I've screwed up Casey's chances with him. Have I blown it or is he just upset? I should've talked to him before saying yes. I knew he needed that from Casey. I knew it and I didn't do it, worried that if I said it out loud to him, then I'd back out. I had assumed he'd be going with me and I thought we'd work things out in New York. I had no idea Ava was going to screw him out of the job. I shudder to think how expendable people were to her. If things didn't go well in New York, would Casey be next?

"Why doesn't Ava want you to be the executive producer? What did she say?"

"That they were going in a *new direction*. Best part? I'm out of a job. Her other plans for me include wrapping things up here at *Gossip TV* and letting me go because she knows she's *holding me back*. It was like she was reading from some bullshit manual on how to give someone the ax." He runs his fingers through his hair. "I've worked for her for eight years. No loyalty. None."

"What a bitch." I fold my arms over my chest. "I wish I had known."

Charlie laughs bitterly. "Why, so you could make a toast to that too?"

I flinch but speak up. "I'm sorry," I say again. "I really am. I took for granted that you'd be going with me."

"But did you want that?" he asks, his eyes now searching mine.

"I did," I answer honestly. Whether Casey or I ended up in New York, we both needed someone like Charlie looking out for us. I feel tears sting my eyes when I think of being there without him, of being all alone and away from my family. That I'll miss all of Charlotte's milestones and Sophie's next big performance. My resolve begins to crumple and I look away and wipe my eyes.

"Hey, don't cry for me, Casey." Charlie stands up. "I'll be just fine."

I know he'll be just fine—but I won't. What have I done?

I have to think fast—how do I do this? Before I know it, I

blurt out: "Will you come with me to John's birthday party tonight?" I have to get the real Casey and Charlie into the same room. I know—absolutely—that this is the first step in fixing this mess.

Charlie eyes me suspiciously.

"I promise: No red carpet. No paparazzi. Only really good people that I love—and that I think you'll love."

"No bad cheese trays?"

Was he cracking a joke? A good sign.

The wheels in my head are spinning wildly. I've got to get them back together; I've got to figure out how we can switch back. "There will be no bad cheese trays," I say aloud. "That is the one thing I can guarantee."

"Then how can I say no?" Charlie says. I pray that I can get the woman he loves back into her own body before it's too late.

CHAPTER 33

....

casey

"You are so not wearing that." I shake my head as I catch Sophie slinking down the hall in a barely there green minidress. Then I realize, it's practically a clone of the one I wore to last year's People's Choice Awards, a dress I also had no business wearing at my age. "Is that the same dress that . . ."

"Aunt Casey wore last year. *Yes!*" Sophie throws up her arms dramatically and lets out an exasperated sigh. I never realized the way I was dressing was affecting young girls like Sophie. I drop down into John's favorite leather chair and rub my temple. What had I been doing? Somewhere along the way, I'd totally lost sight of who I was. I stare at Sophie, who looks so much older than her fourteen years. "Why do you treat me like I'm a baby?" she cries out as John walks by and does a double take.

"You are *not* wearing that tonight," he says with finality. Sophie glances at me and I can tell she's wrestling with wanting to lash out and ruin John's surprise. I stay silent but lock eyes with her and shake my head quickly.

My, how life had changed. I had never thrown a party for anyone else, unless you counted the time I kidnapped Rachel for a birthday trip to Las Vegas when we were still in college. And even that wasn't really selfless; I had been begging her to go for weeks but she had insisted she had to study. So I took her against her will and plied her with kamikaze shots until she agreed it had been a great idea. Annoyed as I had been when I originally took over the planning for John's party, I had to admit it really did feel good to do something special for someone else. I watch Sophie, holding my breath.

Sophie opens her mouth and sighs loudly. "Fine! I'll just go put on one of your old dresses with shoulder pads or something to make you guys happy. Who cares what I want anyway, right?" She huffs out of the room.

"No one's asking you to wear shoulder pads," I call after her. "I'd be happy with anything that didn't look like something a hooker would wear." I look at John and roll my eyes, feeling a million miles away from the woman who wore the same thing less than a year ago.

"Or Aunt Casey," she snaps, her door slamming behind her.

"It's just a phase, right?" John asks.

"God willing," I say, trying not to think about how much Sophie's comment hurts. I push my head down into his chest to avoid the kiss I know he's looking for and feel a renewed sense of urgency to get Rachel back into this body. I won't be able to hold John off for much longer.

He leans down and whispers in my ear. "You know what I want for my birthday?"

"A new putter?" I ask hopefully before he whispers, his breath hot on my ear, what he'd really like. My cheeks flush. I remember the ripped panties from the night I took what's-his-name home. Was John wild like that too? I didn't want to find out.

"Are you blushing?" he asks, his eyes full of amusement.

"No," I stammer and pull away, backing into the wall.

"So, what do you think?" He reaches out for me again. "Can I get that for my birthday?"

Not if I want Rachel to speak to me ever again. Or if I ever want to be able to look you in the eye again. "Sure," I say and force a smile.

"You said what?" Rachel sounds ready to jump through the phone when I call her a few minutes later, hoping the water from John's shower drowns out our conversation.

"What was I supposed to say?" I squeak, still shaken up over the visuals of what he lodged in my mind. "Seriously, Rachel, we've got to get this figured out."

"I'm on it," she says cryptically.

I hear the water turn off. "I've got to go. I'll see you tonight."

"Wait, Case. Two things real quick. Your mom has emailed you several times this week, the last time threatening to fly out if you don't respond. I'm sorry, I missed her monthly call. I was going to email her back, but I thought it might be better if you did."

Rachel had always been slightly intimidated by Natalie Lee and I didn't blame her. My mother was tough and no-nonsense, a stark contrast to Rachel's mom, who was the Martha Stewart of her time, with homemade cookies waiting for us each day when we burst through the door from school. Their home had been just like her, warm and inviting, and I spent as much time there as I could. Rachel's dad often joked that he had two daughters. "Okay, I'll email her," I said. Not a lot of things got past my mother, and I couldn't afford to have her snooping around. "What's the other thing?"

"Promise you won't be mad."

"What?"

"Promise first."

"Fine, I promise. Tell me, Rachel, you're scaring me."

"I'm bringing Charlie."

Silence. "Rachel. Why?" I finally ask, my stomach dropping to my feet. The thought of him, dancing and flirting with Rachel while I played dutiful wife to John, made my heart hurt. To have him a few feet away would be torturous.

"Is there any way you can uninvite him?" I ask.

"It's going to be fine," she answers ambiguously.

"I'm not sure how that could possibly be the case," I say while trying to wipe the visual of them doing the Macarena out of my head.

"Please, Case. Just trust me, okay?" she pleads quietly and I think about everything she's given up for me since we switched.

"Okay," I concede.

"I'm sorry."

"It's fine, I trust you," I say quickly.

"No, I'm not just sorry for inviting Charlie. I'm sorry for everything." She says this softly and I imagine her twirling her hair tightly onto her finger like she used to do whenever I was angry with her in high school.

"I'll live. Just don't make out in front of me. Then you may have a very awkward girl fight on your hands," I say.

"Got it," she says, relieved.

John walks into the room wearing a robe and I silently thank God. The other day, I had to sprint from the bedroom as he began to pull his towel off. "I really gotta go," I say before hanging up.

"Who was that?" John asks. "And who's girl fighting?"

"It was Casey. She was just telling me some celebrity gossip," I say as I slide off the bed and head to the office to check my email.

"Shouldn't you start getting ready?" he calls out.

I run my hand over the glossy blow-dry I got this morning. "I just need to do my makeup and get dressed." I glance at the clock. I've got forty-five minutes, which is all the time in the world now, but only a few weeks ago, it would've barely been enough time to get my makeup done. "Don't worry, I'll be beautiful," I say playfully before shutting the door to the office and firing the computer to life.

I log into my *GossipTV* account and feel like a stranger as I glance at the hundreds of emails that have come in since Rachel's been living my life. We had agreed that it would be better if she dealt with all of them, most of them being work related anyway, her BlackBerry vibrating day and night with scripts, rewrites, and updates on the latest celebrity bad behavior. I peruse the in-box for my mom's email address, locating the guilt-inducing emails she sent. I quickly fire off a short response saying I've been insanely busy and will call her as soon as I come up for air. I'm about to shut down the computer when I see an email from Ava Greenwood, one of the network executives. The subject line says *Welcome to New York*. I click on it.

Dear Casey,

We are thrilled that you've decided to accept the New York job with the network! I have to admit, you had us worried

there for a little bit, but I'm glad you finally came to your
senses. We'd hate to lose you because you were unwilling to
relocate. We'll be in touch with all the details about your
new show, but we're thinking Ellen-meets-Oprah with a
little GossipTV thrown in.

All the best,
Ava

A new show? New York? How could Rachel keep this from me? This is my life, not hers, even if she is in my body! I read back through the chain of emails between them, Rachel clearly uncomfortable with the idea of moving and Ava reminding her of my contract and what would happen if I didn't take the job in New York. They'd have the right to terminate my contract and would have no problem doing just that. Basically they were blackmailing her into taking the job. So many questions swirl in my head that I grasp the edge of the desk to steady myself. How can she leave her kids? Is Charlie going? Why didn't she confide in me?

I click on an email from Destiny about looking online at apartments in Brooklyn. And one from Charlie saying that Ava called a meeting with him and that he thought they were going to ask him to executive produce the show. Tears spring to my eyes as I realize that Rachel was willing to give up seeing her family so that I didn't lose the one thing I had always loved most, my career. It was clear in the emails that she had been trying to buy as much time as possible before finally getting backed into a corner. *I can't let her do this.* I know if I call her, she'll tell me that we'll figure things out before she has to leave for New York, that I should just let her take the job for now. But now that I've fallen in love with all the people who mean the most to her, I know that she can't spend another day without them.

I know what I need to do.

I push send a few minutes later and hear a soft knock on the door. "Mom?" I hear Sophie's voice. "Is this okay?"

I open the door and gasp. "Sophie, you look beautiful." Her lips form a shy smile as I take in the perfect black silk dress she's wearing, her unruly hair pulled into a tight knot, the small pearl earrings Rachel and John had given her for her birthday last year dangling from her ears.

"Audrey helped pick it out." She smiles again and I wonder if she's been acting out because she's craving attention from us, because Audrey's been getting so much. She tucks a strand of hair behind her ear. "I'm sorry about earlier," she says, hugging me.

"It's okay, baby," I answer, more sure than ever that I made the right decision a few minutes ago.

"Are you crying?" she asks, noticing my tear-stained face.

"I'm just happy," I confess. And for the first time in a long while, I truly am. I wipe my face with the sleeve of my sweater. "Do you mind getting Charlotte dressed so I can get ready? Pick her out something pretty to wear? Since Audrey helped you, maybe you can give your little sister some assistance in the fashion department too."

She eyes me warily—I doubt she's seen Rachel cry more than once or twice in her lifetime. "I'm fine, honey, really," I reassure her.

"Okay. I'll get her ready," she says as she heads down the stairs.

My mind is rushing over what I just did. By turning down

the New York job, my career as I know it is basically over. To reject an opportunity like that, well, let's just say it's unheard of, no matter the reason. *It's okay,* I tell myself as I apply moisturizer to my face. *I'll land on my feet. I always do.* I hope Destiny will forgive me. I'll take her with me as soon as I land another job. And Charlie. Will he go to New York without me? And will he still want me if I'm not on a top-rated show? I guess I'm going to find out.

I emerge from the bathroom and examine myself in the full-length mirror. Wearing the sequined black dress that Rachel had picked out months ago for this occasion, I have to admit that she knows her body well. It hugs all the right curves and shows just enough cleavage to make it interesting. I run a brush through my hair one last time, spray Rachel's Trish McEvoy perfume generously, and hope I'll make her proud tonight.

When we arrive at the venue, my heart beats wildly and I'm hoping I'll pull off the surprise. The valet opens my door and I gingerly step out before leaning in to unclasp Charlotte from her car seat. "Come here, baby girl," I coo. I place her firmly on my hip and John materializes at my side and puts his arm around me possessively. "Ready?" I say.

"You bet," he says, having no idea that one hundred of his slightly buzzed friends are getting ready to scream *surprise.* Destiny texted me ten minutes ago and gave the all-clear. *Everything's ready to go here. Maybe we should have waited on the open bar?! LOL See you in ten. xo*

We ride up the elevator in silence, the girls looking at each other nervously. The door dings and opens to two large doors. Beyond them, I can hear a few *shhh*'s and smile. I look at John—he has no clue. "Is this the dining room?" he asks, confused.

"It is," I say. "Go on." I nudge him.

The greeting is almost deafening and I put my hands over Charlotte's ears as John's friends and family yell *"Surprise!"* and break into an uneven chorus of "Happy Birthday." His face turns from confusion, to shock, to joy in moments. He grabs me and plants a sloppy kiss on my lips and I pull away quickly, laughing. I search for Rachel's face in the crowd and am relieved to see her laughing too. My mouth goes dry when I spy Charlie next to her, clapping and cheering for a man he's never met. But knowing Charlie, the fact that John is important to me is good enough for him.

John is engulfed with well-wishers when I hand Charlotte off to his mother and father, who flew in from Arizona and thankfully offered to provide child care for the night. John breaks free a few moments later and grabs my hand. "How long have you been planning this?"

"A long time," I tease. "You like?"

"Yes. More than you know."

"Happy birthday, Dad," Audrey and Sophie say in unison as they wrap their arms around John.

"I love you guys. I don't need anything else for my birthday. This is the best gift ever," he says and I hear the tears in his throat. He looks at me, a softness in his eyes I haven't seen in years, and it reminds me of how John looked at Rachel on their wedding day. "Thank you."

"You're welcome," I say as someone brings over a shot glass filled with what looks like tequila. John downs it in one gulp. The sight of the shot glass reminds me of the high school reunion and I look around at the waitstaff, dressed identically in white shirts and black pants, searching for Brian. My heart skips a beat when I think I spot him, but when I blink, he's gone again. How silly of me to think he'd show up here.

"Hey." I hear my own voice and turn around to find Rachel and Charlie.

"Hey," I say casually as I grab a champagne flute off a passing tray and hope my knees don't buckle underneath me in front of the only man I've ever loved.

CHAPTER 34

....

rachel

Casey takes a long sip of her champagne, her hand shaking slightly as she presses the flute to her lips. "Hey," she says lightly, but doesn't take her eyes off Charlie. "It's Charlie, right?" She extends her hand.

"Thanks so much for having me," he says sincerely as he shakes it, the sleeve of his jacket rising up to reveal a watch he told me was given to him by his father, one he rarely removes. I smile at the many special things I've learned about Charlie since I've known him, only reinforcing my feeling that he and Casey should give it another shot. "Great party," he says, looking around the room, and I follow his gaze.

The large ballroom, not unlike the one where we had our high school reunion, is packed with familiar faces: John's tennis partner, Jeremy, and his wife, Kelly, our neighbors who had become close friends; Sophie's longtime best friend's mom and her husband, whom we befriended after dozens of play dates; John's colleague Martin and his partner, George, whose quick wit and funny stories make them frequent dinner guests at our house. So many people I want to talk to, but can't.

"We're so glad you could make it," Casey answers and narrows her eyes at me slightly, signaling she's still not completely on board with Charlie being here. Before I can offer her an apologetic smile, the catering manager comes over and stage-whispers something. "Excuse me," she says, giving Charlie one more backward glance as she's led away to deal.

"How many years have you guys been friends? You said since middle school, right?" he asks.

"Right, it's been a long time," I say carefully, the past two decades flashing before me, mental snapshots of our first sleepover, secret late-night phone conversations, huddled together next to my locker while I whispered the details of my first makeout session with John.

John. I find him in the crowd just as he reaches for Casey, who's walking by. She pauses briefly as he leans in and says something that makes her smile. She laughs and gives his hand one last squeeze, her fingertips lingering on the end of his until she finally releases his hand and heads in the direction of the bar. John takes a long swig of his whiskey and watches her walk away, a smile on his face I haven't seen in a long time.

What I wouldn't do to have that smile shine on the real me again.

"They seem like a nice couple," Charlie says and I realize he's also been watching them.

"They are," I say simply as I grab a shrimp off a passing platter.

"They must have a secret." The sides of Charlie's mouth turn down and he takes a drink of his scotch on the rocks, his eyes never leaving mine.

"What do you mean by secret?" I ask, startled.

Does he know?

He smiles. "I mean their secret to a successful marriage. Just look at them, after all these years, still gazing into each other's eyes like that. It's like they're just falling in love for the first time."

Falling in love for the first time. Charlie's words linger as I fix my gaze on John, now talking to Jeremy and Kelly. He's making a backhand motion with his arm, obviously replaying a moment from a recent tennis match. I know Casey's not falling in love; she would never do that to me. Plus, he's like a brother to her. And of course she's got to play the part of loving wife, especially tonight. But what about John? Could he be falling in love with her? I know he thinks she's me, but she's not. She's the antithesis of me in so many ways—she's laid-back, she's open-minded, she's even sexier than I am, even in *my body*. She carries herself with so much more confidence than I ever have. Could John be attracted to that? What happens if—*when*—we do switch back? What if he misses those things about her?

"Casey? You're a million miles away. What are you thinking about?"

"What you said about their secret to a happy marriage." I think about what Casey's brought to the table since she became me. "You know, I think the secret is trust. No matter what, they know they can always count on each other." Watching John now, I realize I'd stopped trusting him, stopped believing he had my back, that we were a team.

Charlie looks at me intently. "You know them well."

"Better than you think." I smile.

"Now come with me, there's a couple of really important people you need to meet," I say as I lead him over to Sophie and

Audrey, who squeal with delight when they see me. "You girls look gorgeous," I say, holding back the tears as Sophie twirls for me. "Your mom is so proud," I whisper.

"Who's this, Aunt Casey?" Audrey says playfully as she points at Charlie.

"I'm Charlie," he says as he reaches out and shakes both of their hands gently. "I'm a good friend of your aunt's."

The girls giggle. "I bet," Audrey mutters under her breath and snaps a picture of us with her cell.

"Audrey," I call after her, but they take off, arm in arm.

Charlie wraps his arms around my waist as they huddle over Audrey's cell phone, laughing. "They're adorable."

"They are, aren't they?" I say as I start to gently release myself from his grasp, but he holds my arm firmly.

"You're not trying to pull away again, are you?" He looks down so I can't see the hurt in his eyes. "I thought you invited me here because you want this to work." He pauses and touches his finger to my cheek. "Do you trust me?"

I wish Casey did trust him. I hope Casey will trust him. I know I do. But I don't know what it feels like to have a man hurt you in the way she'd been hurt. And then to have to give up her baby; I might have never recovered from that. How can I expect her to jump into Charlie's arms and ride off into the sunset? I want to wrap my arms around him and wipe away the hurt look on his face, but will Casey understand that I'm doing it for her? I catch John's eye and he waves, having no idea that I'm his real wife.

"Charlie," I begin. "I do want it to work."

"Sure doesn't seem like it."

And then I decide that I have to listen to my instincts and

hope I'm right. I touch his forearm gently and lean in and whisper, "Please trust me. There's no one who loves you more than Casey Lee does."

He looks up, startled. Before he can reply, Destiny prances up, juggling three drinks. She hands one to each of us and we toast. "You never stop taking care of me, do you?" I ask as Charlie recovers from my proclamation of Casey's love, something he's probably been waiting to hear for a long time.

"Nope, that's why you pay me the big bucks!" Destiny laughs.

I smile, having no idea what Destiny actually makes. Will she get a raise when we go to New York? I know from glancing at the contract the messenger sent over that Casey was getting a substantial one. Not that it mattered. No amount of money in the world was going to make up for how alone I would feel.

"Hey, I heard what that bitch Ava did to you. I'm sorry." Destiny smiles at Charlie.

"Thanks. But I'll be fine. I've still got a few tricks up my sleeve." He runs his hand across my back and finds my free hand and I squeeze it. *He will be fine. He's the type of guy who deserves good things.*

We're standing so close that I can feel his iPhone buzz in his pocket. He pulls it out and glances at the number, his face turning serious. "Excuse me, I've got to take this," he says, before pushing through the ballroom doors to the hallway.

"So, are you in an Empire State of mind yet?" Destiny asks as she pokes me in the arm while giving the eye to a tall twenty-something waiter with olive skin and dark eyes. Feeling her gaze, he looks over and rewards her with an inviting smile.

"He's cute," I say.

"For me, not you, missy!" Destiny laughs. "And don't try to change the subject. Why do I get the feeling that you'd rather gnaw your own arm off than move to New York?"

"Not true," I say, trying to muster up some excitement for Destiny's benefit. "I can't wait!" I lie.

"Don't bullshit me," she says.

"What?" I ask as I throw my hands up. "I'm fine," I add as I glance around the room for an escape. This was not the time or place to have this conversation, my heart breaking into tiny little pieces as I imagine leaving Los Angeles and my family.

"Casey, we don't have to go."

"Yes, we do," I say forcefully. "We'll both be out of a job if we don't."

"Hey, don't take this job because you're afraid I'll lose mine. This is your life. No matter what you decide, I'll be okay. We'll be okay." She tucks my hair behind my right ear, something she always does right before I go on air. "Got it?"

My heart fills with love for her. Because I know she means it; she'd rather be out of a job than see Casey unhappy. "I wish it were that simple." I sigh.

"Why can't it be?"

I look over and see John walking toward us. "Long story."

"Little C!" he exclaims with glossy eyes and a slight slur. He's buzzed, I think, and wish he'd place one of his drunk, wet kisses on me. The same kisses I would have pushed off in the past, annoyed by the smell of his whiskey breath.

"Happy birthday!" I put my arms out and let him engulf me in a bear hug, leaning my head against his shoulder for just a beat too long. "There's someone very important you need to meet," I say as I grab Destiny's hand. "This is my very good friend Destiny, and she helped Rachel plan this party." Destiny gives a small curtsy and John kisses her hand.

"I can't thank you enough. This is the best party ever!" His college roommate walks by and they high-five. "Seriously."

"It was my pleasure. Your wife is great; you're a very lucky guy."

"Yes, I am," he says as he searches the room for Casey and I feel my stomach fall. *I'm right here! I'm sorry I stopped caring whether you found me in a crowded room. I promise to never take you for granted again!* I squeeze my eyes shut and make a silent wish. *Please, give me my life back.*

"Let me get you a drink, birthday boy," Destiny offers. "I made sure the bar is well stocked!" John gives her his order and she saunters off, the waiter she smiled at earlier falling in step beside her.

"Open Arms" by Journey begins to play and the memory of dancing with John at our high school prom is overwhelming. I can still remember clearly the smell of the butterscotch schnapps John had been sipping all night out of the flask in his pocket when we danced. I never wanted the song to end, wanted John to hold me with that urgency forever. "Want to dance?" I ask him now.

Looking over my shoulder quickly, he says, "Sure. Rachel might get a little jealous, though!" he says with a laugh, clearly not meaning it.

When was the last time I really got jealous or felt territorial or even got butterflies?

"I think she'll be thrilled," I say, the butterflies I hadn't felt in years swelling in my stomach as I lead him onto the dance floor and he takes me into an easy embrace of an old friend.

"I love this song," I say, thinking about the green taffeta prom dress I begged my mom to buy me, the hours Casey and I spent on each other's makeup.

"Me too," he says as he spins me playfully. "Rachel and I danced to it at senior prom. And then it was our song all through college."

"*You* remember that?" I ask, shocked.

"Of course I remember that! Why don't women give us more credit?"

I had started to think you were the one who had forgotten all the little moments that made our relationship special. Maybe I was the one who had forgotten. Either way, there was no doubt we had lost our way the past few years.

"Sorry!" I say. "I just didn't think guys cared about the little things like women do."

"Let me tell you something," he says seriously. "Your best friend, Rachel? I loved her since the minute I first met her at that water tower. I love the way she gives every homeless person she sees five dollars, even if they look like the biggest crackhead on earth. I love that she cries every time someone gets kicked off *American Idol* and the way she has to fall asleep with her ankle wrapped around mine. Our relationship may not be perfect—in fact, it's taken a freakin' beating the past few years— but it's those little things that remind me of why I fell in love with her a million years ago."

We've stopped dancing and we're standing together in the center of the dance floor, me trying not to fall apart at his words. "That's beautiful," I whisper. "I hope to have that someday."

His eyes glance at something behind me. "You will, Little C. I promise," he says as I feel someone tap my shoulder.

I turn around to see Charlie, an odd look on his face. "Can I speak to you for a moment?" He pats John's shoulder and wishes him a happy birthday before pulling me away to the large window overlooking the ocean. "What the hell did you do? And how long did you think you could keep it from me?" he asks.

He's finally figured out I'm not Casey. "What do you mean?" I ask innocently.

He holds up his phone. "I just got off the phone with Ava. She says you turned down the job." He laughs. "She actually accused me of talking you out of it! Little did she know, I had no idea."

My mind starts racing. What the hell was going on? Last time I saw Ava, we were drinking from paper cups filled with champagne and masquerading as best friends. How could this have happened? "I don't know what happened," I stammer.

"Come on, don't play coy. You had the balls to give the executives the middle finger. At least take some credit for it!" Charlie's smiling.

"But she's lost her job," I say, more to myself than to him.

"Oh, don't worry about her. I think she'll be okay." I look up when I hear my own voice and see Casey, a knowing smile on her face. She hands Charlie her empty glass. "Charlie, would you mind getting us refills please?" she asks as she nods toward the bar. "I need a minute alone with my bestie."

"You got it," he says before practically skipping away.

"He seems pretty happy," Casey says sadly.

"How could you not tell me?" I accuse her.

"I could ask you the same thing," she says quietly.

"I knew you wouldn't let me take the job if I told you about it, and I didn't want you to get fired." I look out at the waves crashing on the beach, feeling incredibly relieved that I didn't have to move to New York, yet worried that Casey had just thrown everything away just so I could stay.

"Rachel, if I've learned one thing since we switched, it's that family is more important than any job. And I could never let you be taken away from them." She leans against the glass and sighs. "Although I have to admit, I'm going to miss Charlie."

"He's not going to New York. He didn't get the job."

"What?" Casey grabs my shoulders. "What are you talking about?"

"Ava fired him. Now you're both unemployed!" I say loudly. Casey starts to laugh and I join in, both of us laughing so hard that tears begin to stream from our eyes.

"Oh my God, I just peed a little bit." Casey looks at me wide-eyed, spitting out some of her drink.

"Ah, that's what giving birth to three kids will do to ya," I say and we break into a fit of laughter all over again.

Casey finally composes herself. "Well, we've really made a mess of things, haven't we?"

I think for a moment before answering. "Depends on how you view it. Some may argue that you've just made the best decision of your life. You can't keep up this pace forever," I add, thinking about how easy it was for me to sacrifice time with my friends and family since I'd become Casey. Maybe it was time for her to take a breather too.

"And I have you to thank for it. You helped me realize what's important. The saddest part? I had no idea what I was missing."

I nod to the dance floor, where John's dancing with Audrey and Sophie. "I know exactly what you mean."

"Hey, you two, don't get all teary-eyed on me." Charlie walks up with two shot glasses filled to the brim with a bright purple liquid. "Are you having a moment?"

"What are those?" Casey asks, glancing quickly at me. *It couldn't be. The shots we drank at the reunion were the same color.*

"The bartender said to tell you he whipped these up just for you guys. He made me promise not to even take one sip! Not that I would. I'd lose all of my man cred if I drank a purple shot. What the hell's in these anyway?"

Our lives, I think.

We both swing our heads toward the bar. Brian's there, quietly wiping down the mahogany counter. He looks up, smiles, and gives us his signature wink.

"Oh my God," I say. "We did it."

"Hold on," Casey interrupts. "We need to take the shot first before we get too excited."

Charlie steps in. "What are you guys talking about? It's just a shot."

"Shh," we say in unison as we take the shot glasses gingerly out of his hands and hold them up, careful not to let a drop of liquid spill.

"To *my* perfect life," I say, thinking of John and the girls.

"To *my* perfect life," Casey echoes, looking at Charlie, who furrows his brow, confused. We clink glasses and I feel the sweet purple liquid slide down my throat and then everything goes black.

I wake to complete darkness and struggle to adjust my eyes. Fumbling around in the dark, I can feel another person in bed next to me. I exhale deeply as I run my hands through the wavy hair that I'd know anywhere. *John.*

I sprint out of bed and make my way through the dark to the bathroom, gently shutting the door and flipping on the light. Tears spring from my eyes when I see my face staring back at me. My crow's-feet. My hair sticking up in five directions.

I grab my belly and laugh out loud. *We did it!* I run my hands over my thighs, and arms, the soft flesh that I had always cursed after having kids now seeming like heaven. I'm me again.

I grab my cell phone off the bathroom counter. *Did Casey switch back too?* I breathe a huge sigh of relief as I click on the picture text she sent me thirty minutes earlier, her face beaming into the camera, her eyes shining with a light I hadn't seen in a very long time. *Woo hoo!* reads the caption beneath it. I hold my phone up and smile as the camera flashes and send my own picture in response. *Best selfie ever!,* I write and hit send.

I crack the door open and take in the sight of my husband sleeping soundly on the bed. Funny how true that saying is— that you don't realize what you've got until it's gone. I tiptoe down the hall to Charlotte's room and stifle a laugh when I see her asleep, her bottom sticking up in the air. I rub my hand along her back and she stirs, turning over on her back to face me. "Hi, sweet pea," I whisper. "Mama's home."

"Mama!" she squeals her first word, her face beaming as I pick her up and she takes my face into her tiny hands, staring deep into my eyes.

She knows. And now she's able to say what she's known all along.

I squeeze her tight. "I promise to never leave you again, baby girl."

"Mama," she repeats, her eyes getting sleepy. I set her down gently back in her crib and pull her favorite blanket over her.

"Night, night," I say softly as I watch her eyes flutter, and then shut. I wait, watching over her until I hear her breathing become heavy with slumber.

Back in my bedroom, I slide back into bed and inch my way over to John, grabbing his long arms and wrapping them around me tightly, wiping the tears from my eyes on my pillow. *I promise to never forget this moment.*

He stirs. "Hey there," he whispers as he kisses my bare shoulder, turning his body and engulfing mine.

"I've missed you," I whisper back, trying to conceal the sob rising in my throat.

"I've been right here the whole time. I was just waiting for you to notice me," he says as he runs his hands through my hair.

I slide my hands under the covers. "Come here. I'm ready to give you your birthday present," I say and kiss him like it's the very first time.

Epilogue

Six Months Later

"Got it, yes. I understand. Thank you!" Casey says before hanging up the phone and spinning her chair around to face Rachel, a huge smile on her face. "We did it!"

Rachel leaps over the stack of *Entertainment Weekly*s and *Variety*s on the floor next to her desk, grabs Casey, and they jump up and down like two schoolgirls who've just won a foursquare match. "I told you we could make it happen. C&C Productions is now officially in the game!" she cheers, referring to the meeting they'd just secured with HBO to pitch their first television series.

When Destiny and Charlie walk in a few minutes later, they're greeted with a shout. "We got the meeting with HBO!" Casey yells and they all embrace in a group hug. "Thank God for Destiny and her contacts!" Casey adds. From her long stint with Casey, Destiny knew the assistants in practically every office from West Hollywood to Santa Monica, and understood they held the coveted key to their bosses. Thankfully, she'd

leveraged many of her relationships and called in several favors that helped get the production company off the ground,
earning her the long overdue title she deserved: vice president of development. "I'm not getting your coffee ever again,
bitch!" she'd said, laughing as she spun around in her new
desk chair, holding her hands over her head like a child riding
a roller coaster.

Destiny had been Casey's first call the morning she and
Charlie decided to go into business together. "We can't do this
without you," Casey pleaded, knowing full well that to make
this work, they'd need someone like Destiny to keep them on
track.

"You can't afford me!" she joked before agreeing to join them
for brunch to discuss coming on board. Casey told her that
she'd be an equal member of the team, giving her a percentage
of equity in the company as a bonus. Destiny had been loyal to
her for years, even when Casey may not have deserved it, and
Casey wanted to repay her with more than just money.

Destiny walks over to Casey's desk and high-fives her. "I still
don't know where you got the idea for this, but I think it's ge-
nius," she says, referring to the series they were pitching about
two childhood best friends who switch bodies at their high
school reunion.

"What can I say?" Casey says lightly. "It just came to me one
day." She recalled the meeting where she and Rachel passionately outlined it to Charlie and Destiny, Charlie staring intently
at her the entire time, prompting her to wonder if he had any
suspicion about what happened.

Casey plops down into her chair and feels Charlie's hands
on her shoulders, expertly rubbing the tension away. He leans
down and whispers into her ear, "Good job, babe," and goose

bumps instantly appear on her arms. Part of her was still pinching herself that she was with Charlie after everything that had happened. But when she admitted as much to Rachel the other day, Rachel had encouraged her to never stop feeling that way. "Then you'll never forget how lucky you are to have each other," she had said, thinking of the mistakes she'd made with John.

Waking up in her own bed the morning after John's party, Casey muffled her screams with her pillow after discovering Charlie curled up beside her and then her own naked body under the sheets. (Although she did slightly miss the comfort of Rachel's Ebenezer Scrooge–like nightgown and made a mental note to invest in one.) She may have been out of a job, but in her eyes, her future had never been more exciting. She lay in bed for hours, watching Charlie sleep and contemplating her next career move. When Charlie finally stirred, she leaned over and kissed him deeply, realizing it was the first time in more than a year that she had done that. It felt good—damn good—but more important, it felt right. "I have an idea," she announced. C&C Productions was born that morning, Casey feeling more than ready to be on the other side of the camera and Charlie, still smarting from his experience with the *GossipTV* network executives, wanting to be in charge of his own career for a change.

Rachel glances up at the C&C PRODUCTIONS sign they'd hung last month on the wall in their humble office on Santa Monica Boulevard, bursting with pride all over again at the perfect logo designed by Audrey. She had shyly handed over a draft and asked if they'd please consider it. Rachel, taken aback by Audrey's talent, had run her hand over the intricate design: two C's intertwined with an infinity symbol underneath it, signifying eternity. "It symbolizes Aunt Casey and Charlie's love and also your friendship with her," Audrey had said profoundly, sounding so much older than her years. Rachel had secretly slipped her design into the pile with the others, not wanting Casey and Charlie to know who'd created it, understanding that Casey would instantly choose it if she knew it was Audrey's. Rachel wanted them to select it because it was the best, and she felt confident that it was. When she came to work the next day to find Audrey's design sitting on her sleek black desk with a Post-it note stuck to it that read, *LOVE this one, what do you think?*, she fingered the paper in her hand, her heart swelling with pride.

Rachel's cell phone buzzed and she looked down. "I've got to run in a few minutes," she says as she grabs her jacket off the chair. "John's taking me to see Coldplay tonight," she says, a happy smile playing on her lips. This makes Casey smile too. She'd been enjoying watching the two of them fall back in love, John fully supporting Rachel's decision to accept Charlie and Casey's offer to work with them. She'd refused a title, saying that she was too green, instead wanting to dig in and learn every aspect of developing and producing projects first. Turns out, not only was Rachel a natural in front of the camera, she was also a mean negotiator, joking that dealing with her two teenagers had taught her how to play hardball. She'd been responsible for getting them the fantastic deal on the cozy office space in Santa Monica where they'd set up shop, later confiding in Casey that she couldn't remember the last time she'd been so happy. Casey had smiled and said, "I know exactly how you feel."

"How's your *other project* going?" Charlie asks Casey.

"Great! All the paperwork is in, and they'll be out to interview me in a few weeks," Casey replies.

"I still can't believe you're actually going through with it,"

Destiny interjects from across the room. "Not that I don't think you'd be a great mom. But who would have thought?"

"I know, right?" Casey reaches up for Charlie's hand and squeezes it. She had made her decision to begin the adoption process after one too many nights of stepping inside her empty high-rise apartment to nothing more than the sound of the buzzing refrigerator. She'd felt an ache as she observed the silence—deciding she had to do something to fill it—tired of missing the sound of Charlotte's laugh and even the girls' bickering. She'd stayed up half the night researching adoption, and when Charlie showed up the next morning, her vanilla latte in his hand, she told him her plans, nervously detailing the process and even reading him the email she sent the director of the most reputable adoption service she could find. Did he think she was crazy?

After she'd become "herself" again, she'd taken Charlie for a walk on the beach and told him about the date rape, her mom, the clinic, everything. She'd begun to cry as she declared she was sorry she'd never confided in him; she was sorry for freaking out on him; sorry for it all. He'd grabbed her elbow as she paced in the wet sand, spun her toward him, and said, "No. I'm sorry that ever happened to you. I'm sorry that you ever had to go through that." She hadn't realized how much she needed to hear those words.

She held her breath as she waited for Charlie's reaction to her decision to adopt. She was completely committed to moving forward with or without him. So much so that she'd already asked a Realtor to put her condo on the market and was searching for houses in Santa Monica. She loved him—yes, she'd finally said it back—but becoming a mother was something she needed to do, regardless of his response. If she had learned anything from losing her identity, it was that she had to be true to who she really was.

Charlie stood silent for a moment and finally turned to face her. "I think anyone would be lucky to have you in their life," he said simply before kissing her softly. "I know I am."

Casey blushed and rested her head on his shoulder. "I just feel like it's something I have to do."

"Then do it," he said, his eyes bright, remembering Casey's recent confession to him about what happened to her in high school, understanding why she needed this. "I'll be there for you every step of the way."

Relief flooded her body. *He is the man I thought he was*. "Thank you."

Later that day, she called her mom and told her what she was planning, speaking so rapidly she had to slow down and start over. After she finished speaking, she was met with silence. Then she had heard the tears. Her mom, who had never been emotional, not even when Casey was bedridden and sobbing for three days after what happened to her on prom night, was now crying. Loudly. "Oh, honey. I think . . . I think that's the best news I've heard in a long time."

"Do you think I'll be a good mom?" Casey asked in a small voice.

"I think you'll be a much better mom than I've been." She sighed. "And I can't wait to be a grandmother." She called out for Casey's dad and put the phone on speaker, and for the first time in as long as she could remember, neither of them asked one question about whatever celebrity was topping the headlines that week.

The pop of a champagne cork jolts Casey from her thoughts and she ducks as it comes flying past her head, an embarrassed Destiny shouting, "Sorry!" from across the room.

For her part, Rachel was surprised by how easy it had been to go back to work, especially considering she'd never had a job outside of the home before—at least not as Rachel Cole. Charlotte was thriving with the nanny and things with Sophie had changed dramatically since Rachel took her for a girls' day out and told her she was sorry for not noticing how much of her attention Charlotte had consumed. Rachel couldn't believe how quickly Sophie's entire demeanor had changed after hearing those words. Rachel glances in the mirror in the kitchenette just a few feet from her desk and runs her fingers through her hair, the short, sassy bob that Casey's hairdresser, Jose, had talked her into getting last week still feeling foreign.

Do it! Casey had texted her. *If we've learned anything this past year, it's that taking risks is good for you.* And so Rachel had nodded her head yes and squeezed her eyes shut as the hair she had coveted for twenty years fell to the floor. When she walked into the office later, she stood nervously next to her desk, clutching the bag filled with styling gels, awaiting Casey and Destiny's reaction. But they'd loved her new 'do, marveling at the way it brought out her cheekbones. "It's like you're a completely different person," Charlie finally uttered after a long silence. *Yes,* she thought. *I am.* And John had loved it too, scooping her up in the doorway when she'd arrived home that night and taking her straight to the bedroom. "Wow, I guess you like my new look." Rachel laughed through John's kisses. "Maybe I'll dress up for you next week!"

"I'm out of here," Rachel calls as she grabs her sunglasses and places them on her head.

"Wait!" Casey calls. "We haven't toasted yet!" she says as she quickly fills each champagne glass, trying to stop the foam from spilling over. Rachel grabs a glass, Destiny and Charlie joining them.

Casey gives Rachel a quick glance. Toasting would never be quite the same experience for them after what had happened.

"To us!" Rachel calls out as they clink glasses before she looks over at Charlie. "And to Charlie finally winning over Casey's Facebook fans," she says with a laugh, referring to the latest poll there, *Do you think Casey and Charlie should get engaged?* More than 80 percent of them had answered *Hell, yes!*

Charlie smiles widely. "I'll drink to that!" he says before leaning closer to Casey. "And to love," he whispers, clinking his glass to hers.

"Yes," she agrees. "To love."

Acknowledgments

Thankful. No other word seems to sum up this experience quite as well.

None of this would have been possible without our incredible editor, Greer Hendricks at Atria Books, who is just as smart and kind as we thought she'd be and didn't seem to mind that we had been harboring a *major* girl crush on her for years. Thanks also to our publisher, the wonderful Judith Curr! And we also appreciate Sarah Cantin, who is an absolute delight to collaborate with.

We are *still* pinching ourselves that we get to work with Elisabeth Weed—she had been at the very top of our agent list for years and has far surpassed our expectations—she's gracious, lovely, and insanely talented. And to Dana Murphy, you're the best!

We owe a huge debt of gratitude to those of you who have followed our journey for the past five years on our website, *Chick Lit Is Not Dead.* You have no idea how much your unwavering support has propelled us to keep following our dream.

And a huge high-five to our fellow book bloggers—we feel lucky to know you all.

Thank you, Emily Heckman. Your incredible editing notes and cheerleading were just what we needed. And you performed a miracle by helping us work through our unhealthy obsession with dashes! For those of you in need of a sharp freelance editor—look her up. You won't regret it.

We've also had the pleasure of getting to know several authors who have been incredibly supportive and whose own books have inspired us. Much thanks! And an extra-special shoutout to the amazing Sarah Pekkanen, who believed in us from the beginning. Simply put, we wouldn't be here without you.

Big love to our beautiful families and close friends, who cheered us on for years—we can't put into words how much we've relied on your support. To our moms and beta readers, thank you for always giving pointed feedback, even when you knew we didn't want to hear it. And to our children—we hope our journey inspires you to believe anything is possible.

To Kenan, who uttered the first line of this book after a *very* memorable girls' night out many years ago. Thanks for the inspiration!

And to Mike and Matt, our two good men who have stood by as we doggedly pursued our publication dream, "thank you" doesn't seem like enough. You believed in us always—even when we had lost faith in ourselves. Your loyalty has meant everything and this moment belongs to each of you, as well. We love you.

We're also incredibly grateful that our friendship has withstood the test of time—over twenty-five years of door slamming and hugs, of tears and laughter. We hope this novel makes you want to pick up the phone and catch up with an old friend who knows you better than you know yourself.

xoxo,
Liz & Lisa

your
perfect life

liz fenton
and
lisa steinke

A Washington Square Press
Readers Club Guide

QUESTIONS AND TOPICS FOR DISCUSSION

1. How did you interpret the title of the novel? Did switching lives show Rachel and Casey that the other's life wasn't as perfect as it seemed, did it make them see that their own life was pretty perfect as it was—or is the answer somewhere in between?

2. What do you think the book is saying about "having it all"? Is such a thing attainable? What does "having it all" end up meaning for each of the protagonists?

3. Who are the people in Casey and Rachel's lives who seem most attuned to the shift in their behavior and personality after they've switched bodies? Who seems to most recognize that something is not what it should be? Consider the significance of these particular individuals—what does it say about each woman's relationship with them?

4. As Rachel and John enter the reunion holding hands and smiling, she thinks, "It's funny how quickly we can transform into the people we ought to be" (page 12). In this moment, Rachel "pretending" to be a version of herself that she doesn't feel seems to have negative connotations. But when she and Casey switch lives, "pretending" becomes a necessity, and even leads to positive things for each of

them. How does "faking it" ultimately prove to be empowering for both women?

5. On the surface, Casey's life might seem more glamorous than Rachel's. What are the cons of being Casey that you wouldn't have anticipated? And what are the pros of being Rachel that you might not have recognized?

6. What are some of the hard truths about themselves that Casey and Rachel are only able to see once they switch places?

7. As her relationship with Audrey blossoms, Casey remarks, "The one thing I've learned since being her mom is that having a teenager is a bit like dating a new guy; you can't let them know how bad you want it" (page 143). In what other ways do Casey and Rachel use experiences from their "real" lives to help inform the decisions they make while they are switched? What unique skills are they able to bring to their best friend's life?

8. When Casey and Rachel visit Jordan, the psychic, she says, "You already have the answer to switching back and it's right in front of you. You need to think about why you switched in the first place and that will lead you to how you switch back" (page 110). Discuss what enables Casey and Rachel to finally switch back. What had to happen for this to become possible?

9. Consider how certain dynamics and fixed roles can develop in long-term friendships. How did this apply to Casey

and Rachel at the beginning of the novel, and how has it changed by the end?

10. Which of your friends would you most trust to take over your life? What is it about this person—perhaps their personality traits, or your shared history—that makes them the best suited for the job? Which friend's life would you most want to test out—and do you think your answer is different having now read *Your Perfect Life*? Are these two friends one and the same, or are they different?

11. There's an old adage that you need to walk a mile in someone else's shoes before you can really understand them. In the case of *Your Perfect Life*, could it also be said that you need to walk a mile in someone else's shoes to really understand yourself?

ENHANCE YOUR BOOK CLUB

1. Bring your high school yearbook to your next book club meeting. Share how you feel you have changed since high school—and what you feel has stayed the same.

2. Rachel makes Casey a very detailed "How to Be Rachel" list to help her get through the days. Make your own "How to Be Me" list and consider sharing with the group. Try to think of everything that even your best friend might not know about your routine, your home, or your family.

3. Pretend that you are the casting director for the film version of *Your Perfect Life*. Who would you cast as Rachel and Casey? Who would play John and Charlie? What about Destiny and Audrey?

4. Speaking of films, consider watching one of the many movies that take the idea of "switching lives" as their central theme (*Freaky Friday, Sliding Doors, Trading Places, The Change-Up,* etc.). As a group, consider what it is about these kinds of stories that fascinate us so much. What desires do these narratives tap into? What do the common lessons of each seem to be?